Deception of Lies

Michael J. Balian

DEDICATION

I dedicate this book to all. To remind you to believe in yourself...

Surround yourself with people that believe in you, and when you find yourself around those that tell you not to quit your day job, then jettison them as quickly as possible.

Thank you to my children, McKenna, John and Vaughn, without whom I would not realize all the joys and wonderment of this World.

We the peoples of the United Nations determined to save succeeding generations from the scourge of war, which twice in our lifetime has brought untold sorrow to Mankind, and to reaffirm faith in fundamental human rights, in the dignity and worth of the human person, in the equal rights of men and women and nations large and small, and to establish conditions under which justice and respect for the obligations arising from treaties and other sources of international law can be maintained, and to promote social progress and better standards of life in larger freedom, and for these ends to practice tolerance and live together in peace with one another as good neighbors, and to unite our strength to maintain international peace and security, and to ensure, by the acceptance of principles and the institution of methods, that armed force shall not be used, save in the common interest, and to employ international machinery for the promotion of the economic and social advancement of all peoples, have resolved to combine our efforts to accomplish these aims.

Preamble to the Charter of the United Nations
1945

CHAPTER ONE
AUGUST 2ND

"I didn't think it could be done, but, my boy, you've accomplished the impossible." Garrett held out his rough stocky hand and tightly grasped Alex's palm. "Son, you've done a wonderful job of hosting this fund-raiser. And look at this turn out, far beyond any expectation."

"Well, sir, it was honoring you which seemed to spur people to attend," Alex replied. As chairman, he had to be present. Sometimes, he felt invigorated by events such as this one, other times it was more obligatory, to be seen. Tonight, it involved a little of both.

"Where's your beautiful wife?"

"She wasn't feeling too well, so she stayed home." Laurel was expected to attend, but their sitter backed out. Alex suspected she invented the excuse. He knew she did not care for the political scene and would usually sit or stand near the entrance of events while he made the rounds, shaking hands, working the room. If he glanced over to her, he would see the look of disdain on her face. Laurel's expressions were not discreet. One knew exactly how she felt just by observing her.

"That's too bad." Garrett Baird, the Chairman of the Republican Party for Virginia, was in his mid-sixties, noticeably short and stocky. If you stuck a pin in his barrel chest, he would explode like a balloon. He had no real discernible manner of dress, except for two things, he loved to wear vests and whatever he wore cost a lot of money. A cigar always protruded from the corner of his mouth, and a glass of Glenmorangie was ever present in his left hand. "Son, we all are thoroughly impressed with your efforts here."

Alex felt like an impostor. He delegated most of the work to a committee and made a few phone calls. He nodded graciously. "Yes sir, it wasn't really all that difficult."

"Your modesty is refreshing. Listen, this fundraiser is scheduled to finish at nine, however, afterwards I and a few others are going to the Chart House and I'd like you to join us."

"Well. . ."

"I won't take no for an answer. I believe it would be to your benefit."

If Garrett took a liking to someone, believing he or she had a future in politics, one would go far with his guidance. There were always prices to pay for his assistance, though. Some questioned whether it was worth it. "I would be delighted to attend," he said cordially, inasmuch as he did not like to burn any bridges, since he never knew when he would have to retreat. Treat people nicely on the way up and you will be cushioned on the way down was Alex's creed, especially since politics ebbed and flowed. It seemed all time consuming.

"Good. Well, Alex, it's time for you to introduce me so I can give a brief talk and let these fine folks do what comes naturally for them - socialize," he laughed.

The event, a black tie affair, was held at the Torpedo Factory Art Center in Old Town Alexandria, to raise money for Virginia's Republican Party's General Fund. Alex proceeded to the podium set in the middle of the atrium. Garrett tagged behind, stopping every now and then to quickly shake someone's hand and then stutter step to catch up.

"Ladies and gentleman, distinguished guests and fellow Republicans, I would like to welcome you to this event honoring a man who has given so much to our political party. I'm sure you don't realize it, but this building and Garrett Baird have much in common. The Torpedo Factory was just that at one time." Alex paused and looked around as people stood around the stage. "It was a factory used during World Wars I and II for the manufacture of torpedo casings. Old Town Alexandria, in keeping with the tradition of maintaining its history through the renovation and maintenance of its historic buildings, had the foresight to renovate this old plant, remodeling this wonderful three story building, keeping an open atrium throughout, looking skyward to the greatest artistic Creator. The studios which you all have visited and, I promise, will stay open late, are leased out to over 150 various artists. This facility enables artists, who go through a meticulous screening process, to have studios to work from and a place to sell their creations. And for them to be here, adding color to our conversation, we are extremely grateful." Alex waited for the applause to diminish.

"I am proud to tell you that this effort tonight has raised over five hundred and seventy five thousand dollars. . ." The applause grew as Alex continued to talk. ". . . which will be used in specially earmarked elections. Those are campaigns selected by the party seen as crucial or winnable. None of this would have been possible without your support, and none of this would have happened without Garrett Baird."

Garrett acknowledged the applause, lifting his glass of scotch.

"There's a lot to this man," Alex continued. "He started out his career in the public sector; however, his success came only after he left civil service thirty years ago, after becoming, and I quote, 'disenchanted with the federal bureaucracy and the lazy parasites which thrive, unseen, but ever feeding off of the host - our hard earned tax dollars'. Garrett has been an entrepreneur since. He turned to insurance, leaving his mark and earning his fortune. The man is a natural salesman and could sell sins to a sinner. For those of you who don't know it, Garrett is also a political animal, an integral part in the structure of Virginian politics, and has been for as long as anyone can remember. Many people, tongue in cheek, refer to him as the 'Godfather' of Virginia's Republican Party." Alex paused and looked toward Garrett, who let out a belly laugh. "And as my wife Laurel would quip, 'Many a truth is said in jest'."

Actually, when Garrett's name was mentioned, she would comment, 'I don't know how anyone can put up with such an egotistical, self-centered cad.' Never one to hold back her dislikes or prejudices, once she had something in her mind, she became stubborn, unwavering from her original opinions. Having grown accustomed to her preconceived notions, he would let her have her say, and then she would let him go on his way. Alex continued, "He had the vision and foresight to resurrect a party which most of the media said was dead. The political pundits wrote Virginia was a one party state and would stay that way. Oh how they were wrong, for they never met Garrett Baird and Garrett has never met a challenge he wasn't up to. And now without further ado, the man we are all here to see and pay our respects, Garrett Baird."

Looking every part the consummate politician, Garrett walked up to the podium, placed his drink down and raised his arms in appreciation. "I'll tell you, he's a tough act to follow, especially when he took my best lines. Before I start, I would like you all to give Alex Westcott a big round of applause for making this possible." Garrett waited briefly, holding the cigar in his left hand as he talked. "You all have to know that I'm really known as the George Burns of politics," he hesitated. "I smoke cigars, like to be surrounded by beautiful young women and I'm older than God, or at least it seems like it. I'll tell you something else, to have these artists present while politicians, community leaders and others mill about has made this a memorable event, adding to the atmosphere of this evening. And while not everyone may share the same ideas about art, I know it when I see it, and there are quite a few gifted and talented artists in our presence, and for that we are grateful. I have just one more comment before you all can get back to socializing. I've been leading this party in Virginia for some time and my theme always remains steadfast," Garrett paused for emphasis. "We need a new direction in our nation and the current administration does not seem to believe we are serious about our future. We should stop being an island. We are at the pinnacle and now is the time to expand our global influence. We are the greatest and strongest nation in the world and we must make our voices heard. Your presence and generous contributions tonight will allow our party to take that step to making our voices heard." Garrett acknowledged the loud applause, and then he looked toward Alex.

The first shot crashed into the podium, sending splinters in every direction. The sound caused most people to cease all movement, as each tried to comprehend the reality of the situation. The second shot ripped through Garrett's left arm with such velocity he just stood and looked at the wound in disbelief.

Alex looked up and could detect a shadow of a figure on the third level of the building, firing into the atrium. Pandemonium broke out with people scattering in different directions. People were falling. Others, without a care as to whom they injured stepped on bodies to escape harm's way. Sensing a third shot, Alex immediately ran toward Garrett and threw himself into the rotund man, as another shot rang forth, striking Garrett in his abdomen. He cried in pain from the bullet and Alex's weight being thrust into him. All that could be heard was screaming as Alex used his body to shield Garrett. Alex looked up and saw the figure quietly leave up through an open skylight. As quickly as the gunfire started, the shots fell silent.

If the United Nations once admits that international disputes can be settled by using force, then we will have destroyed the foundation of the organization and our best hope of establishing a world order.

Dwight D. Eisenhower
34th President

CHAPTER TWO
SEPTEMBER 10TH

"Who do you think the best person for this would be?" Garrett asked while inhaling deeply on his rich Cuban cigar, swirling the smoke around the inside of his mouth before pulling it deep into his lungs.

"Well," she paused. "I guess it would depend on what you're trying to accomplish."

"That's what you're here for." Reclining in the overstuffed chair, he exhaled, blowing the smoke up and away from her. "You've been briefed. You know the possible candidates, some of them intimately," he said watching for her reaction. She did not flinch, so he continued, with the cigar dangling from the corner of his mouth. "You know their capabilities. I want your opinion, and I want it now."

She flew in late from Miami and now it was almost 3:45 a.m. "My selection would be either Vickers or Henry. They are both capable and qualified." She chose her words carefully.

He scowled, "I know Vickers and he's not qualified to take out my trash. Who's Henry?"

"His name is Thomas, Thomas Henry," she said.

The sound of the alarm pierced the quiet of the early morning. Alex stirred slowly, groping for the annoying noise. Saturdays were usually a time for him to sleep in, a luxury which, at times, seemed more like a necessity. On his third swipe, out of repetition, he hit the snooze button. Shifting his weight, he could feel the warmth of his wife sleeping next to him. He took comfort in knowing she was there. He slowly opened his eyes. Rays of the rising sun pierced the curtains. Their bedroom, traditional in design, with a sleigh bed, matching dressers and nightstands, was very light. Laurel believed a bright bedroom was an important way to begin each day. Light depravation would lead to depression, she thought, so she insisted on white accessories for them, including not blocking out the morning as it drew near. It was nature's way to wake up. He rolled over, away from the approaching daybreak, knowing full well his slumber would be short lived and he would be forced out of bed before the alarm sounded again.

"This better be important," he said in a muddled voice as he placed the phone to his ear. "Do y'all know what Goddamn time it is?"

"Thomas Henry, please," came the unconcerned reply.

"Speaking. Who's this?" Henry annoyed, asked in his southern drawl.

"That's not important right now. Are you willing to handle cleanup?"

He stirred more upright in bed as he reached over to flick on the light. "Yea. I'm willing. Where do y'all want me to be?" He wiped away the crusted sleep from his eyes, then rubbed his hand on his shirt. He looked around for a pen and paper. The pen was on the floor next to his bed. He picked it up.

"D.C. Plan on meeting with Garrett Baird, tomorrow at noon. He'll tell you what his needs are. The instructions will be in locker 2732 at the bus station, your plane ticket and some cash will be in a cab which will pick you up this evening, at 6:00. Be ready." Click.

Henry busily scribbled down all he was told on the palm of his hand before he hung up the receiver. He looked at the information, then situated himself back down and fell quickly to sleep.

Alex faced the back of his wife. They had been married for almost fifteen years and settled nicely into a system. Familiar settings were comfortable. Laurel divided herself in several ways. First, and of most importance to her, she was a mother, taking care of their two sons, Jeremy and Christian. Next, she was a supportive wife, allowing him to expose his imperfections without being critical. Finally she indulged herself artistically. During her creative periods she would sequester herself in her studio, behind their house, painting, molding clay, experimenting with different mediums, as her mood permitted. As she sculpted or painted, Laurel would feel as though she was removed from her body.

Alex felt her move toward him. The bed creaked as she stirred. She gently caressed his shoulder, running her hand up to his hair. He pulled away, slightly, instinctively, knowing this was her method of forcing him from bed.

"Honey, it's time to get up. You told me to make sure you were out of bed so you could get to the office early."

Alex let out a slight grumble. He had to finish preparing for his argument opposing a motion for summary disposition. His client, Ameritrend Chem Company, was a major contributor of legal fees to the law firm. They always paid on time and they never questioned their bills. That attitude was a plus for any attorney handling billables and collectibles. Ameritrend was result oriented, much more so than most other clients who realize principle is expensive. To Ameritrend cost was never an issue. Alex nurtured the company along from its inception at the firm, giving sound advice and stringing a list of impressive victories. Because of those accomplishments, the Board of Directors increasingly gave Alex and the firm more responsibility, work and money.

"You know I don't care for your weekend jaunts into the City," she whispered. "The firm takes up too much of your time, time which should be spent with me and the boys." Laurel nibbled on his ear. "I've always told you work is your mistress, just don't neglect us."

Alex moved the pillow up around his ears.

She wished he would take on more of the parenting responsibilities with their two sons and while his concern was little when they were young, Laurel would now acknowledge her husband was spending much more time with them as they grew older. "Why don't you just work here today? We all would enjoy it. You know your boys would be quiet while you work." The father-son bonding was evident, especially when they would mimic their father's words and mannerisms.

Alex groused. He rarely went into detail of any case he was handling for his law firm, MacClennan, O'Brien, Dougherty & Ernest, only explaining to her, in laymen terms, the basics of what he was working on. The legal profession was an industry unto itself. An understanding of the language took years to master, beyond a mere law school or textbook comprehension of issues. Laurel never expressed an interest, real or otherwise, as to the finer aspects of law. He never had the patience to explain the subtle nuances. Perhaps his wife sensed his opposition to communicating his work to her. It had more to do with the fact that whatever Alex accomplished was in the abstract. When Laurel created, she made something that could be observed and admired. It could be from a piece of artwork, to cooking a meal, planning a project for her sons, or even in giving birth, all of her accomplishments were visible. He was of the belief they, as individuals, could and should each grow outside of one another's shadow, holding true friendship occurred when one was comfortable in silence when the other was present. Alex knew, while silence showed friendship or comfort, communication offered stability, keeping their relationship on an even keel. He always made it a point to communicate, forcing Laurel to deal with their marital issues which would come into play occasionally.

"You're not going to stay in the condo tonight, are you? We have plans to spend it together." Laurel said.

When Alex had to prepare at length for hearings or meetings, he would stay in the firm's condominium at 1212 New Hampshire Avenue, N.W. located just south of DuPont Circle. As for this condo, the firm drafted the legal documents transforming an apartment building into condominiums. They exchanged their attorney fees for three condos. The partners sold two, making a nice return on their money, and retained this one. Apartment conversions were highly profitable deals. Alex researched transactions and drafted the initial documents to allow the transfer. It was his first real corporate contract experience as a fledgling attorney. He had to evict most of the tenants, to allow the transition to take place. Not an activity he liked, but one in which he was proficient. The apartment was provided by the firm for the convenience of staff attorneys, encouraging them to stay late and arrive early when they were working on important matters. Many of the firm's attorneys looked to the apartment as slave labor, putting in many more hours than they would otherwise, just because of its convenience. The condo allowed him the means to work hard to achieve partnership status.

"I'll be home tonight," he grumbled.

"Honey," she said in a voice firmer than before. "It's time to get up. You made me promise last night I'd have you out of bed by 7:00." She ran her fingers through his hair, gently pushing out the twisted, tangled strands which sleep seemed to force in all sorts of random direction. It pulled slightly at his scalp.

He moved slightly, other than that, he did not stir.

"Alexander. I don't like you leaving on a Saturday any more than you do, but I had nothing to do with you getting home so late," she continued trying to prod him from his slumber "Plus, I don't control your work load. I'm just doing what you asked me to do."

He could feel the warmth of her breath on his ear. He knew she was close. Murmuring, he placed the pillow over his head, muffling the sounds, along with closing the light of the world from his heavy lids.

"What's that?" she said as she got up.

The bed shifted as she left. He moved over to her side where it was warm.

"Well, one of us better get going." She grabbed an old George Washington University sweatshirt from the top of the dresser and put it on over her T-shirt. The sweatshirt, which belonged to Alex at one time, was ample enough to cover most of the boxers she scammed from her husband.

Alex was counting on fifteen minutes more of precious sleep, before the assault of the day's activities.

Christian sniffled "Jeremy, are ya up?"

"Yea."

"Led's go watch television.' Christian said toward the bunk bed above him.

"Mom and Dad are sleepin. We'll get in trouble if we make too much noise." Jeremy turned his head to the side, then he reached under his pillow and grabbed a Night Warrior comic book. He leafed through the well worn pages.

The boys shared a bedroom. Alex figured this would be the last year before Jeremy, who was the older son at 8 years, asked to be moved into his own room, asserting the start of his independence. Their room was on the opposite side of the house from their parents. The distance between the boys' room and theirs gave Alex and Laurel some privacy. The boys had bunk beds that were rocket ships. Their room was decorated in an astronomy motif, with different planets, solar systems and constellations set about, all created by Laurel. She believed in order for her children to learn about the world around them, they had to see it as an adventure. Every night, when the lights were turned out, the stars painted around the room and on the ceiling would come out, and they could believe they were sailing along in their rockets to chart new territories.

Christian kicked his feet out from under the covers and placed them under Jeremy's mattress "Come on," he said as he pushed up, giving his brother a mild bounce.

"What do you want to watch?" Jeremy asked as he followed the story in his comic book. Night Warriors told about the good and evil of King Arthur's court, with events taking place in the present.

"Night Warriors"

"Alright." Jeremy closed his comic book and placed it back under his pillow, which was decorated with a bright yellowish orange sun. Christian's was of the moon, more subdued in a pale blue color.

"Just a minute you two."

The boys turned and looked toward their doorway where Laurel was standing. Her arms were folded over one another in a motherly fashion. She looked around their room, noticing how it was still relatively neat. Christian and Jeremy's friends loved to spend the night in since sleeping there was a truly visual experience. She looked over to her sons, each in their own bed.

"Mom. How long have you been there?" Jeremy asked. "Don't you know you've gotta knock first. I put a sign up." He pointed toward the door.

"So you did." The neatly stenciled and colored sign at waist level. Jeremy was creative, not artistic. His talent did not flow freely from him and had to be coaxed. "However, you should know by now that all signs and their posting must be cleared through me first, otherwise, I don't have to pay attention to them. I am the house manager and permits have to be obtained through me."

"Oh Mom," Jeremy said, which caused her to smile.

"Mommy. Jeremy and me want to watch Night Warriors."

"Jeremy and I," Laurel instructed.

"Jeremy and I want to watch it. Can we? Please"

"I'll let you boys watch it under one condition." Laurel looked at each of her sons. They were growing up fast, too fast as far as she was concerned. She and Alex would talk about their sons' development and life's plans. To them it seemed it was only yesterday they were changing diapers and now their sons were real people, each with his own personality, separate and distinct from each another. It intimidated them. "You have to wake up your dad."

"Let's go," Jeremy said.

Christian mimicked, "Led's go."

"Wait a second," she said after they flung off their covers and were standing right in front of her.

"What"

"I'm going to time you. I want to see how long it takes you to run from here to your daddy, however, to be fair, I want you both to get a running start. Okay?"

"Aw right."

"On your mark," Laurel instructed as she held the boys back. They were like horses in a gate, ready for the race, straining at her arms. "Get set. Go!" She moved away from the door creating an open straight-a-way to their father. She watched them run and yell and their hair flop up and down as they raced each other to their dad.

"Ahhhhhhhhhhhhhhhh." The sound gained in volume as it approached. There was a brief silence, followed by the loud crash of his two sons flopping on top, causing the bed to bounce and creak.

"Daddy, Daddy," they yelled in unison. Alex bolted upright in bed, grabbing them both. Christian squealed in laughter as he was tickled

14

and roughhoused. Jeremy, as he begged for forgiveness from his dad's torture, managed to get out in gulps "Daddy, Daddy - Mom - mie made us - wa – ke you up - Pleeease don't - Daaaaaaad." Tears were coming down the boys' red faces.

"Do you know what time it is?' Alex asked.

"Donnybrook time," Jeremy responded at the same time his father pulled the back of his pajama top over his head, creating a situation where he could no longer see, forcing his arms downward, giving Alex complete control over his son.

"You are now at my mercy, Jeremy. Do as I say." Alex pushed his son down, face first, onto his bed, then grabbed Christian and tossed him on top of his brother, They each struggled to get away from their father's control, taking delight in it all that much more. They were creating such a racket they did not hear Laurel approach.

"Okay, okay. That's enough playing and riling up for my three boys," she intoned with motherly inflection. "Jeremy. Christian. Leave your Dad alone. It's time for him to get ready for work."

"Nooooooooo!" Christian retorted. "You said we could wake him."

"Yes. And you've done such a good job now you can watch Night Warriors."

Jeremy grumbled, "Dad, please don't go."

Alex suppressed his remorse. "It's okay - I promise I'll be back tonight and then we'll all go to China Inn for dinner." That would occupy the boys' thoughts and go toward making up for not spending much time with them lately. He was not around much during their first few years, more so with Jeremy than Christian, due to the long hours he had to put in at the firm to achieve partnership status. Alex was on the fast track, and made it in record time. Now he had some amends to make. Jeremy developed a love for eating with chopsticks since, in school, he was studying Asian culture. He developed a knack for submerging himself one hundred and ten percent into whatever he was studying. A trait he inherited from his dad, along with his father's physique, dark hair and eyes, which was combined with a slight hint of his mother's fragile facial features.

Christian was the exact image of his mother. Slender, frail, almost delicate, blond hair and blue eyes. He was a mimic. One had to be careful what was said or the tone. Next thing you knew, your words were coming right back at you from this innocent looking child. His older brother could do no wrong. He wanted to do whatever Jeremy did. Christian was along for the ride. As a parent, you only had to control one child and the other would fall into line.

"How does that sound?" Alex asked as he pulled each son up to either side.

"Can I use chop sticks?" Jeremy inquired. "I know how. They showed us at school."

Christian echoed "Me too, Daddy."

"Sure. Whatever you want to do, but on these conditions." Alex made his voice sound as stern as he could. He was not one who was much for strict discipline. He believed in a more humane approach to his children, one where the strap gives way to reason. Unreasoned violence spawns brutality. Intonation, Alex discovered, worked just as well, if not better, on his children.

"What's that?" they asked eagerly.

"The conditions are you'll let me get up and get ready, and you'll help your mother out today. Whatever she wants you to do, do it. If I hear you didn't listen to her and do as she asked you to do, then the deal is off. Okay?"

Jeremy said, "Okay."

"Yea, me too," Christian repeated.

"Now get out of here and go watch TV while your mother gets

16

breakfast ready." He gave each son a kiss, sent them on their way downstairs. His joints ached as he swung his feet onto the floor. He stood up and stretched his body, feeling the years of tension in each muscle. Alex ran his fingers through his hair, pressing it backwards. He knew he looked like a mad scientist, with how wild his hair was. "What are you waiting for?"

"Just making sure you're up," Laurel responded.

"I'm going to the bathroom to get ready. Do you want to join me?" Alex still was not used to their home, even after living there for over two years. Laurel decided it was time for them to move from the hustle and bustle of City living to quieter confines. She reasoned Jeremy was getting older, ready to start in the public schools, which was something she would worry too much about. Plus there was no room for the kids to play. As they were getting older, they were becoming more rambunctious, and wanted to explore their surroundings more. While their neighborhood in the Adams-Morgan District of Washington, D.C. was not inadequate, it was a part of the City which gave her reasons to be concerned. When living in a major city, one always has to be on guard. They lived in a row house, which they purchased as newlyweds during Alex's final year of law school at Georgetown University. It was convenient for both of them while Laurel was finishing her Master's in Art History at George Washington University.

"You're a grown boy. You can do that all by yourself."

"Really?" It was a joint decision to place the house for sale. They enjoyed the area and the commute to work was reasonable. There was no real need for a car and every imaginable need, from food to entertainment to hardware, could be met within a five-block radius. The housing market in greater Washington, D.C. had grown by leaps and bounds. It did not take long for their home to be sold. The quick sale of their home was unexpected and the outlying areas were somewhat foreign. Alex grew up in Leesburg. Laurel was from Trenton. Soon they settled on Old Town Alexandria. Laurel fell in love with the abundant history and quaintness of the town. It suited her artistic nature. When she would visit Old Town, looking at homes, she would come back ecstatic. Old Town, it was decided then, would become their new address.

"Yes. I have younger boys to see to."

Alex rubbed his eyes. "Okay." That decision was followed by the next big one. Finding a house they not only liked, but also could afford. As they searched the area, a brick colonial came onto the market. It was a beautiful home nestled on an almost an acre, with a small cottage in the back yard. The home was constructed in 1937. Even though Old Town was over two hundred years old, the area was developed as an outreach community for D.C. The house was over 3,000 square feet, comprising four bedrooms, a Master suite, the usual accommodations downstairs, wood floors throughout, including a library with a fireplace. The previous owners renovated the house extensively. Laurel thought Alex would use the library as an office, allowing him to be around his family more often. The library, which was quite adequate, did not suit him. Alex was never one to take his work home. He had to leave it at the office. By the time he would get home he would be too tired, mentally, to think about his clients' cases and their legal issues. The main feature, which sold Laurel on this house, was not the size of the yard, but the cottage out back. It was a small carriage house built with the original home. She envisioned that as her studio, a place where she could create without being disturbed.

"Alex."

"Yes?"

"Remember, tomorrow, we have to rake the yard." The home was on Princess Street. A mature tree lined neighborhood near the Lee-Fendall House, the boyhood home of Robert E. Lee. The neighbors were mainly professionals, slightly older in age than they were. They all took pride in the beauty and quiet charm of their neighborhood. The

Westcotts' were welcomed with open arms. Their house was located eight blocks from the Braddock Road Metro. Alex would take the Metro to Farragut Square, which was close to his office. While the jaunt did not take long, it was another adjustment he had to make, since his travel time more than doubled.

"All right."

"How are you getting to the office?"

"MG," Alex said as he turned toward the bathroom. Driving to the office was a luxury he afforded himself on weekends, and once or twice during the week. He limited his car travel around Washington during the week. His 1974 MG was a car he took much pride in, having restored it to its original condition. Alex noticed from their bathroom window it was going to be another beautiful day. He took off his T-shirt, stepped from his shorts, and then into the shower, adjusting the temperature warmer, and then letting it pulse down on his scalp.

He looked up at the steady stream of water pulsating down. He opened his mouth, letting the water massage his teeth. His client, Ameritrend Chem Company, was embroiled in a patent infringement lawsuit. Ameritrend had been good to the firm and Alex was doing everything in his power to keep them happy. They were accused of white collar espionage, which translated to stealing a deep oil well drill bit design and applying it to various off shore and intercontinental oil drilling ventures. Adco Bit Fabricators, Inc. was the company suing them. His client was being screwed by a larger company out to corner the market. When one company could not compete against a smaller more efficient company, they hit the smaller enterprise with numerous suits, golden parachutes, whatever it took to monopolize the industry and snuff out competition. This was Adco's fourth lawsuit against Ameritrend in the past year. They were putting a financial squeeze on and Alex was hired to stop it. He turned, letting the water beat a rhythm on his back. He pushed his hair back from his eyes, blinking several times. With the technology his client developed, it would push their stock through the roof. With the company mired in litigation, the opposite effect would occur. That would undervalue the business and make Ameritrend susceptible to a hostile takeover. The next six months were make or break.

He shut off the water and reached out past the shower for his towel, hanging on a hook behind the bathroom door. Steam escaped from the shower, evaporating quickly as it did.

"I'll be there shortly," Thomas Henry said into his phone. On the late flight from San Antonio, there were few people aboard, so privacy was not a concern. That, coupled with the drone of the engines and the buzz from the pressurized cabin, no one heard his conversation. He nodded in agreement, while pressing the phone as close to his ear to better hear what was said.

"Yea. Y'all are right about that. I know." Henry paused. "Yea. He's got to get back in line. We checked him prior and are surprised by the about face. I know it's within. Right, details will be later. I know, okay," Henry finished without acknowledging the end of the conversation and snapped the phone back into its clip. He typed a few more entries on the laptop he had perched on the tray in front of him.

"Flight Five Seventy Two will be landing at Washington's National Airport in ten minutes. Please return your seats and trays to the upright position and store any items you may have brought to the overhead compartments or under the seat in front of you. On behalf of the flight crew we would like to thank you for flying Southwest Airlines. It has been our pleasure to serve you tonight. Remember the local time in Washington is Nine Fifty p.m."

Thomas Henry looked at his watch, then reset it to reflect the two-hour time change. He took his lap top computer from the tray, closed the top and placed it in its case, placing it on the floor beneath him. He reached his arms over his head and stretched. He knew he was called in for some unusually heavy responsibilities, especially with Garrett Baird setting up the meeting. Money would not be an object. Henry smiled. He liked the edge and he expected a few thrills. He moved his seat forward, settling in for the landing.

In the months after victory, probably nothing characterized the times more hopefully for Americans than did creation in 1945 of the United Nations. The UN would provide, its American supporters believed, a solvent for national rivalries. It would be the Parliament of the World of which poets long had sung. An American president in 1919 had revealed a vision of world government which failed to obtain popular support. Woodrow Wilson, his supporters were saying while the Second World War was still being fought, had been "ahead of his time." By 1945, time had caught up with the prophecy.

American Diplomacy

CHAPTER THREE
SEPTEMBER 12TH

The air had a sweet smell to it this early fall morning. It reminded one of the impending change of seasons. The scheduled hearing on the motion Alex had worked on so diligently was set for this morning. He stayed the night at the firm's condo, then arose early and decided to go for a run. Running relaxed him. He believed he could argue better if he could exercise. He decided on the zoo course. There would be fewer cars to deal with. Running toward the State Department meant he would have to contend with the bum hurdles - his reference to the homeless sleeping on heat grates, blocking one's access to the sidewalk. The homeless seemed as if they were multiplying due to social program cutbacks and the tightening economy. It was en vogue to help only those who help themselves. The bootstrap philosophy was making a resurgence. Alex did not look down on them; however, he did not like to be bothered by their pandering. Most were unkempt, unshowered and rough in appearance. While Alex would leave cans of food, in boxes, around various Metro stops, he refused to give money when asked.

Upon returning to the condo he noticed the message indicator flashing on his phone. He went over and picked it up, pressed listen. He wiped the sweat from his forehead on the sleeve of his sweatshirt. Underneath, his T-shirt was soaked.

"Good morning honey." Laurel's voice was cheerful. "I missed you last night and wanted to make sure everything was all right since you didn't call me when you finished, like you said you would. I tried you at the office, but your voice mail came up, and now you're not here. I hope I didn't miss you. Please call me when you get this message. I love you."

Alex promised to call, but the preparation and tying up other loose ends took longer than he anticipated. He walked to the kitchen and dialed home. Two rings.

"Hello," Laurel said.

"Morning," he replied. "I'm sorry I didn't call, but I didn't finish until very late. I didn't want to wake you."

"Alex, please. We've been through this before. I'm always concerned. You know me, I think the worst. You can thank my mom for that, besides, I always like to hear from you.

"I know."

"By the way, where were you when I called?"

"I went for a jog." Alex was not one for small talk over the phone. Sometimes, he just did not want to be bothered by the weight of the phone. "Down to the zoo, past the bears. I thought of you. Then I realized I forgot to call." The zoo was always open from the back. Even though it was closed to the general public, anyone could mill around inside if they really wanted too. Some people took advantage of the back gate, and enjoyed the animals during quieter times. It gave him something to see as he ran.

"Did you think of yourself when you went past the snakes?"

"No, but several attorneys and judges did come to mind. I

thought of your sisters at the Water Buffalo," Alex answered. They both laughed. "Look Laurel, when I finish up tonight, let's have a late dinner. After the boys go to sleep, you can give me one of those long massages I love. Perhaps, we can even get a movie. I don't have to be at work until late tomorrow."

"That sounds great. It has been so long since we've had some time to ourselves. I'll make sure to wait for you."

The motion was scheduled for 9:30 a.m. Judge Connally was not known for his mild temperament, nor for his promptness. From a prominent Texas family, his Grandfather, who made much money from fields of black gold, was in Congress, around the turn of the Century. At one point he held the longest tenure for any Congressman in the history of the House of Representatives. His father followed in his Grandfather's footsteps, only on a higher level, was a Senator and, continuing on in the tradition of the Connally longevity, served from the 1930's, through the 70's. He was an FDR Democrat, riding on his coat tails to victory in 1932. The Depression was an easy time for Democrats to get elected to public office. The Connallys' were a well oiled political machine for over five generations. Growing up, Michael Connally spent most of his time outside Texas. Summers and holidays in Washington, while attending boarding school in Massachusetts during his formative years. His education continued at Harvard, where he lettered in two sports. Law school followed. Michael Connally, almost ten years older than Alex, was athletically gifted, who seemed to excel, not only in any sport he played, but also in any venture he undertook. He had a Midas touch. Alex got along with him due to their love of hockey, reinforced through the practice of law. Both played in college and agreed it was the only sport that encompassed both total coordination and peak fitness. Each was drafted by minor league hockey teams, but each decided not to sacrifice his education. They were members of an unspoken brotherhood, longing to have turned pro, but never admitting they regretted their decision.

Whenever he was scheduled in court, Alex prepared thoroughly. Judge Connally expected and respected that. It was important, if not necessary, in today's age of litigation to know all sides, including judges - their perception, idiosyncrasies, likes and prejudices. It gave the attorney who amassed this knowledge an advantage. Sometimes that was all one would need to prevail. Michael Connally had been groomed for the federal bench all of his life. First, as a research clerk to Justice Douglas, then he was an assistant U.S. Attorney General, then Federal Magistrate, before being appointed to his lifetime post.

Briefcase in hand, Alex left the condo.

"Good morning Mr. Westcott." Raul, dressed in his full regal outfit greeted him and held the door open for him.

"Good morning Raul, another nice day."

"Yes indeed sir. Enjoy."

Walking north on New Hampshire Avenue, toward the Metro at DuPont Circle, there was a genteel feeling to the morning. The sidewalks and streets were a combination of brick and cement, a convergence of two eras. The DuPont Circle fountain glistened as the water gracefully arched upward, before gravity pulled it back. Trees lined the circle with individuals playing chess or checkers. Alex especially enjoyed mornings this time of year. People were in better moods. The summer heat and stifling humidity were subsiding.

As he approached the Metro, he paused at one of the street vendors hawking various wares near the escalators. "Washington Post please and this." He picked up an apple.

The vendor quickly folded the paper in half and handed it to Alex. "One seventy five."

He gave him two dollars. "Keep the change."

"Thanks."

The metro system in Washington D.C. always impressed and

amazed anyone who saw it. Alex was a child when the system was first being constructed. Traffic would be halted and rerouted while trucks scurried about. Detours were inexhaustible, leading cars in the opposite direction from which they desired to go. The masses, grudgingly, put up with the inconvenience with the hope and belief the traffic congestion would abate. The system, even though it was a generation old, appeared modern. It was clean, absent of panhandlers, grime, graffiti or trash. A painstaking effort was made by the City, daily, to maintain the beauty and integrity of this mass transit system. It was the showcase for the World. As one approached the escalator heading down toward the metro, a rush of musty tunnel odor would come up, invading one's sense of smell and being the only true indicator of how old the system was. Alex enjoyed this mode of travel. He felt like a warrior battling as he descended the stairs. Everything in this underground environment had a futuristic look. The ceiling and walls, honeycombed in design, formed a gentle arch, stretching from one platform over the tracks, to the next. Lighting was recessed. Everything was machine operated, from Metro card dispensers to entries and exits. Platform lights flashed, notifying a train's arrival. Security was more vigilant, and less obtrusive, through cameras, all seeing, recording any suspicious movement.

Sensing a train approaching, it was a feel and a sound, faint, but detectable, he hurried down. It was outbound, so he walked to the half wall surrounding the backside of the platform, away from the tracks, which hid more lights behind it. Leaning against it, he bit into the apple. He set his briefcase down next to him and looked through the day's paper. The headline to the left read that **The Federal Reserve took steps to tighten the money supply by raising interest rates for the fifth time this year.**

Alex felt fortunate they had locked into their mortgage when they did. Many sectors of the economy have been on a downward trend for the past two years, and that did not include the weakening of the U.S. dollar abroad. Gloom and doom does not happen often, but when it does the naysayers rejoice in their pessimism.

The platform lights flashed. He could feel the cold swirl of air from the tunnel. People moved toward the platform's edge, everyone eager to get a seat. The crowd was not too bad. Alex was not in any real hurry and did not have to transfer from the red line. This Metro went directly to Judiciary Square, where the District of Columbia's local and federal courts were located. He boarded the metro and sat in one of several unoccupied seats, pumpkin orange in color. The cabin, well lit in fluorescent light, gave everyone a stark, ghostly appearance.

Chewing on his apple, he glanced at the front page. There was mention of violence worsening in Syria. President Hassad was in Damascus meeting with Jordan's King Hussein, regarding the Palestinian uprising in both respective countries. They were both asking for calm. The Palestinians were now a majority in Syria, and exerting some control in Jordan. Fighting had escalated. The Syrian Ambassador to France was just assassinated.

The train arrived at the Judiciary Square Metro stop at 8:23 a.m. There was a certain ritual Alex followed to be relaxed. After getting to the courthouse he would review the motion, briefs and his argument one more time to be thoroughly prepared. Judges sometimes asked off the wall questions which had no bearing on the hearing at hand, but an attorney had to be prepared for any possibility.

"Judge Connally, Thomas Henry is here to see you." There was no response to Marion's page. She looked at the man standing in front of her tidy desk. She was the gatekeeper. The Judge made it clear to her, when she started, no one disturbed him unless she cleared them first with him. No surprises, he would stress.

"It's this phone system," explained Marion. "It's new. I'm not used to it." That was her excuse for any mix-up. It did not matter if she knew something inside out if she was flustered she would make up an excuse.

He shook his head. "I'm in the book, am I not," he declared in his thick southern accent. "I've had this meeting planned for quite awhile now."

"Yes sir." Marion was tight lipped. "I know he's here cause I saw him earlier. He was here at 8:15. I'll try him again." She did not like his rough approach.

"Please do ma'am. That would be greatly appreciated."

Marion pressed the intercom button on her phone. She hung up the receiver. Her phone rang loudly, so she picked up the handset. "Hello? Yes Judge," she paused. "I'm here with Mr. Henry. Unh huh." She nodded her head as she listened. "Okay. Yes, Um hm. Bye."

"Am I ready to go?"

"Yes Mr. Henry. Through that door, down the hall, to the double doors. The Judge will be waiting for you."

"Thanksalot," Henry said in one quick slur.

He followed Marion's directions, to the double wooden doors, which opened up into a very posh, large interior. Berber carpeting, a large mahogany desk, with a high backed burgundy leather chair behind it. One wall was covered with a full legal library. A couch and table were at the opposite end. The view outside was of the Capitol Building, a radiant white, as the morning sun glimmered upon it. Various pictures were of old British horse hunting scenes. The room had an appearance of aristocracy.

"Thomas, it's good to see you. It's been some time," Michael Connally's voice boomed out. He stuck out his hand. Henry returned the gesture. "How about a three day old cup of coffee? Marion hasn't made a new pot yet. Please have a seat over here," he gestured toward the two chairs in the corner of the room separated by a table with a lamp on it. Henry sat down first, then the Judge.

"Michael, I guess we can cut to the chase. Y'all know why I'm here."

"I could guess, but why don't you tell me."

"Who have you contacted, so far?"

"Garrett Baird. He called me and said to expect a visit from you today. He gave me no other details."

"No other details?"

Judge Connally felt uncomfortable with his tone, but glared back. "Nope. Only that you're here for cleanup."

Henry smiled a wide grin. "Well, there y'all go. Y'all say nope, and then y'all add something. Now I'm going ask one more time, Michael." He glared, his nostrils flared. "Are there any other details y'all have gone over?"

"No, nothing else." Michael's voice was more subdued.

"That's more like it. Let's get down to business."

The Federal Courthouse in Washington, D.C. was not unlike any other Federal Court building. Money was not a consideration when it was constructed. Government always took care of its own. Federal judicial positions were for life, so judges were tended to well. Their surroundings had to be more than adequate. When individuals are given life sentences, the government wants to make sure they stay put. The Courthouse was opulent - marble floors and walls throughout. Courtrooms were furnished in mahogany. It was magnificent.

Almost as impressive, but on another spectrum, was the security system installed within the past year. There were two metal detectors to maneuver through. Bags, purses, briefcases or any hand carried item, for that matter, were placed flat on a conveyor belt, moved through a machine, and then X-rayed. Any further suspicions, then packages and people were searched individually. No act of violence had occurred in a D.C. court building since the tax court was fire bombed by Constitutionalists in the mid 1980's. The last time anything exciting happened was in 1969 when an offshoot of the Weathermen held the building hostage, setting a few fires, destroying many files, before the police forced the group into a retreat mode, lobbed in tear gas and then made arrests. Two planned violent acts in twenty years made courts the safest areas to work in Washington.

The added security was from the perceived notion of threats and due to judges believing they were a vitally important and integral part of society. The judges reasoned they were more prone to planned acts of violence than the average person. They suffered from a misconception that people cared about the impact of their rulings. Only individuals affected by their decisions cared what the judicial system was doing. The general population did not have a clue or a concern; most people did not know the name of their local judge, let alone a Federal one.

After passing through security, Alex retrieved his briefcase from the conveyor belt.

"Mr. Westcott." Andy Vassily, the attorney for Adco, approached. He was an impressive figure. Tall, well over six foot four, he stood out in any crowd and was permanently tanned. His dark hair, graying at the temples, was worn slicked back. He exuded confidence, but he was also the reason Alex spent so much of the past week away from his family. The Motion for Summary Disposition was brought by Andy Vassily. He stated they had shown their allegations were true regarding the patent infringement. Vassily further argued there was no material dispute of fact, so they should be granted a Judgment against Ameritrend for an amount exceeding several million. "I was wondering if we could discuss some of the issues with the Judge, prior to my motion. I don't want to prejudice Judge Connally against my client, for if he's inclined not to grant the motion, I'll withdraw the request for consideration, at least until discovery is over, because I feel I can win on the merits." Andy paused, engrossed in thought as to what he should say next. Looking squarely at Alex, he continued. "I also heard you are tight with this Judge. It's obvious the home field advantage goes to you, but if you glanced at today's sports section, you'd see the Redskins were favored, but got trounced. Anything can happen."

Andy was the consummate attorney. He would try to win at any cost. He was not above lying to win and serve his client. The managing partners told Alex, from the case's inception, he was not to be trusted, and everything had to be in writing. Andy Vassily began a new breed of legal practitioner, wanting to win at any cost, with truth and ethics casualties of greed. The practice of law was now akin to guerrilla warfare.

Alex held his brief case up between them. "I'll go back in chambers with you on one condition. If you decide not to go forward with your motion, due to whatever intuition you have, then I want my costs associated with preparing this. This was something you could have decided long before today. I have a telephone, voice mail, email, texting and secretary, yet I don't seem to recall getting a message from you. A considerable amount of time was spent researching your brief. Follow that up with drafting a response and prep time. Plus I had to neglect my wife and kids and now, all of this was something you now tell me I didn't have to do."

"But I. . . ." stammered Andy as he swayed back a little.

"Did I say I was finished?" Alex cut in coldly. "If this is the way you want to handle this case, then I would suggest you march to a different beat, starting now." He paused and looked straight at Andy. "I'll tell you how nice I am going to be. Instead of asking for two times my hourly rate, if you decide not to go through with this motion, I want one and a half my hourly rate, three hundred fifty dollars, at ten hours of prep, and two for today, for a grand total of four thousand two hundred."

Andy was still. After a few moments, they proceeded to the elevators. There was an icy silence as the elevator ascended to the fourth floor. Andy was the first to speak. "How about fifteen hundred?"

Alex laughed. "No way in hell. Don't make me repeat what I said. It stands." They exited the elevator, walking to the end of the hall,

31

where a sign was posted.

AUTHORIZED PERSONNEL ONLY

Alex opened the door leading to the back corridor, Andy followed. The hallway walls were paneled wood. Portraits of preceding jurists lined them, appearing to gaze at each person as he walked past. People swore they could see the eyes move on the portrait of Thomas James Stallworth. He was one of a handful of judges barred from the bench for tax evasion because of accepting bribes. He committed suicide, in chambers, the day before his Senate impeachment hearing. His act allowed his family to continue to receive benefits, with his wife able to maintain his pension. Judge Connally was appointed to replace him.

"Hey, where you going?" A voice boomed, startling them. Alex spun around. It was Gus Peterson, Judge Connally's Bailiff. Gus was old. That was the only way to describe him. He had been a Courthouse fixture for as long as anyone could remember. He was a former professional boxer, back in an age when people participated in the sport due to their love for the action, not for any monetary incentive. Gus had lived a variety of lives, most were hard. He looked considerably older than his years, with a rumpled face, weathered skin and shuffled motion. His knees were damaged long ago, as was his vision, wincing when he would enter brightly lit rooms. His hands dwarfed those of any average person. He was quick with a story and had thousands. He would tell you every one if you let him. You never knew where they would lead, but he would always entertain. Occasionally, if he had an old fight program in hand, the conversation would last even longer. He would flip through showing pictures of himself in his prime, telling stories of other boxers who appeared on the pages with him. Once in a while he would explain about how his wife and only child, a daughter, were both killed in a car accident some twenty-five years earlier. Old Gus seemed to start his shuffle at about that time. He never got over the loss, remaining a widower.

"Hi, Gus," Alex replied. "We're going to see the Judge prior to Mr. Vassily's motion this morning. Do you know if he's in yet?"

"Well, as a matter of fact, he is," Gus said in his loud gruff whiskey voice. "He's meeting with Thomas Henry or Henry Thomas, or some guy whose name sounds like someone I read about. Something' political, you know."

"Yes, I know all about that." It was strange but even though they were in the same political circle, and it was a small group, Alex never heard of anyone named Thomas Henry.

"Well, why don't you see Marion, she'll take it from here," Gus instructed. He turned from them, shuffling down the corridor. "You know where the office is," his voice echoed back.

They walked into the reception area for the Judge's chambers. Marion was pleasant, in her late fifties. She had been the Judge's secretary for the past few years. She was sitting at her desk, sorting through the weekend's mail. She heard them approach and looked up. A smile came quickly across her face. She took an immediate liking toward Alex. She was always helpful whenever he had a question or issue to discuss, getting him back to see the Judge. "Good morning Mr. Westcott," she said. Her formality was ever present out of respect to others. It was something her mother taught her when she was young during a time when others were just as courteous. She was never told about the cold realities of ill-mannered lawyers, though. "The Judge is in a meeting with Mr. Thomas Henry. He asked he not be disturbed, but I'll ring back to let him know you are here." She turned to her telephone.

"No. That's really unnecessary Marion. Mr. Vassily has some questions to ask the Judge, regarding his motion. It may take some time, so it would not be wise to interrupt him."

Andy shifted back and forth, a sign he realized the futility in his request prior to the hearing. "Alex, you know what. I'm not going through with my motion."

"Don't do me any favors."

"Well, I know when the home field advantage will swing the pendulum. I've been there, on both sides. The Summary Disposition will not go my way, since it may be somewhat premature. I'll prepare an order denying the motion, without prejudice, and award you costs as requested. That way I can get out of here and be more productive back at the office."

"That's fine with me," Alex replied, amused by Andy's change in demeanor. "I have an order already prepared, just sign stating you agree with the form and I'll have the Court enter it this morning." He opened his brief case, battered and seasoned from years of use and abuse. When he first got it, it was tan in color, but now it was more of a weathered dark brown, a sentimental favorite. His parents bought it for him when he passed the bar exam and started to practice law. He looked to it as a good luck charm. Alex shuffled through the file and pulled out the folder marked with the heading ORDERS. He was always organized in such a manner. He had a place for everything. He looked through the file and pulled out the prepared order, handing it to Andy. "I haven't filled in the amount yet, so why don't you write it in and initial it. I'll do the same."

Grabbing the order in a hasty manner, Andy placed it on Marion's desk for support, filling in the amount, initialing it, and then signing his name. He left the document on the desk, making no effort to hand it back, and turned to leave. Turning back, he said sternly, "We're not finished yet. I'll see to that," thrusting his long index finger into the air for added emphasis.

As the conversation ensued, escalated, temporarily halted, began again, then ended, Marion appeared to be in her own world. She was active in the civil rights movement of the 1960's. Time, failed of expectations and various personal tragedies left her drained. "Alex, I have to run over to Judge Thomas's chambers. Some mail of ours was delivered there by mistake. If you'd like to wait here until I get back, it won't be a problem. I'll page the Judge to let him know you're here." Before Alex could say it was unnecessary, Marion pressed the intercom button on her telephone. It caused a high-pitched noise, followed by silence. They glanced at each other. "I can't get use to this new phone system," she explained.

"Perhaps Judge Connally put his phone on do not disturb," he said, trying to put her at ease. "When we had our telephone system installed, a while back, I didn't receive a single message for three days."

Marion looked blankly at him. "Well, I'll be back in a few minutes. If Judge Connally comes out and wonders where I am, just let him know about my errand." With that, she got up from her chair, turned quickly on her heels, earrings clinking as she left.

Alex wandered to Marion's desk, where the signed order had been left. He bent over and signed his name. He picked up his briefcase, set it upon her desk, flipped the latches open, and placed the order into its file, until the judge signed it.

"Michael, things need to change."

Instinctively turning toward the door leading into chambers, he noticed it was closed. The next sound came from the speakerphone on the desk. It was the same voice he just heard, but did not recognize. He looked at the phone, as if someone would appear.

"We can't continue on our present course."

The accent was southern, nasal in pitch. Alex tried to envision a mental image of the person talking if he could not see their actual appearance. This started as a child, while listening to the radio and it carried on through to adulthood.

"It's something we've discussed numerous times before. . ."

"I know, I know," Judge Connally interjected.

". . . that the system is breaking down. We've seen it evolve and change course. This is something many people have worked toward, sacrificing their time, ambitions, families and lives for, and now, now we are so close to achieving all our families have pushed for. We are not just discussion ideology here Michael, we are talking about a way of life." His voice was not one of reason, but conviction.

The image conjured up by Alex was that of a man in his late thirties, with the onset of a receding hairline, overweight, as he stereotyped most southern men. He had a mustache and, due to the tenor of his nasal southern accent, he was probably about five feet seven inches tall. He always pictured southern people to be shorter than the average. His manner of speech indicated he was well schooled.

Thomas Henry continued. "The last thing we want to have happen is for Congress to take a protectionist stance toward the world. Especially as to trade and military involvement. Those people don't know what is best for us even if it jumped up and bit'em on the ass. They react with their standard knee jerk manner. Perception and form over substance every time." He paused, to make his point stronger. "We've been placed into these positions to ensure the course continues. The New World Order is bigger than both of us. Y'all and I both know that."

"I'll concede that."

"And if we look to the course taken by President Lawton, if he follows the line as to public sentiment, he will sign protectionist measures placing tariffs and quotas on foreign products, along with pulling back U.S. troops from their commitments overseas. That cannot occur. We've got to straighten out the President, even if it means resorting to past procedures and protocol."

"You know we've tried," Judge Connally began. "Communication with the President has been somewhat nonexistent for the past several months. We have Cutter and Walters on the inside, monitoring. They say he's being influenced by Richard Wheeler."

"Is that so?" Henry asked. "What else have your references told y'all?"

The quick steps of Marion could be heard coming down the corridor. She was humming an unrecognizable, but happy tune. Alex looked for the volume control on the telephone and quickly turned it down. Marion walked in, moving toward her desk where he was standing. She gave him another one of her patented smiles. "Did the Judge come out yet?"

"No. Not yet."

"I don't know what they're talking about, but it must be important. Let me try to page him, to let him know you are here. Hmmm," she said out loud. "It seems the volume is set too low." Marion pressed the intercom button, then picked up her hand set. "Judge Connally, Mr. Westcott is here to see you." There was a slight pause. "Okay. I will tell him. Yes. All right." She placed the phone back in its cradle. "Judge Connally said they are finishing their meeting right now. He'll be with you shortly. Can I get you a cup of coffee?"

"No thanks. I've already had my allotment of caffeine today. No need in wiring me up too much. So what do you know about Thomas Henry?"

"Not much, really. The Judge has been talking to him on and off over the time I've been here. It seems their conversations have become more frequent recently. This is the first time I can remember he has been here. Usually, they meet for lunch or dinner." She looked at Alex, but past him. "I thought you were politically active. Don't you know Mr. Henry?"

"I am somewhat politically active. You know, given the time I have to spend at work, with my family, the occasional workout, not to mention my hockey therapy, I am able to fit politics in, on occasions" he jokingly replied. "But I don't believe I've ever had the opportunity to meet him."

"I was of the belief he was involved in the same scene as Judge Connally. You know, beyond what I care about. I seem to tune those things out."

Several minutes passed before the chamber's door opened. Thomas Henry preceded the Judge from his office. He was not as Alex pictured. In his late twenties, he looked much younger, as though he were waiting for his first shave. His appearance was dark, almost Mediterranean, but with Anglo features. At five foot eleven, he was a little shorter than Alex and there was no girth about him. He was lean and powerful looking. He wore round tortoise shell glasses that gave him a bookish quality.

Usually impeccably dressed, Judge Connally's appearance was disheveled. He looked as though he had been in a hurry this morning. It was unusual for his appearance to be amiss. His tie, always coordinated to his suit, was out of place. His usual starched white shirt had been replaced with a wrinkled blue oxford button down. He looked more like a fraternity member than a jurist. His graying hair was mussed, pushed forward, and in dire need of a comb.

"Good morning, Judge."

"Alex, good to see you. Anyway, I read over the motion and your reply, so I'm ready for arguments. Remember to keep your comments short." That was his way of saying he had already decided. "Before I forget, Alex, I'd like you to meet Thomas Henry."

Henry outstretched his arm toward Alex. They grasped hands and shook firmly. The grip was steady, but not overly assertive. Pressure was an important gauge, the basis of first impressions. Alex worked on his hand strength, by keeping putty around at home, in the car and at the office.

"Nice to meet y'all, Alex."

"Likewise. So, what brings you here?"

"Well, the Judge and I go back a long way," Thomas Henry drawled. "Both of our families are originally from Texas, only Michael stayed away from there once he left. I guess he couldn't stand the heat. Anyway, I was in town on some personal business, so I figured I'd pay my respects."

"That's right," Michael said. "Thomas comes into town once in a while. We talk about our families and brushing up on current events. We enjoy each other's company. The only problem I have with him is his inability to play, or for that matter, not even try hockey. Can you believe he's never even laced up skates? God knows I've tried to get him to do that since he was a kid." He directed his attention toward him. "You know Thomas, you could always join in the ultimate exercise."

"That's just fine," he chuckled. "But I believe I'll stay with those country club sports. Y'all know them as tennis, golf and swimming. Thanks a lot for the offer though."

Alex intoned "If you ever change your mind, I'm sure you'd become addicted to it, like both of us. We try to play four times a month. Wanting to play even more but constraints keep us from doing that."

"I'm too old."

"Nonsense," replied Alex.

"Three things you don't mess with in Texas," he paused and looked at Alex. "A mad steer, a rare steak or sports that originate north of the Mason-Dixon."

"Thomas did you know that Alex is a hero?"

"Really."

"Judge, please." Alex looked down. "Must you always bring this up? It wasn't anything, really."

"No room for modesty here, Alex."

"What did y'all do?" Henry asked.

Alex remained silent, shifting his feet, then straightening his tie.

"Well, he saved Garrett Baird's life," Michael Connally began to explain.

"Really?" Thomas Henry said.

"We were at a fundraiser, and if I didn't see it with my own eyes I wouldn't have believed it, when all of a sudden shots start coming from everywhere. Alex was on the platform with Garrett Baird."

"With Garrett?" Henry asked.

"Yes, with him."

"Do you know him?" Alex asked.

"We're recent acquaintances," Henry replied. "So what happened next?"

"Garrett was shot three or four times, just standing at the podium, when Alex got up the nerve to throw himself into the old man, taking him out of harm's way. He probably saved Garrett's life, plus many others."

"Judge, please. It wasn't all that spectacular. I was just doing what anyone else would have done."

"Did they catch the shooter?"

"No. No one has been caught, but I imagine it's only a matter of time," Judge Connally replied.

"What was the reason for going after Garrett?" Henry asked.

"I suspect it was his economic beliefs," Alex said matter of fact.

"Really?" Judge Connally said as both him and Henry looked at Alex.

Alex continued, "Yes. His political agenda to reignite the economy has caught grass root support. Let's face it, no one was getting more publicity around here recently, than Garrett."

Do y'all believe that would be enough to take someone like Garrett down?"

"Yes I do, especially with the way the economy has been going recently," Alex continued. "In fact, that reminds me. In today's Post, an article indicated President Lawton is leaning toward those protectionist measures supported by Congress. It indicated he was considering tariffs against the European markets, quotas against the Orient and a move to repeal the North American Free Trade Agreement. The reasoning was due to losing jobs, compounded with higher overall inflation here."

"Is that so?" Connally asked.

"Not only that," Alex continued in the same vein, "but the article went onto say much of the statistical numbers being bantered about, supporting the opening of barriers, are wrong or extremely misleading. An example given was that Mexico, on a per capita basis, spends over Five Hundred Dollars per year on U.S. products. Based upon those numbers alone, Mexico should be a debtor nation to us. However, there is always a 'but' with numbers like that, those figures, as supplied by the government and applied to our gross national product, contain items purchased from us, to be used in products manufactured in Mexico. Those finished products are then shipped back to the U.S. for consumers to buy here, at a higher finished price. The same is said to hold true for the Asian markets."

"So what does it matter if trade flows freely between nations and jobs do the same?" Thomas Henry asked.

"We're losing jobs. Higher paying jobs, I might add, to other less developed countries. Look at Mexico. It benefits from free trade with us in the long run, while our benefits are of a short duration. Just look at what happened to Germany and Japan after World War Two. Their economies were destroyed along with much of their infrastructure. We came in and rebuilt them, new. Coupled with that you can't forget Japan's strength. It's not when they improved upon a product they really took off. Anyone can do that. What they had the insight to do was purchase scrap steel, transform the raw material into a finished product and sell it back to us at an extremely high profit."

Thomas slurred, "I still don't see where the problem is."

"Let me go about it another way. As I perceive it, not only do Multi-National Corporations make a bigger profit from cheaper labor costs associated within developing countries, and we can use Mexico here, but Mexico more than makes up for any costs of importing items and the perceived deficit. They can now run a surplus with the U.S., in turn causing us to owe them money. The big companies aren't going to use profits for reinvestment in the U.S., or for paying hard working trade salaries here. All they're going to do is use profits for improving factories and production elsewhere, improving developing countries infrastructure and standard of living, consuming more energy in the process, driving up energy costs, weakening the dollar against other currencies, causing higher unemployment and inflation."

"Don't you have a motion to argue this morning?" Judge Connally tried to interfere and deflect the conversation.

"Not any more Judge. All I need is your signature on a stipulation to dismiss Mr. Vassily's motion, and I am out of here."

"May I suggest if you want me to sign that order, you cease this mode of conversation right now." The Judge frowned. "I thought you were a true Republican, Alex. Complete with the understanding of how our system works. Trade flows freely between nations, with no aid or intervention by government."

His abrupt demeanor took Alex by surprise. He heard part of the conversation between him and Thomas and figured he was in the same mode of argument, however, he was not at all familiar with the New World Order. He thought he could explore the issue in a back door manner with the Judge and Thomas, but he seemed to be getting all sorts of wrong impressions this morning. To stall for a few more seconds, he looked for Marion. She was nowhere to be found, having stepped out during some segment of their conversation. He could not remember when.

"Judge, I guess I just like to play the devil's advocate on occasion. I feel, as a lawyer, who's better suited for that, than I am?" All three laughed.

"I better be going or I won't make my appointment," Henry said to them. He then held out his hand to Alex. "It was nice to meet y'all. Maybe I'll see y'all around sometime soon. A real life hero, huh. Not that I get to meet one."

"It was nice to meet you too. If I had known you would have such an adverse reaction to what I was discussing this morning, I wouldn't have brought it up. One more thing Thomas, remember the press is extremely liberal in its outlook. I was just talking about what was written in this morning's Post. You know, conversation for the sake of conversation."

Saying nothing more, Thomas turned and faced Judge Connally, cutting Alex off from making any more statements. "Michael, it was nice to see y'all this morning. I'm sorry for such short notice. Next time it will be lunch, my treat. Remember, get back to me on what we were discussing."

"No problem. Say hi to your family."

"I will." Henry turned and left the outer office, leaving the Judge and Alex alone.

There was an uneasy quiet between them for a few moments until Judge Connally spoke. "Alex, it's somewhat difficult for me to get on the bench if I don't have a secretary to get me organized and going in the morning. Where is that order you wanted me to sign?"

Alex opened his briefcase, which was still on Marion's desk. He took out the order Andy and he had signed, handing it to the Judge. Connally looked over the stipulated order, laughed to himself and then looked up at Alex.

"How did you manage to get him to agree to all of this?"

"It's my subtle persuasion, Judge. I demonstrated this morning with you and Henry," Alex grinned.

"That's Thomas, Thomas Henry."

"I stand corrected, your Honor. I will not let that happen again. You know, the more I've been involved in this political game, the better able I am at remembering names. I figure if you have two first names, using one as your last, then they should be interchangeable. That would save a lot of confusion and embarrassment."

"You still didn't answer my question Alex. What got Mr. Vassily to withdraw his motion and pay you costs?"

"Well Judge, it seems Mr. Vassily was of the impression I had the home field advantage and he may have been untimely in bringing his motion."

"I see. What gave him that impression?"

"Just some rumors were circulating that you and I are involved in the same political things, plus we share the same affinity for hockey, including playing together on occasion."

"I believe that, as a judge, I try to leave the impression I'm impartial, that there is no impropriety. I've done that. Respecting Mr. Vassily's motion, I was going to deny it today, since discovery has not been completed. He really should have known better. I feel you may have gotten the better of him though. He should have stayed and argued the motion anyway because, even though I would deny it, I wouldn't have awarded that much."

"How much?"

"Maybe one quarter of the amount."

"Really? Why?"

"We are a litigious society and, if you didn't respond, then Mr. Vassily would be sitting with a judgment this morning, collecting from your client and the docket would be cleared by one more case. However, this forces both of you to proceed with discovery expeditiously. It's part of the process"

"Judge, I am not trying to change subjects here, but are you going to play the charity hockey game on October Fifteenth?"

"You mean for the Battlin' Barristers, when they take on the NHL old timers?"

"Yes sir."

"I signed up for it. I like playing in those charity games. I may have lost a step or two from my younger days, but I figure they have too."

The UN was to be the government of the brave new world; the mistakes of 1919 would not be repeated. Because of the United Nations, so carefully established before the war had ended, there would be no muddle and descent into international anarchy such as had marked the two decades after the armistice of 1918.

American Diplomacy

CHAPTER FOUR
SEPTEMBER 16TH

It had been a few months since Alex had seen Bill Weylyn. They quickly became friends during their college days at George Washington University, during their freshmen year while rooming on the same floor in Strong Hall. Bill telephoned Alex on the afternoon of the 12th, to reminisce about old times and catch up on what was new. Plans were soon set to meet at 6:00 p.m., at their old stomping grounds, the Tune Inn. It was a quirky bar located near the Capitol, on Pennsylvania Avenue between Third and Fourth Streets, in the Southwest quadrant of the City. The City is divided into four sections. The Northwest quarter is where George Washington University, the White House, the State Department and numerous government buildings were located. Northeast contains the Capitol, Gallaudet and Catholic University. Southeast comprises, mainly, middle and lower income families.

They first experienced the Tune Inn during their sophomore year. Upper classmen showed them various nightspots to try out and it was one of those places. It was there where Bill earned his nickname, Sniper. It came about during one of their drunken sojourns when several of the ever present, but now forgotten, group of college youths noticed Bill's capacity for finding a female in the crowd, moving in on her and then coming back to the dorm the next day talking about his conquest. His accuracy in obtaining what he sought was always impressive.

The name stuck through college, then law school, and even with him to his present position as a special agent with the FBI. When he was in training, however, his nickname was believed to be from his accuracy at the range. Only his true friends, those present on that evening, so many years before, knew for sure.

Running late, Alex tried to phone Sniper at the FBI headquarters where he was working on an assignment, but he was in a meeting. Laurel approved of their friendship. Sniper was part of Alex's world before her and she encouraged her husband to see him whenever their schedules permitted. Alex phoned home to remind her of his plans. "Hi honey. How are you this beautiful day?"

"Hi," she replied. "What a pleasant surprise to hear from you."

"Just a reminder that I'm meeting Sniper."

"I know and you better behave yourself. Remember what happened last time. You were hung-over for two days, complaining of the cigar taste in your mouth."

"I learned my lesson."

"When you two get together you behave just like children. Will you ever grow up?" Laurel mockingly chastised her husband.

"It's all his fault," Alex joked. "He's the demon seed. I'm only along for the ride."

"I don't know about that. Sometimes I think it's you who is the bad influence and causes things to happen."

"I promise it won't be a late night,"

"Right, I know about that promise, I've heard it before, Alex. Just go out, have fun, and call me if you're going to stay in the City."

Alex appreciated it when she encouraged him to let off some steam. Her response to him spending time on political happenings was always more reserved. Laurel was of the impression politics made him uptight. She sensed there was something wrong with him all week and thought it was due to the fund-raiser.

"I'll see you later."

"Good-bye, and be careful."

"I will." Alex hung up the phone.

It was closer for Sniper to be at the bar, since he could forgo the traffic, and walk from the J. Edgar Hoover Building to the Tune Inn. Alex glanced at his watch as he left his office. It was 5:50 p.m. He closed his office door and proceeded down the hallway toward the firm's reception area. The building was empty for a Friday. The firm's staff always made it a point to leave quickly. Even attorneys would endeavor to schedule appointments outside of the office at around 3:00 on Fridays. That way they could abandon going back. The only one present, apparently, was the receptionist.

"Good night, Mr. Westcott."

"Good night, Sara. Have a great weekend. What time are you out of here?"

"6:00, sir," she said.

"Is there anyone here to accompany you out?" The firm issued a new office policy that came about because of an increase in assaults around the building. It was nothing to be concerned about, the memo said, however, there should always be two people leaving when the office closes for the night. The last attorney present had to make sure the clerical staff was cleared from the office. Senior partners were concerned about liability. They wanted to provide a secure environment to work in and it was believed this new policy would protect employees the best way possible.

"Yes. Mr. Colton's still here. He said he'd walk me to the Metro."

"That's good. I'll be going then." Alex was relieved. It meant he would not be too late. It had been a long week. He had not had a decent night's sleep in some time. Tossing and turning throughout the night, then getting out of bed at three or four in the morning and going downstairs to read the paper or watch TV, He was looking forward to unwinding. As he left the building, he welcomed a beautiful, warm, and clear evening. Mindful of the time and mission he was on, he hailed a cab. The taxi, with him situated inside, set off.

Twenty-five minutes later, they pulled up to the bar, packed with Friday night regulars. Those out this early were weekend venerators, a religion onto itself. Alex knew about it firsthand. He was a member of that crowd once before, a long time ago.

Three forces immediately assaulted his senses, as he opened the door. First was the noise. The crowd was loud, festive. No one seemed depressed, for if they were, the alcohol and atmosphere wore away everyone's worries. Alex then noticed how strong the smoke was. It gave the room a faint appearance. This bar was the last bastion of unadulterated smoking. Passive smoking was not an option. If you were there, you were smoking. Clean air did not exist. The patrons felt if you did not like it, then you could leave. That summed up how the regulars felt about personal choices too. No one should interfere with anyone's life. Self-centered and ill-mannered was Alex's impression. Finally, one could not help but feel the warmth generated by all of the bodies. The togetherness of people created a moist heat.

Taking a deep breath, he worked his way into the bar. It seemed much smaller than the last time he was here. The giant tuna was still hanging above the bar. The music was old rock and loud. The wait staff seemed cantankerous and old as ever. Those items did not change. The essence of its personality was intact. Near the center of the bar was Sniper, standing. He waived Alex over to him, trying to direct him through the maze of people congregated about. He had a beer in front of him and another one in an outstretched hand in Alex's direction. Sniper had a presence. He was taller than Alex, at 6'2", with fair characteristics, sandy blond hair, steel blue eyes and chiseled facial features. The FBI kept him in great shape. Working out was not only encouraged, it was mandated. Each agent had to pass a yearly physical. Alex was never in doubt that, by just looking at him, Sniper would hit the mark.

"Talk about a mob scene," Alex said as he grabbed the cold beer from Sniper's hand. He yelled above the din, "Snipe, you old dog. I couldn't help but notice you standing here alone. I figured if I were late you would be heading out the door with some chick at your side, making up some excuse about how you had a big covert operation to get back to."

"Well, if there were a babe at my side, it would be an undercover investigation, not covert. How many times do I have to explain that?" Sniper shouted back. "Alex, it's good to see you. It's been too long." He held up his beer to Alex's. "Cheers!"

"Cheers," Alex returned, clinking bottles together. They took long drinks.

Sniper continued, "Since I've been in D.C. for the past month, I've been meaning to get together, but I just haven't had the time. Sorry. You know how the Agency is, you marry it instead of someone else."

"There's less agony that way," Alex replied. "Besides, I am sure Hoover wouldn't have wanted it any other way." They both laughed.

"Yea. Hoover liked his boys. That's why the agency was always all men."

"Yes he did, however, I hope no one is listening to your unfriendly remarks Snipe."

"You never know." Sniper burst into a loud laugh, adding to the roar around them. "I think it's time for another beer. Your treat Alex, I may get to play James Bond occasionally, but the pay sucks. It's nowhere near what a partner in a prestigious Washington law firm makes."

"How about a shot?"

"Sure. Make it something I can tolerate. I can't do tequila or that liquid heroin stuff anymore."

"Boy, you are getting old. I find it hard to believe we're the same age. Please don't let me down," Alex stated before he ordered two more beers and kamikazes.

"Here's to old times," Sniper shouted as he raised his shot glass, spilling some as he did.

"And to new times. May nothing and no one stand between them," Alex finished.

Both downed the sour dose in one gulp. "Boy, was that smooth. I hope my liver can process this stuff like the old days." Sniper paused, smiled. "Remember the time you got us kicked out of that bar in Georgetown when we were in undergrad? What was it called?"

"Must you always bring this up?"

"Com'on Alex. What was it?"

"If you must know, the place was called Slide One By. You had to launch yourself down a slide to get in. That's how they determined if you were sober enough to be there."

Sniper laughed, "Most times we weren't."

"And, by the way, I must correct you. You got us kicked out. I was just an innocent bystander. You kept dropping your beer bottles."

"Only after the ten shots of whiskey," Sniper added.

"Between us. You wanted to drink your last beer before they threw us out."

"It was the principle."

"And I stood up for your right to do that and, as I was slurring my words telling the bouncers to let you finish your beer," Alex acted drunk, swaying from side to side and over emphasizing his gestures. "You dropped your beer. Glass shattered everywhere. The bouncers grabbed our arms, thrusting them behind our backs and then kicked us

51

out into the middle of M Street."

"Ah yes, the good ol' days. Sometimes, they seem just like yesterday. Are you sure about that incident, though? I don't quite remember it that way, but who am I to argue. You're the one with the memory." Alex was one to remember details. He could recite cases and dates with no problem. Law school came easier for him than it did for Sniper. Sniper was more of a generalist with his memory, form over substance.

They had been at the bar for over three hours and still, there was no sign of the crowd letting up. People jammed all around them. There was a definite party atmosphere existing. "Look at this place," Alex said. "Are the stars, planets and moon all lined up to cause this phenomena, or has it been so long since I was out without Laurel that I'm just caught up in the excitement?"

"Speaking of which, how's your lovely wife doing?" Sniper asked above the noise.

"What?" Alex asked not hearing the question. He was letting his mind wander to all of the surrounding commotion.

"Your wife. Laurel and the boys. How are they?"

"They're all doing just fine. I haven't been able to spend as much time with the boys, but with work, hockey every other week, and dabbling in politics, something has to suffer, and right now it is the family. We are thinking of going to Florida over Thanksgiving, to spend time with the in-laws. That should give me some time with my little guys, and I don't mean it as Hoover would."

"Yea. Right. That should be fun."

"The boys are getting so much bigger now. How long has it been since you've seen them?"

"I think it was before I left D.C., for an assignment in Topeka. I guess it would have been about fifteen months ago."

"You wouldn't recognize them now. They've gotten so much bigger. Christian's six. He follows his older brother around and mimics whatever he does. They are really into the Night Warriors. It doesn't matter what type, they just like that ancient armor coupled with lasers and Merlin Magic stuff. Jeremy is somewhat temperamental, though. He throws himself into everything he does, at least one hundred and ten percent."

"I wonder where he got that from." Sniper asked facetiously. "He sounds just like you. Whenever something interests you, you pursue it until you've worn it out. Then, you find something else to turn your attention toward."

"Bull."

"Seriously?" Sniper asked.

"Seriously," replied Alex.

"Let's start with college. When you liked something you stuck with it until you mastered it, then you'd move on. Your major. You started in Political Science, until you felt you knew it all, and then you moved to Economics. How many people have a double major. Plus you minored in Art History. That's not altogether easy. We then move onto your dating life. No one really interested you until you met Laurel. The pursuit was relentless. There was also the legal aid program you ran while in law school, to help the underprivileged. Once you got tired, look out corporate world - associate to partner in record time, then. . . ."

"Okay, okay. Enough, enough. I believe you. You make me sound much brighter than I thought was possible," he chuckled. "Maybe I should watch over Jeremy a little closer. I don't want my clone running around, looking for a better way of anything."

"You better keep an eye on him."

"So Snipe. What do you feel like doing? Do you want to stay here or head somewhere else?"

Sniper glanced at his watch. It was 9:30 p.m. "Alex, before we make that decision, there's something I have to tell you." Alex looked downhearted. "Don't go puppy dog on me. I just have to get up early tomorrow. I have an important meeting at Headquarters, 8:30 sharp. I've been staying in Reston, and the commute could take a while. I guess what I am trying to say is, I can't get too drunk tonight."

"Why don't we stay downtown at the firm's apartments? I signed it out for tonight, just in case things got too out of control. I have to phone Laurel and everything will be fine."

"If that's the case, then let's get out of here, get a bite to eat, and if I'm in bed by midnight, I'm there."

"Why don't we grab a cab, get a six pack, order a pizza and head to the condo. It would be nice to get out of crowds and smoke."

"Smoke still bothers you?"

"I truly believe it has only gotten worse with age. So how about it? Shall we order a pizza and get some beer?"

"Sounds like a plan."

They made their way out of the bar, excusing themselves past the sea of bodies. Once outside, everything seemed extremely quiet, except for the high pitched ringing noise Alex heard. He took a deep breath, to clear his lungs, then rubbed his eyes, trying to get relief from the smoke induced dryness. "It feels good to breathe fresh air."

"Not that the quality went up," Sniper said.

"Yes, but the diffusion is greater."

They hailed a cab to take them back to 1212 New Hampshire Avenue.

"I don't know what it is, but I don't like the feel of this Henry." Garrett Baird took a long sip from his scotch. He kept a few cubes of ice in his mouth to temper the drink. "He's come highly recommended, his credentials are beyond reproach, but I don't know, damn it. Something's not right."

"I imagine that's why I'm here."

"Can't slide one past you, eh, Michael." He laughed. His body rippled up and down.

"So, what's your question?"

"Don't grow impatient with me. I've been around far too long for you to have an attitude like that. While you're knowledge is important remember I am the one who showed you the ropes. Do you understand what I am telling you?"

"Yes," Michael Connally replied.

"I want to know if this boy can be trusted."

"I would trust him."

"With your life?" glared Garrett.

He thought about it for a little while, not wanting to overreact to the question, for one could never tell what Garrett was up to. "Yes."

Garrett looked for a sign of wavering. "We'll see."

"What do you have him doing right now?"

"Just some preliminary work. I want to see if he can walk before I have him run."

Connally nodded.

"Can I freshen up your drink before company arrives?"

"No thanks. I'll wait."

"Suit yourself." Garrett went to the bar and poured himself another glass.

The cab approached the entrance to 1212, a six story, rust colored brick, seasoned, but stately building. Expense was no object when the conversion took place. The lobby was plush.

Sniper looked at the building as they exited curbside from the taxicab. "This doesn't compare to the type of places I get put up in. You can tell it's bad when rooms are rented by the hour."

"Good evening, Mr. Westcott," Raul, dressed as though he belonged in the eighteenth century British army, said as he opened the door.

"Good evening, and good night, Raul," Alex greeted. "When the pizza gets here, please send it up. We've already called."

"Yes sir, Mr. Westcott," came the reply.

They proceeded to the elevator, beer in hand. "Hit six," said Alex.

Once inside the condo, Sniper sat down on one of the couches that were directly across from the other, in the living room. "Catch," Alex said as he tossed him a beer, without warning. Sniper grabbed it with one hand. Out of their past experiences, he knew exactly where it would be.

"Thanks."

Alex went to the kitchen and placed the remaining beer in the refrigerator, which was void of anything else. He came back to the living room. Just then, there was a knock at the door.

"Ten to one it's the pizza guy." Sniper said.

Alex opened the door. "What kind of bet would that be to take?"

"A good one for me."

"Pizza," said the young delivery person. "It'll be fourteen seventy-five," he added as he gave the box to Alex.

Alex handed him a twenty. "Here you go. Keep the change." He shut the door, setting the pizza on the coffee table between them. "Need any napkins or plates?" Alex asked.

"Napkins would be nice."

On the second try, Alex found the cupboard where they were kept. "Is there anything else you'd like me to get while I'm up?" he called.

"No thanks, I'm all set."

"Give me a minute and let me call Laurel, so she won't worry. I'll be right back."

"Okay."

Several minutes later, Alex emerged from the kitchen. "Laurel said to say hi."

"Was she okay?"

"She wasn't upset, especially when she found out we were not out gallivanting about."

"Bless her. Give her my love when you see her tomorrow. We all must get together sometime soon. My treat. I'll behave and even bring a respectable date."

"Like that'll ever happen. It'll be about the same time as hell freezes over."

Alex turned on the stereo with a flick of a button, which also caused the lights to dim. "Like that?" Alex laughed.

"You know, today's technology is truly amazing. You'd be astounded at what we can do," Sniper replied.

"Such as?"

"Personally, I am not at liberty to say. You never know when I may need your services. But if you want to know, off of the record, we have developed a device for decoding computer language over the Internet. I've been working with that lately."

"What?" Alex asked incredulously.

"Computers are the avenue for criminal activity. I'll even preface that with 'The Biggest Current' criminal activity taking place today is through the use and manipulation of computers. The technology is outpacing our ability to monitor events. So much happens with computers. We virtually have no control over them. Their activity is very difficult to detect. Even if you pick up the output source of a computer being transferred over the phone, you can't decipher what is being transferred."

"Tell me what activity we are talking about. How much criminal activity can take place by computer?" Alex interrupted. "Where's the harm?"

"Where do you want me to start? Let's start with pornography, including child pornography, being transmitted by computers via the telephone lines. We're not only talking about the written word here either, but pictures and movies. We'll follow that up with the old standard, gambling, betting, whatever you want to call it. Then there's the white-collar crime of corporate espionage. A new trend of criminal activity. Drug trafficking has become extremely sophisticated and mobile through computer usage. It keeps track of shipments, suppliers, dealers and users. I'll finish all of this off with credit card fraud. Telephone calling cards, credit cards, the same old stuff which once had to be transacted in person is now made easy and impersonal. Couple this all with the understanding that criminal networks are established nationwide. Plus, through fiber optic transmission, you can't overhear conversations anymore. Wiretaps don't work. And if you delay the computer transmissions to decode them, it raises suspicions immediately."

"Jesus. I never realized it was so extensive. What steps or measures are needed to stop this?"

"This is pretty classified Alex, but since I've known you for most of my life, and I've run a background on you." There was a slight pause.

Seeing no reaction from Alex, Snipe continued. "Just kidding. This goes no further, though. All new computers have been modified so they come with a special chip encoded in them. It allows us to pick up computer transmissions and decode them while they are being transmitted over the phone lines. It's accomplished without delaying the transmission. It is amazing. We have developed technology to monitor about ten percent of all computer transmissions, to look for key words. Once we pick up on it, we record the transmission, trace the call and build our case."

"No shit? That's incredible Snipe. Here I am a lowly attorney. . ."

"So am I," Sniper corrected him. Alex and Sniper had followed the same educational path. Undergrad at the George Washington University, followed by three years of law school at Georgetown. Only then did their career paths diverge. Alex went into the private sector and Sniper entered public service under the tutelage of the FBI.

". . . just arguing for certain equities in the existence of a corporation. Motions to enforce orders," Alex said as he waived his beer about in front of himself. "Always getting stressed out about an upcoming trial, which never occurs? Yet, there you are, James Fucking Bond!"

"Now, now," Sniper cautioned Alex with a laugh. "So, what's been bothering you lately. I don't talk to you for a while, and here you are, all depressed. What's up?"

"It really isn't anything. It's probably more of my active imagination than any manifestation of a psychosis. But since we're on this, let me ask you a question." He took a bite of pizza, washed it down with his beer, then continued. "Have you ever heard of the New World Order?"

"In what way?"

"Well, I'm not really sure it exists. My knowledge of it is limited. I remember studying world history and current events while in school, twenty years ago, but, in spite of that, I have no recollection of learning about a World Order. I was sort of wondering if it's somewhat new. Have you heard of it?"

"To be honest with you Alex, I don't recall whether I have heard of the term. I suppose I could theorize what it means, though."

"I could do that, too, Snipe. I thought, maybe, you'd know more about it than I do."

"How did you come across this?"

"I've heard it mentioned on occasion, you know, fanatic talk radio stuff. Never anything in detail, but brief references here and there. I would say more subconscious memory than anything else. Then this past Monday, I was talking with a judge, and we got into a heated conversation about the New World Order, its strengths and underlying currents. He even accused me of not being in the true Republican mode of freedom and capitalism. I couldn't argue the points with him, especially since I didn't know what I was arguing. I was arguing for the sake of argument, trying to provoke more information from him."

"Flush the bushes, much in the same way as Professor Lear," Sniper said.

"Yes."

"When in a position of unfamiliarity, turn the situation around with a question, to get your answer. Use the Socratic method," they recited in unison.

"It's the one thing I remember from Lear's class," Alex said.

"I still use that advice on a regular basis."

"I did discover a couple of things, though," Alex said. "It seems this force has been around for some time. I believe it was created within the United States and, based upon this judge's reaction, I would guess it is well entrenched within our social structure."

"What do you mean?"

"How much more basic can I be, Snipe. Here is a well entrenched and highly respected judge."

"What kind?"

"Federal. One appointed for life. The kind that doesn't have to play the political game anymore, or try for reelection. He has no constituents, or for that matter, other attorneys to be accountable to. He's set, detached from the real world. But in the same instance, he must be, or should be in favor of maintaining the status quo. He would want to keep his power base. To make it simple, he isn't going to belong to any radical organizations. He's not going to be an extremist."

"Well, what else did he say?"

Alex took a sip of beer, then placed the crust of his pizza in his mouth. He continued talking while he chewed. "He intimated the New World Order has been around for quite some time, and its purpose is to maintain and expand the global position of the United States."

"What's his name?"

"Michael Connally."

"Did he say anything else?"

"That's about as much as I could get from him. He abruptly stopped the conversation. His entire mood changed drastically. I have spent some time with him, personally, and I have never seen him react in such a manner." Alex grabbed another slice of pizza. "Oh, yea."

"What?" Sniper asked.

"There was someone else there, too. All of this drinking made me almost forget."

"Who?"

"His name was Henry, Thomas Henry, supposed to be very politically active, from Texas, yet I never heard of him before."

Sniper got up from the couch and headed toward the kitchen. "I think we're getting too deep here about nothing." He turned and faced

Alex from the kitchen doorway. "How about joining me in another beer? My treat."

"Sure," Alex responded in an unresolved voice.

As he returned, Sniper handed Alex a beer, and sat next to him on the couch. "Look Alex. If you want my opinion, I don't think anything is there. And while this New World Order may exist, it's probably nothing more than a term placed upon a belief. I don't think it's a movement of any kind within the United States, or I would have heard of it. Subversive stuff within the U.S.? I'm in charge of investigating it, you know."

Alex laughed casually. "Yes, I suppose it's true. Maybe I'll do some research on it. You know, just to see what we're talking about."

"It's getting late. I have an early day tomorrow, so I'll head to bed. I hope the boss doesn't recognize the same clothes, though."

"Don't worry. The bedrooms are stocked with some suits, shirts and ties for just that occasion. Help yourself. Your bedroom is down the hall to the right, I'll take the one to the left. And Snipe. . . ."

"Yes?"

"If you need anything else, just let me know."

Sniper got up from the couch and proceeded toward the bedroom. He turned back. "Don't worry about anything. I'm sure there is nothing there. Sometime this week I'll investigate a little as to this New World Order thing. Once I come up with something, I'll let you know."

"Thanks, Snipe. Goodnight."

Sniper turned back, heading to the bedroom. Alex took another slug of beer and rested his head against the back cushion of the couch, hoping he would soon tire.

The United Nations is the creation of appropriate international machinery with power adequate to establish and to maintain a just and lasting peace, among the nations of the world.

Representative J. William Fulbright
Fulbright Resolution (September 21, 1943)

CHAPTER FIVE
SEPTEMBER 24TH

It was 6:45 a.m. as Sniper finished reviewing some detailed reports at the FBI headquarters. He was exhausted after spending the past twenty-two hours working his detail. As he got up from his desk, he looked at a note he had written to himself a week earlier.

NEW WORLD ORDER - ALEX/MICHAEL CONNALLY/THOMAS HENRY

"Shit," Sniper said as he logged onto the FBI's computer system, a vast network of confidential information, acquired from decades of investigations from within and outside of our shores.

ACCESS CODE:

He typed

23425122514

The screen showed, instantaneously,

WILLIAM WEYLYN

FBI ID 23425122514

LOGIN TIME 06:49

SEPTEMBER 24

PRESS ENTER FOR MENU

Sniper moved the cursor and hit **MAIN MENU**. From there he selected **GENERAL INFORMATION**. The system was set up so if one word was entered, describing the information desired, then the computer program would access any listing which contained the material. The more words entered, the research became expanded, more focused. Sniper entered

NEW

The screen showed

--1257493672 FILES

Then he added

WORLD

--481239 FILES were listed

ORDER

--31246 FILES

Sniper then re-entered the words as

NEW/WORLD/ORDER

That informed the computer the information desired had to do with those three words in consecutive order, not interspersed throughout any report.

--375 FILES

He pressed **CONTROL/ENTER** on the keyboard. General Tract Information was listed. He highlighted and clicked open the file.

The New World Order is a general term, referencing a perceived political movement taking place throughout the world. This belief is unfounded, with no substantiation of a movement to a world government; however its concept is postulated upon the idea that industrialists, bankers, philanthropists and politicians support the position [of a one world government] to best maximize resources and to raise every individual's standard of living. The United Nations has long been rumored to be the means by which this

objective is to be accomplished. Recent mention of a New World Order was pronounced by President George Bush in a State of the Union Address. His reference was to the pecking order of countries. With the dominance of Asia and the demise of the Soviet Union and Eastern Europe, there was a new political order. Strength had weakened in one area of the World, while increasing elsewhere. No inference was made that the U.S. subject itself to a consortium government.

Sniper checked on Judge Michael Connally. He clicked the cursor over to the prompt, typing

MICHAEL CONNALLY, FEDERAL JUDGE, DISTRICT OF COLUMBIA

Pressed **ENTER**. The screen flashed.

ACCESS INFORMATION DENIED - NO AUTHORIZATION

"How about this?"

THOMAS HENRY, REPUBLICAN, TEXAS

He moved the cursor to **ENTER** and clicked. The screen flashed.

ACCESS INFORMATION DENIED - NO AUTHORIZATION

The monitor went blank. "No shit. What's wrong with this damn thing?" Sniper stared at his black screen.

"Where are you going at this hour?" Laurel complained. "How many weekends are you going to be away?"

"I promise this will be it for a while."

"Alex, today's Jeremy's soccer game."

"I'll be back before then. That's why I have to get going now, bright and early, before the boys are up," he explained.

"Let me guess, the Ameritrend case."

"I just have some research to complete on it. I'll be home before noon, in time for Jeremy's game." He did not want to tell her he was going to the Library of Congress. There would be too many questions. Ameritrend Chem Company had cases pending in New York, Texas and California. Alex was heading up the litigation in D.C. and San Francisco. A lot of preparation and research had yet to be completed, but not today.

"Are you sure that's it? You seem preoccupied."

"Just thinking about the case, nothing more." Alex pushed her hair back off of her forehead then kissed her on the cheek. There was something more to the conversation he had with Judge Connally and Thomas Henry. It nagged at him. It was intuition, but it was something he was usually right about. He set aside some time to undertake a little investigation. Sniper had not yet called him. Maybe there was nothing there and he read too much into the conversation. He wanted to do some preliminary research on his own. What better place to begin than the Library of Congress. If there was nothing there, then the New World Order did not exist.

"I'll see you in a few hours. I promise." One aspect of the Library of Congress worried him. He had never mastered the card catalogue system in college. Research was always difficult. Now, with millions and millions of books and articles to sort through, Alex believed the task would not only be intimidating, but like finding a needle in a haystack.

"You better be or you'll have some pretty big explaining to do."

Approaching the Library of Congress in his MG, with the top down, the weather called for it, he found a parking space within two blocks of the entrance. As with most landmarks in the Capitol, Alex no longer needed a map to find his way. He knew, innately, where places were. He parked the car, acknowledging this as a sign of something good, a day better than anticipated.

He locked the steering column, shut his door and then started in the direction of the Library. As he approached the main entryway, the majestic beauty of the building was evident. He gazed at the copper dome, aged to a distinct green appearance. It was one of many architectural marvels that existed within the City. He paced himself up the marble steps surrounding the building. The bronze doors were big, imposing. They were constructed that way to show the importance of knowledge. Doors, like knowledge, are difficult to open, but once inside, you are exposed to so many new and exciting realms. He grasped the handle and pulled. It opened grudgingly. Alex took four steps inside the atrium, stopping as the door closed behind him. Adjustment to the dim light took a few moments.

During all of his years of living in Washington and the surrounding area, he had been to the Library of Congress only once, and that was as a youth. He never had a need or desire to go. Any past research project was handled through school libraries, and now through the firm's legal library or computer hookup to their legal information provider.

He took a few more steps forward. Each stride caused an echo throughout the atrium. He looked above, to the massive ornate dome, with its subdued lighting, then down. The marble floor had a geometric pattern to it. Different colored tape ran in every direction. He stopped at the information booth, situated away from the main flow of traffic.

"May I help you?" a young man asked.

"I don't quite know where to start."

"Well, The Library of Congress contains more than just books, millions and millions, it also has a film archive, historical artifacts, music and other items pertaining to our nation's history. The entry way is also an exhibition hall, giving the history behind the Library and its various collections."

"It's like an historical cultural menagerie," Alex replied.

"Pardon?"

"Nothing." He glanced at the diagram behind him. "How about the main reading room. It seems like as good as a place to start as any."

"Follow the blue line through those doors over there," he instructed.

"Thank you." Alex looked along the floor and saw the blue tape leading in the direction of two smaller glass doors, about fifty feet away. He strolled by the cases and various exhibits, following the blue line as he did. A group of scouts were being told about the history of the building. Their young eyes wide with awe, amazed at the world and all it has to offer. Alex remembered that time in his life. He would take the world on. It was his oyster and there was nothing to stand in his way for fame and success. Anything could be his if he worked hard for it, was constantly impressed upon him by his teachers and parents. He soon came to realize success took more than hard work and intelligence. It also took connections and luck.

MAIN READING AREA

He opened the door and walked toward the main desk. A woman, somewhat older than him, was looking down, shuffling some books around as he approached. "Excuse me." Alex interrupted her concentration. She looked up, tilting her head somewhat forward, which enabled her eyes to peer over her half reading glasses fastened around her neck with a chain. "I need to do some research and I was wondering if you could direct me to the card catalogue." He smiled.

"Sir, we no longer use the card catalogue system here, as you may have known it," came her snide reply.

"Well then, how do I go about it?" Alex was slightly taken aback.

"Here is a form which explains what needs to be done." She

handed a one-page sheet of canary yellow paper to him. He glanced at the document marked **LIBRARY OF CONGRESS - USER FRIENDLY**.

"We have moved our catalogue system to computers. Now we are prepared for the twenty first century." The librarian continued, "With the vast number of material we get here on a daily basis, the only way we can keep track of everything is to be computerized. They are a godsend."

Alex looked at her then back to his paper.

"The computers are to your left, against the back wall. If you need to see some material, just fill out the request sheet, bring it back here and we'll get you those items. If you have any questions, please refer to your form." She looked back down and sorted through the stack of books again.

"Thank you for all your help," Alex said as he headed toward the bank of computers which emitted an eerie green glow. He had his choice of over thirty computers. He sat down at a terminal somewhat to the left of the grouping.

"I think I'll start with that last item there." Alex typed **NEWWORLDORDER.GENE**

He punched the enter key and waited, not knowing what to expect. The screen had a slight flash. Two entries were listed.

NEW WORLD ORDER

HARROLD WILLIS, AUTHOR

FOREIGN QUARTERLY NEWS

APRIL 1973

VOL. 132/SPRING ISSUE/PAGE 275

NEW WORLD ORDER REVISITED

HARROLD WILLIS, AUTHOR

FOREIGN QUARTERLY NEWS

APRIL 1986

VOL. 184/SPRING ISSUE/PAGE 114

The Foreign Quarterly News was familiar to Alex. Various politicians, professors and ambassadors would express their perception about political, military, social and economic developments and changes in the world. The Quarterly, well respected, was still being published.

Alex pulled a request slip from a box attached to the side of the computer. He filled it out. He went back to the main counter. The librarian took his request.

"This will take a few minutes," she informed him. "Publications older than five years are stored on microfilm. Those machines are to your left." She pointed with her crooked index finger to an area immediately to his left.

Alex turned his head and saw the machines she was indicating. He turned back and watched as the librarian typed some numbers into the computer. She looked up and seemed to scrutinize Alex. He turned away from her glare and looked around the vast building. It was incredible to conceive of all of these vast resources, knowledge and information that anyone has access to. That, and it is provided free.

"Here you are," she said as she handed him the film. "I need an ID to hold onto while you have this checked out."

He took out his wallet, a black Coach breast billfold. It was a Christmas present from his children. He opened it and handed her his driver's license.

She took the license, looking it over closely. "It's a good picture of you Mr. Westcott. Not too many people smile. It will be here when you finish."

Alex walked to the viewer. He threaded the film through the sprockets, and then felt around the side of the machine for the on switch. He flicked it back. The projector came to life.

"Time to sort the mail." Alex spun the hand crank, moving the microfilm along. He stopped the film, focused the machine. He was still in the Winter issue. Alex continued to unwind the film, stopping after a sufficient amount of film had been exposed. Spring issue 1973, page 211 appeared on the screen. He gave the crank two quick spins then slowed the film speed down to a crawl.

"Page 272, Page 273, Page 274, Page 275. That's what I've been looking for."

THE NEW WORLD ORDER

By Harrold Willis

The bottom of the page listed the author's biography. It would give him some insight to the person who wrote the article.

Harrold Willis had been a correspondent for the Associated Press for twenty-five years, having retired in December, 1972. He lives in Portland, Oregon, where he is a freelance political journalist and is working on his memoirs. Mr. Willis followed President Nixon during his re-election campaign. In this Article, he writes about what he perceives is in store for the future of the United States, as indicated by his Presidential tour of duty in 1972.

He read.

Is the United States moving in the right direction? During the tumultuous campaign of 1972, accentuated by protests, parades and parties, that was a question posed by me as I crisscrossed the United States. President Nixon's re-election campaign was an enigma. He appeared concerned, overtly, about the election. I would hear many advisors reassure the President that no one gets off a horse in mid-stream. Many people not connected with the every day events of a political campaign do not get the type of awareness afforded one who becomes a true listener of all that a candidate states, both on and off the record.

71

During this campaign, the President and his staff were readily accessible. They had a true belief in their cause, but their course and message appeared uncertain. They believed they would win, but were not sure how. The campaign focused on the positive aspects of the President's first four years in office, especially expressing the President's depth in foreign affairs.

Nothing has propelled this administration like its assertiveness in the world milieu. President Nixon has had numerous successes outside of our boarders and, if we look closely at his agenda through speeches and action, one is privy that he sees the world in a new light, as a world leader, pulling all nations in one direction. Creating a new order of political power, with the United States as the superior force. I have bestowed the title "The New World Order" to this movement. While this title may seem ominous, it really is not. It is an inevitable outcome of the direction which the United States and other nations have been travelling toward during their evolutionary process.

President Nixon is a man for our times. He is the catalyst to spur the United States into its proper position as leader of not only the free world, but also the entire world. The move toward a one world government, with a pre-established hierarchy, has a broad mass appeal to it.

In pushing for the establishment of this new political order, we must break down existing barriers. President Nixon stresses the free flow of ideas, goods and people between nations. As an admirer of St. Thomas Aquinas, Richard Nixon believes in change and taking the chance for transformation.

St. Thomas Aquinas observed "If the highest aim of a captain were to preserve a ship he would keep it in port forever". Richard Nixon expounds that premise by saying, "The sea may be stormy, but conflict is the mother of creativity. Without risks, there will be no failures. But without risks there will be no successes. We must never be satisfied with success, and we should never be discouraged by failure. The key is the call, the commitment, the power of a great cause, a driving dream bigger than ourselves, as big as the whole world itself."

The main challenge presented to the creation of the New World Order is how to establish and maintain a viable form of world government and control. The answer is simple. It is right before us, as clear as day. We use an already established government. The United Nations.

"Incredible," Alex excitedly whispered under his breath. "I wonder why I didn't see the creation of the United Nations as the means to the end. Look at all the power it is amassing now." He glanced around to see if anyone heard him.

I would endeavor to state it has been some time since we have had a futuristic president. President Kennedy may have reached for the moon, but he forgot the Earth. It was not a united front. It was competition to see who was better, them or us. There was a fraternity mentality to the Kennedy Administration. Sometimes you do not see the forest through the trees. President Kennedy was of that disposition.

Many other leaders have taken the approach of U.S. domination through military might. However, might does not make right. It makes resentment. It creates hostility. It fosters insurgency. If we look to all great warring nations of the world throughout history, the Romans, Britain, Russians or Japanese, their victories and domination were short-lived, in an historical perspective, due to them not controlling the hearts and minds of the conquered peoples. Vanquished people still had their identities. They held onto that inherently. It is not the way to maintain world domination. Nations and people must be lulled into a sense of security to create a one world order. There must be a mutual benefit to all concerned.

Richard Nixon realizes this. The expression of wanting to open doors to the East, break down barriers, exchange ideas, people and products will lead, ultimately, to a new creation of political power. This will be accomplished through conventional means already in place. While this may not happen in one or two generations, it will not be much beyond. Fifty years from now this concept will become rooted in reality.

He stared blankly at the screen. "If this were true," he muttered as he tried to comprehend the idea of a movement to create a new political order through existing conventional channels, "it would be incredible." He fed the second tape through the sprockets, quickly turning to page 114.

THE NEW WORLD ORDER REVISITED

By Harrold Willis

The author's biography showed what Mr. Willis had achieved since his last article.

Harrold Willis was a correspondent for the Associated Press for many years before he retired in 1972. He moved to Portland, Oregon, where he was a freelance political journalist. Mr. Willis agreed to review his 1973 article and provide insight to events since then. Regrettably, Mr. Willis died prior to the publication of this, his last political perspective, in December 1985.

The Willis article started.

Is the United States moving in the right direction? That was a question I posed over a decade ago and much has happened since then. I would never have thought I would bear witness to the resignation of a Vice President, then the President of the United States. One could not but be impressed with the Global outlook of Richard Nixon, what I characteristically referred to as the New World Order. Is it fact or fiction? I would venture to say a little of both. I had immaturely believed this movement to be a restructuring of the World, but it was a new political structure to ensure our nation's survival and dominance through a world political body. The United Nations was the means to accomplish this.

Let's go back a few years, to 1943, when both houses of Congress passed resolutions -- the Fulbright Resolution in the House (September 21, 1943), and the Connally Resolution in the Senate (November 5, 1943), to forge ahead with a world governing body. Then, in 1944, the United States invited Britain, Russia, and China to meet in Washington to plan for the new organization. The meeting was held from August 21 to October 7, at a mansion known as Dumbarton Oaks.

"Dumbarton Oaks. Hmm," Alex said. The mansion was in the Northwest portion of D.C.

I asked myself, why invite China and Russia. While they were large nations and we were linked through treaties as a method of safety in numbers, they were not dominating the world. Where were other countries, like France and Canada, and why were they not represented in Washington, D.C.? Those countries would be included later in devising the new order, but they were not in on the ground floor.

The Senate of the United States advised and consented to the U.N. Charter by a vote of 89 to 2. It was astounding. 89 to 2. Even the most simple of legislative issues have more dissent than that, especially one outlining the creation of a new parliament which our nation became a part of. And yet, Americans seemed to regard the U.N. as a kind of super government.

Super government is right. It is amazing the U.S. would agree to this, affording everyone equality. Consider that segregation was not ruled unconstitutional for another ten years. Women only voted for twenty-five years. Why did not anyone test the constitutionality of the U.N., which, apparently, our government willingly submitted to?

The San Francisco Conference, in 1945, had established the Security Council in a belief that in this select body of eleven members, dominated by five great powers possessing permanent seats and the right to veto any action deemed detrimental to their interests, the world of watching over the world could easily be accomplished. The Security Council was to be the true governing body. A consortium of five main nations. That was the future for us. Those countries were to determine what we, as a sovereign nation, were able to do and accomplish. How was this possible?

In the early postwar period of 1945-1946, faith in the U.N. was coupled, as we have seen, with a dominant American mood of letdown, relaxation. The world should return to its prewar habits, nations "standing on their own feet" without American aid and sustenance. The nations should "get off the U.S. taxpayer's back." If this were done, so Americans thought, everything would be just fine. There was enough to do without thinking of foreign countries, which is interesting, since it appears there was some resistance to this belief. The resistance must have been short lived though. International relations continued, whether most Americans saw any value in them or not.

One aspect our leadership did not consider was the expense of running a world government. Since the U.N.'s founding, the U.S. has contributed more than $17 billion to the various U.N. bodies and agencies. Seventeen Billion. That is a huge investment which we, as a nation, have made. It is too big to let fail. I cannot believe we have been so financially supportive and it will only get worse.

The Reagan Administration has moved the U.N. up in priority, significantly changing the U.S. policy toward the U.N. From 1981 to 1985, Ambassador Jeane J. Kirkpatrick repeatedly warned that "business as usual" at the U.N. was not acceptable. It was her view, fully supported by Reagan, that the U.N. had to be taken seriously. Now Reagan supports this body, a parliamentary government, subjecting us to its power and control.

Enough is enough. It is time to wrestle away this approach to world government. Each nation must be independent of one another. We strive for our autonomy and the U.N. does not allow or recognize it, believing the whole is better than the individual. It is an unsuitable philosophy to live by in our ever-changing society. We must, as a nation, urge the dismantling of the United Nations as a method for world dominance, control, policing, and financially supporting any extravagance it undertakes.

The New World Order was us seeking the Holy Grail for total world control. Let's hope we can wise up and see the folly in this, before it is too late, otherwise we, as a nation, are doomed to live a subservient existence.

Alex realized, as he was instructed through law school, the best way to understand something was to discover how the idea was created. With law, all he had to do was Shepardize a case to see where it came from, who followed the Court's decision, who dissented and whether it was overturned, to get an understanding of a rulings creation. This would be a little more difficult.

Alex took out the film, trotted back to the bank of computers. There, he pulled up numerous books on the United Nations. He selected a few, at random, to give him an historical understanding. He took the request form back to the counter. There was now a young man working. He was young, bookish, looking as though he was barely old enough to be in college.

"Here's the microfilm."

"What name was it under?" he asked.

"Westcott. Alex Westcott. But, before you give me back my license, I would like to look at these books."

"Sure, no problem."

Within a few minutes, he was handed his selection of books. Alex sat down at one of the communal conference desks set up throughout the main reading room. The quiet struck him as odd. There was quite a reverence for libraries. One is instructed as a youngster to not talk in hospitals and libraries for the fear of disturbing others. People need quiet to concentrate on learning and healing. Those processes must be one and the same. He picked up the first book and read. "I need to get more information on President Wilson. The notion of this Brave New World must have been his brainchild."

"Who accessed those items?" he asked, nodding as he listened to the response. "When was that done?" There was a slight pause. "I see, yes. Well," he interrupted. "You are well worth your weight in gold for finding out this information, I believe we should keep this situation monitored to see how it develops. If there are any further inquiries, then we'll address it at the appropriate time. Right now it's just a needle in a haystack." Garrett slammed down the receiver. "Shit!"

The general international organization should be based on the principle of the sovereign equality of all peace loving states.

Senator Thomas Connally
Connally Resolution in the Senate (November 5, 1943)

CHAPTER SIX
OCTOBER 6TH

Alex moved the mouse so the arrow pointed to the electronic mail selection and clicked down. A flashing mark appeared on the screen. He typed,

OUTSIDE OFFICE CONSULTATION, THURSDAY, OCTOBER 6, 3:45 P.M.

He then pressed the enter key and turned off the computer. Alex got up from his chair and pushed it to his desk. He liked to straighten up and organize his office before he left for the day. He went over to his office door and grasped his suit jacket hanging from a hook on the back. He pulled it on, straightening his cuffs so they were exposed below the jacket sleeve. He opened the office door, his right hand flicked off the lights, as his left closed the door behind him.

Shaking his left hand, Alex's watch moved down his wrist. 3:30. He was right on schedule to meet Morris. Morris Braxton was the curator at the Woodrow Wilson House. Alex would not say they were friends, but acquaintances. They went to college together, now only seeing each other by chance.

"Maura, I have that outside meeting," he said as he walked past his secretary's cubicle. "I've posted my e-mail. Also, I have forwarded all direct calls to you. I'll check back with the message center, at five thirty, to see if any fires need to be put out." She looked up from her computer screen. Dictation earphones hung around her neck. He wondered whether she heard him. Whenever he suspected she did not, Maura would surprise him with her accuracy.

Alex inherited Maura when he started at the firm. She was a new employee. He was an aspiring attorney, ready to conquer the world. He saw Maura as his project, to mold her into his legal secretary. It gave him a reason to look out for her, especially since she started to work after her marriage failed. Her husband left her and their three children to find the greener pastures in life. She was down on her luck, trying to use skills she learned in high school, fifteen years prior. The only factor she did not consider was that technology had changed greatly since then. Her lack of experience was a concern to the firm, however, so was turnover. Eventually it was decided the lowest level attorney would have to deal with new secretaries. Alex was it. Maura was in her early thirties then, had skills, would listen to what he had to say, was always willing to learn and would stay late without complaining. No one could ask for anything more. Alex knew it, which is why he took a special interest in her.

Now, in her mid forties, Maura had mellowed from experiencing life. Nothing seemed to faze her. Her output was steady, efficient. She never complained about her job duties. Alex believed they suited each other well in the hierarchy of the firm's rigid structure. "Good night, Mr. Westcott." She was formal with him, even though he was younger. She had a deep respect for him. Alex showed her what to do, was concise in his directions and she benefited from the position with him

"Any questions?"

"No. I'll leave a list of messages with the message center and I'll indicate those with priority."

"Thanks Maura. Have a good night, and I'll see you in the morning." Alex continued down the hall, past the main reception area and proceeded to the elevator. Taking advantage of the balmy weather, Alex walked to Woodrow Wilson's home. He had never been there before even though it was close to his office. He headed north down Connecticut Avenue to DuPont Circle, then followed the traffic circle to Massachusetts Avenue, up to S Street.

He saw the address out front. Above it was a sign indicating - President Woodrow Wilson's Residence. "That's the place," Alex said. The architecture was Georgian Revival. It was a townhouse near Embassy Row. He glanced at his watch. It was a little after four. The last groups of visitors just left past the front door, down the steps.

President Wilson lived at 2340 S Street after he left the presidency, from 1921 until his death in 1924. Woodrow Wilson was in frail health when he left office. He suffered several strokes during the final two years of his presidency, never regaining his strength. Wilson was responsible for the League of Nations, which was, Alex believed, the foundation for the New World Order. He was convinced President Wilson was the championing force behind this phenomenon, but he had to be sure.

He did not know what to expect. Something drew him to this house. Whatever the instinct was, Alex felt he had to satisfy his curiosity. Maybe it was to try to get an understanding of where Woodrow Wilson was coming from. Maybe it was for additional insight into what he perceived to be the force behind the movement. It was not something he could articulate. Alex walked up the steps leading to the main entryway.

"Alex, how you doing? It's been long. When you called I couldn't believe my ears." The voice was as loud and robust as he remembered. Morris Braxton was heavyset. In school he was torn between art history and American history. He found a nice position for himself as the curator in an historical setting.

"It has been a long time. Let me look at you," Alex said as Morris held the door open for him. "Have you lost some weight? You seem to have slimmed down since the last time I saw you."

Morris let out a guttural laugh. "No, no, I haven't. I don't think I have ever weighed more than I do now. It's the good life," he said with a wink. "Now, what brings you here. I knew you were a history aficionado throughout school, but when I got the phone call to arrange a tour of the Wilson home, I couldn't help but wonder why the sudden interest," he looked inquisitively.

Standing in the foyer, it seemed as though Alex had been there before. There was an ease in being there. He looked at Morris closely and could still see the acne scars on his cheeks. Braxton had a full beard now, which covered up most, but not all of his marks.

"I've been thinking about certain aspects of our history lately," Alex started. "Something came up where my knowledge was limited. That was regarding President Wilson. There were certain questions dealing with his involvement in the League of Nations. I knew he had formulated that governing body to end all future confrontations, but my knowledge was limited in its scope. You know how I get Morris. If I feel trapped, I retreat, gather more information, then wait for the next encounter."

"I see. Here's a booklet, which tells the history of the building, with a map. It describes each room as it existed while President Wilson lived here. Mrs. Wilson gave the home to the U.S. government in her will. Upon her death, we took over and opened the home to let others see how President Wilson spent his final years. When the Parks Services took over the building, much of the President's personal belongings and writings were left as on the day he died."

"Really?"

"Not only that, but it seems as though Mrs. Wilson couldn't endure going into the rooms which were occupied by the President. His death really shook her. I don't believe she ever got over the loss. It seems, even though she was considerably younger than President Wilson, she lived out her remaining thirty-seven years in near seclusion, becoming a recluse of sorts. The information and presidential paper work was a literal treasure trove of information."

"What happened to those items which were left here?"

"It depends upon the item," Morris started. "Many, if not most or all of his writings were catalogued. Most of the non-personal items were placed back in the sites where they were found. We wanted to keep this home in as near a condition as when President Wilson lived here after leaving the White House."

"How were the various items catalogued," Alex's interest was raised, "and where are they now?"

"Well, most of Wilson's important personal documents are here because there isn't a presidential library for him. Some historians come here and rummage about, but those people are few. No one has had any real interest in him since the start of the United Nations, when a movie about his presidency was made." Morris took a handkerchief out from his sports coat and wiped the perspiration from his forehead. "The air conditioning only works in our main area, boy it sure's hot in here. That's something I've never gotten use to. Anyway, in the annex, we've kept his personal notes, fully marked and catalogued."

"Is any of this on computer?" Alex asked.

"We haven't been funded for converting that."

"Would it be possible for me to look at those items?"

"Sure. I don't see a problem. However, I have to go over to the annex to make sure everything is in order. In the meantime, why don't you look around here. It'll be quiet. Our two docents have gone for the day, so you can have the entire home to yourself, for a little while. I'll lock up the front here, as I leave, then I'll be back in about twenty minutes to take you to the annex."

"That'll be fine."

"One more thing. I hope you don't get spooked easily, but the old man has been seen here occasionally. I've yet to experience it, however, other people swear to have seen him. Usually in his study. Sometimes in his bedroom, peering out the window, to the street below."

Alex did not know what to make of Morris' comment. He was not one to believe in superstitions and apparitions, especially dead Presidents. "I think I can handle an encounter with a deceased President. It would be fun to hear what he has to say."

Morris went back to the main door and opened it. He glanced at Alex, as if to say something, then turned, closing the door behind him. Alex heard the turn of a lock. It made the hair on his arms stand up.

On the cover of the pamphlet was a picture of a handsome spectacled man. He looked the part of a President. The brochure read:

WOODROW WILSON
TWENTY EIGHTH PRESIDENT
UNITED STATES OF AMERICA

Welcome to the home of Woodrow Wilson (1856-1924), the Twenty-eighth President of the United States. President Wilson lived in this house from the time he left the White House in 1921, remaining here until his death, in 1924.

Many of the items contained here are from President Wilson's personal collection. Every effort was made to establish the authenticity of all furniture, books, pictures and documents.

President Wilson became our 28th President in 1912. He was nominated as a Democrat and won the general election, beating the incumbent, President William Taft, and Teddy Roosevelt, who ran as an independent on the Bull Moose ticket.

President Wilson was a political neophyte when he was nominated for President. His first political office was Governor of New Jersey, having been elected to that in 1910. Prior to that, Woodrow Wilson was President of Princeton University from 1902-1910.

President Wilson was nominated for President again in 1916, promising to keep the United States out of World War I. He ran against Charles Evans Hughes, the Republican candidate, and went onto defeat him by a three percent margin.

During President Wilson's second term, he suffered a stroke during his push for the League of Nations, in 1919. His health was in decline from that point, until his death on February 3, 1924. Many of the items around the house, you will notice, were designed to accommodate the President, aiding him to get around enabling him to meet with guests and dignitaries.

In 1923, President Wilson explored the prospect of obtaining the Democratic Presidential nomination for 1924, however, his health proved too frail.

The back page had a diagram of each floor of the townhouse, listing every room, along with what President Wilson used it for. Alex folded the pamphlet, placing it in his breast pocket. He breathed deeply, as he looked around, trying to breath in the history which existed all around. Everything smelled sweetly old, musty. It had a gracious air about it, though. At one time, this was one of the most powerful men in the history of the world. Here he was, standing in the foyer of Woodrow Wilson's final residence - humbled.

"This is stupid," Alex said out loud, not one to feel inferior to the past. "This was just a person. It's not like this is judgment day and I am kneeling before my maker."

Proceeding up the stairs, he decided to work his way from the top down, taking a systematic approach to finding out more about the 28th President. The carpeting covering the stairs, oriental in its pattern, looked strained and worn, from years of use and tours. Many of the steps creaked under his weight as he ascended.

At the landing he looked around. The foyer was exceptionally large, used to greet numerous people at once. The home was well illuminated. Alex had the impression the building would be dimly lit, allowing a man to convalesce after the bitter defeat of his most worked for project, the League of Nations.

President Wilson was a man hailed by millions of people, worldwide, after World War I. Yet, after that, the United States took on an isolationistic approach, Alex remembered from his political history classes. Woodrow Wilson was forced to campaign for the League of Nations, throughout the United States. The League was the predecessor to the United Nations, and now the discussion is leading to the New World Order. He must have been an enigma. There had to be some other force behind this man. He rose from obscurity to become President of one of the strongest nations in the world, even in 1919. He beat out President Taft, an incumbent, who, even though struggling through some party infighting, was a formidable opponent.

Teddy Roosevelt, many believed, purposely split the Republican ticket, by running as an independent, allowing a Democrat to be elected President. It would not be for the good of the party. Wilson's election forced the nation into a liberal mode, something no true Republican would allow. Third party candidacies always allow a non-incumbent to win. It happened at least three times, in 1912, 1980 with John Anderson and 1992 with Ross Perot.

Walking into the President's bedroom was as though time stood still. The bed was freshly made. Flowers were on each nightstand. A book was opened on the far nightstand, with glasses next to it. Alex glanced at the book. Holy Bible. Its black leather cover was faded and well worn. A man heavy in thought would grab it and read it for inspiration and motivation.

He continued to look around the room. It had a yellowish, almost golden glow. On the wall closest to the bedroom door were two oil portraits. President Wilson was looking straight out, while Mrs. Wilson was directing a loving glance toward her husband. The bedroom was large. There was a mahogany armoire against the wall, centered directly across from the bed. The four post mahogany bed was high off of the ground, about waist level, befitting a President.

There was a small table with two chairs around it, in the corner of the room. There, a diary was opened. Alex went for a closer look. He touched the diary, half expecting the President's ghost to tap him on the shoulder, and looked at the entry. It was dated January 23, 1924. The ink was now a pale watercolor blue. The penmanship was uneven and large. It was the last entry made by Wilson before he died.

I have not the strength to carry on the battle. I have suffered too many losses, both political and personal. Some of my political losses I have taken personally. Probably more than I should have.

I am not long for this world, and another journey yet awaits me. Somehow, though, my work here is incomplete. Hopefully, those to whom I have expressed my knowledge and vision will carry on

the torch from here. I realize one thing, though, and that is there are many good men who I tutored, who understand the vision of one world, a vision of peace and prosperity through strength and conviction. It's a world uniting under the capital concerns of industry, production and ingenuity.

Franklin came by to pay his respects today. I have always admired him and his support, starting when he was the Under Secretary to the Navy, until he ran for Vice President in 1920, supporting the League. It's too bad we lost the edge that year, he said. I told him not to lose the inspiration. To make sure our ideals are carried out. He said he would. I also told him he should watch out with the new government and to remember what happened to Harding.

Well, I am tired. It seems I tire easily now. This body of mine is frail. I find it frustrating to have one's mental intellect, while losing one's physical abilities. I thank the good Lord, every day, for Edith. She has been a true jewel, a gift from God. Until tomorrow. -W-

---

"Is the house all shut for the night?"

"Well, I've got to get back to meet with a friend, who's there now," Morris replied.

"Who's there?" Kathleen Korte asked.

"Alex Westcott. I went to college with him. He's a good guy," he explained.

"What on earth is he doing in the Wilson home while you're here in the annex?"

"What do we have to do, keep tabs on everything? Do you want me to frisk him once he's left the building to make sure no spectacles are taken?" Morris asked sarcastically. His big presence towered over her petite frame, yet she stood unyielding. "This guy's a respected attorney.

He's always been on the up and up since I've known him. There is not anything to worry about."

"I want him out of there now."

"I told him he could come here once he's done."

"No. That would not be wise."

"You've got to be kidding." Morris wiped the sweat from his forehead.

"No," came the stern response. "Now get out of here and close the building."

"What am I going to say?"

"Easy. You're going out of town tomorrow, right?"

"Yes."

"And we were supposed to meet before, right?"

"Yes."

"Tell him you're sorry to cut his time short, but your trip prevents you from showing him anything further. Just give him a rain check and send him on his way."

Morris looked down. "Okay."

"Good. Now get going. I've got some calls to make."

"What are you doing?" The voice startled Alex. He turned from the table toward the door in one swift movement, knocking the diary off as he did. The book made a solid thump as it landed on the wood floor. He noticed the older lady, housekeeper in appearance, from her dress. His heart was beating in his ears, she had so greatly startled him. He did not even hear her come up the stairs.

"Hi, I'm a friend of Morris Braxton's."

"So?"

"He gave me permission to look around."

"I don't know that," she abruptly responded. "How am I'm to know you're telling the truth. You wouldn't be the first person wandering around where you're not supposed to, after hours and all."

"Look, I'm not asking you to believe me, but Morris will be back here in a few minutes and he'll explain everything." He was pleading for no reason. "Or if you want, call him and ask if it's okay for Alex Westcott to be here."

"Maybe I should call the police." She emphasized the second syllable of her words. "You don't look like the typical person who wants to take things though."

"I certainly hope not." Alex straightened his tie as he looked at her. It was a nervous reaction he had, making sure his tie was straight when he felt under pressure.

"Why don't we all go down to the parlor an wait for Mr. Braxton, and he can straighten this out?"

"That's fine with me," Alex said as he kneeled down to pick up the fallen diary. He stood up and placed it on the table from which it fell. He flipped open the book, effortlessly, letting it unfold to where it naturally would. He glanced at the entry. The handwriting was steadier and neater than before.

AUGUST 5, 1923

I met with Tom Connally. He informed me Franklin is feeling better and assured me he would see me shortly to discuss the 1924 Presidential campaign. Tom attests to supporting the one world concept. He is of the belief all Americans would prosper from it. He knows, rightly, we cannot remain as isolationists in our view of the world.

Also, we discussed placing certain government created operations

90

into effect to ensure our direction is maintained, once we get beyond this perception. Tom further informed me this view of the world will transcend political boundaries and social barriers.

"Excuse me, but I'd thought we would head down to the parlor," she motioned with her arms, directing him out of the room.

Alex glanced up at the weathered lady, then looked back down at the diary. He talked to her as he read, a tactic he learned during law school with the Socratic method, and then expanded in courtroom skirmishes.

"Yes, we should head down now. What is your name? I've told you mine," he said as he read more.

The key is to continue the push toward global expansion if it can be accomplished. The industrial base and Mason's are backing it, now we must get the masses behind it as well. Capitalism and U.S. forces must expand.

Edith has complained that she does not trust Tom. Absent my wife, however, there is not another soul I would trust more than him. I have tried to explain how I perceive him and his pressures, but she does not understand. Politics is not for the faint of heart, nor should a woman be involved in any aspect of it. It is too undignified for them to dirty their clothes.

Today was also a somber one. Edith and I attended President Harding's funeral. I felt as though I was out of the political loop for too long, however, I believed I was well received. Edith said it was as though many Senators were apologizing for not fulfilling the prophecy of the League. They were saying Warren betrayed them in his Presidential campaign by straddling the fence on this issue. Tom Connally said there were rumors President Harding's death was not natural, but a result of opposing the League. Harding's words still ring in my ears like it was yesterday:

A world supergovernment is contrary to everything

that we cherish and can have no sanction by our Republic. This is not selfishness, it is sanctity. It is not aloofness, it is security. It is not suspicion of others, it is patriotic adherence to the things which made us what we are.

The man was extremely shortsighted. If what is said is true, then I cannot blame those forces that be for eradicating the problem. The salvation of the world is a small price to pay.

Tom also said that whatever governmental arm we place over the U.S. to ensure the continuing new world direction, it must be undeviating and able to direct the executive branch. If you control the mind, then the heart will follow. It is time to prepare for. . . ."

The page ended. Alex knew he would be pressing his luck if he asked to stay or delay a little longer. He waited for Morris to come back, that way he could finish his tour.

"Let's go. I can't allow you to wait here or else I'll get in trouble."

He walked out of the bedroom, past the irritation and down the stairs, which were just as giving on the way down. The housekeeper followed quickly behind him, but not before giving the room a quick once over to make sure everything appeared to be in order.

Once in the foyer, he looked for the parlor, turned left and sat down in one of the Queen Anne chairs. The cleaning lady stood guard.

"Are they paying you by the hour?" Alex asked her.

"What are you talking about?"

"You do realize if I was doing something wrong, I wouldn't stay here and wait. What do you say? I just want to have a look around. Honestly, I have permission."

Not responding, she continued to glare while leaning against the archway.

"It's going to be a long tour," he said as he looked at his watch.

Thirty minutes had passed. The front door was unlocked and Morris entered the home, looking to his right, and saw both of them in the sitting room.

His voice resonated throughout, "May, what have you caught here? I hope Mr. Westcott hasn't given you a difficult time, as he does occasionally."

"No, Mr. Braxton," she responded. "He did say he had permission to look. . ." She hesitated, a loss for words. Her eyes looked as though they were searching for something, then they seemed to find them. "We've been having stragglers lately."

"Your dedication is much appreciated," Morris said.

"Who needs a security system when you have this pit bull working for you," Alex joked. "I don't think my tour was complete. It was cut rather short. And, while I appreciate May and all the great company she provided, I was wondering if, perhaps, I could continue, then go to the annex, as promised."

"Well Alex, I have some regretful news. I'm leaving tomorrow for the west coast. Anyway, while I was on the phone, back at the annex, my boss said she needs to meet with me, pronto, to go over some items, getting her up to speed as to various events, while I'm gone." Morris wiped his brow with the back of his hand.

"What can I say? You're the boss. I appreciate the time. You've really gone out of your way, beyond the call of duty. When are you going to be back in town?"

"I'll be back in ten days. I'm going to San Francisco for a week of conferences, then some R and R. I'm looking forward to it. Besides this Indian Summer heat is killing me." Morris took out his handkerchief as the sweat beaded down and wiped his face, in a full sweeping motion. He then ran his hand back through his hair, pushing it flat with his perspiration.

"Call me when you get back so I can reschedule my tour. Also, I may be heading to San Fran to take care of some legal matters in about a month, so any insight, places to go, things to do which you'd recommend, would be greatly appreciated."

"It would be my pleasure, after all, I did set this up and now you're left without anything you were hoping for. It's good to see you," he boomed.

"It certainly was," Alex said as he got up out of the chair and proceeded toward Morris.

"Hopefully, you'll find the answers you're searching for. Don't look too hard, though. Sometimes many of the explanations are all around you," Morris said with a gruff laugh.

Alex shook Morris's hand. It was warm and wet. He waived to May. "Good bye Morris. It was nice to meet you Attila."

"It's May," she responded emphatically.

"I know," Alex winked.

He walked to the foyer and out the front door, without closing it.

"Enough time to go back to the office and look at my messages," Alex said softly, as he looked down at the sidewalk before him. "I'll be home in time for dinner with Laurel and the kids." His pace quickened.

The United States invited Britain, Russia, and China to meet in Washington to plan for the new organization, a meeting held from August 21 to October 7, 1944, at a mansion known as Dumbarton Oaks -- the meeting thereby becoming known as the Dumbarton Oaks Conference. Its draft proposals became the basis of the UN Charter which the latter was drawn up at the San Francisco Conference of the following year.

CHAPTER SEVEN
OCTOBER 7TH

Ameritrend's office was located within the National Chemical Building, an imposing new structure at 14th and G Street, two blocks from the White House. Much controversy surrounded its construction. MacClennan, O'Brien, Dougherty & Ernest helped to obtain the necessary construction permits. Washington's building restrictions stated no building could be taller than the Capitol, limiting all buildings, within the District of Columbia, to ten stories or less.

National Chemical Building was a remarkable legal achievement. Not only did it double the height of the Capitol, it created an imposing eclipse of 1600 Pennsylvania Avenue. Its construction violated two commandments. It was more than twice the size of any previously constructed office building. The structure's windows allowed quite a view of the White House and its grounds, creating a problem for the Secret Service, whose job is to protect the President.

Federal Courts held the height restriction was too limiting. The Courts relied upon fundamental constitutional rights of property ownership in their decision. They said there was no basis for restricting the height of a building just because it was near the White House. The exposure to the White House was defused by allowing the Secret Service to interview tenants along with giving them a floor for their offices and placing them in charge of securing the building.

Today's meeting went well for Alex. He explained the progress of the lawsuit pending in Washington, along with reviewing upcoming depositions and hearings in San Francisco. The Directors were impressed and pleased with the status of all matters.

"What kind of car?" the attendant asked as he was handed the claim ticket.

"1974 MG convertible." Alex added, "Its green."

"Be right back."

Alex pulled out the cellular phone from the side pocket of his jacket and called his office. "Maura, please," he said when the receptionist answered. After a few moments the call was transferred to his secretary. "Hi. It's me."

"Hello. Do you need your messages?"

"Not right now. Tonight Laurel and I are celebrating our anniversary and I promised we'd go out to dinner - Some place nice."

"Where would you like me to call?"

"How about making dinner reservations for tonight at 8:00 in the Willard Room. Also, phone and reserve us a room there."

"Yes Mr. Westcott. I'll handle it when we hang up."

"Also, make sure champagne chilling in the room, along with some flowers."

"How can anyone say you aren't romantic?"

"Easy Maura. At least I remembered this year. I'll be in my car for the next twenty minutes, so call me when everything has been confirmed, or if you run into any problems. Bye." He returned the phone to his jacket pocket. The squeal of tires could be heard as the attendant drove up from the underground structure. The MG came to a quick stop next to him. Alex admired the look and preservation of his car. Its design was copied, but never duplicated.

"$8.50."

Pulling out a ten, he gave it to the attendant. "Here you are, keep the change," Alex said as he placed his briefcase in the passenger seat, while situating himself in the driver's seat. He buckled up, put the car in gear, then disengaged the brake.

"Thank you. Be good." The attendant tipped his baseball cap.

Alex waived back to the attendant as he turned right, heading north on 14th Street. "How can I be anything but good?" He glanced at the clock on the dash. 2:10, enough time to head to Dumbarton. 14th to Massachusetts Avenue, which runs into Dumbarton.

Dumbarton Oaks contains 27 acres of unspoiled park land within the City, just north of Georgetown. Most of the grounds are accessible only by foot. The property, once an estate which was originally part of the Port of Georgetown Land Grant given by Queen Anne of England in 1702. Numerous buildings are on the property. The mansion is where the groundwork for the United Nations took place. The Garden Library contains many books, photographs, articles and assorted memorabilia about the commencement of the United Nations. For Alex, it was worth an attempt to investigate the U.N. to understand the events of today by looking at what happened yesterday.

As he maneuvered the MG left, from 14th Street onto Massachusetts Avenue, the phone rang. While trying to concentrate on the heavy traffic, which engulfed his tiny car, he placed the phone to his ear.

"Hello."

"Mr. Westcott. The reservations are set." The static on the reception made hearing Maura difficult. "I told the receptionist you'd check in between 6 and 7. Dinner is at 8:00."

"Thanks," Alex said gratefully. He knew Laurel would not expect this from him on their anniversary. "I owe you one."

"Okay, I'll see you later. Just one request, though."

"Yes?"

"Please finish my dictation on the Ameritrend brief today. I want to review it over the weekend."

"Yes Mr. Westcott. It'll be on your desk."

"Thanks. Bye." He phoned home.

"Hello Laurel."

"Hi Honey. I've been trying to get a hold of you since this morning," Laurel was charged as she conversed.

"Why? What's up?" he asked innocently.

"I want to get ready. You promised you'd call and let me know. Where are we going?"

"I thought we'd stay home with the boys and order some take-out," Alex laughed.

"That's fine with me, however, the boys are with your parents, as you requested," she paused. "This isn't like last year, is it Alex? You remembered to make reservations somewhere, didn't you?"

"Okay, okay. Laurel, how could I forget our anniversary?"

"Like it's so farfetched, and you haven't done it before."

"You know I love you more today than when we were first married."

"I know you love me. Now, where we are going," her voice grew impatient.

"You need to know I have changed plans, somewhat, for tonight." There was complete silence on the other end. "I've made reservations for us at the Willard Room."

"Oh, Alex, that'll be wonderful. I hope I can find a dress."

Alex replied, "You look great no matter what you wear."

"Enough already, tell me."

"Before you say anything else, pack a weekend bag for both of us, because," Alex's voice started to crescendo, "we'll also be spending the night at the beautifully restored Willard Hotel."

"Sounds marvelous. But what about the boys?"

"Don't sweat it. I've already cleared it with my parents. I told them we'd pick them up on Sunday."

"It seems as if you've taken care of everything. So what time are you picking me up?"

"I have one more stop to make. It's 2:25 so," Alex busily calculated how much time he would spend at Dumbarton Oaks, along with time for traffic, and crush of rush hour, "I'll pick you up by 5:30. We'll go to the hotel, check in, get ready for dinner and make a night of it."

"I'll be ready," Laurel said warmly. "I love you."

"I love you too." He placed the phone in his lap, then opened his briefcase sitting on the passenger seat and put the phone inside.

"Richard, are you all right. You don't seem yourself, just staring into space like that. You're becoming too complacent for your own good."

Richard Wheeler continued to stare blankly out his living room window, watching the trees rhythmically sway in the wind.

"Honey, if I don't get some sort of response from you, I'm going to make some phone calls."

Coming out of his trance, he looked toward his wife. "I'm fine dear. I just am a little run down, that's all," he responded in his thick southern dialect.

"Are you sure it's not from all of the pressure from work. The press has been rather hard on you lately."

"No. That's just part of the game. Hell, we've been use to that from our days starting in Stone Holler. They only magnify things here, that's all."

"Are you sure?"

"Yes. Look at the beautiful weather here. Please come and sit here." He patted the couch. "I want to enjoy this view with my wonderful wife before I have to head in for a few hours."

"Why don't we just go back to our lives, you know, how we were before? Things were just so simple then. We weren't scrutinized under a microscope like we are now."

"You know that can't be done. You have your job with the Red Cross and I've mine as chief advisor to the President of the United States. It's not so simple anymore. Living in the past can't be done. Everything will be fine, you'll see."

She sat down and placed her arm around him. "Let's get away for a while."

"Can't."

"Why not?"

"I'm committed to William until December."

"There's nothing you can do?"

"If I don't have my word, what do I have?"

"Well then," she sounded upbeat. "We'll just have to make plans for a great vacation in December, now, won't we." She kissed him.

"Yes, we will."

"In the meantime, I'm going to make sure we have another outlet. You know, some people we can socialize with outside of the executive office."

"Sure honey, you make the plans for it an I'll be there," he twanged.

"Is everything else all right?"

"Sure. Everything's just fine. Don't worry that pretty lil' head of yours." He kissed her. "Now let's enjoy this view and the solitude of the moment."

Towering oaks queued along the drive to Dumbarton Oaks, majestic in appearance. Alex surmised they must have been planted over 200 years ago. Some long forgotten individual, who could see the trees through the forest, undertook the endeavor and lives on through his legacy. Their leaves, now tinged with hints of autumn, rustled hypnotically in the soft fall air. It had a soothing effect on one's being. Alex pulled into the parking lot closest to the mansion. It was still a considerable walk to the manor's entrance.

Exiting his car, he grabbed his briefcase and placed it in the trunk. With a convertible, there was little one could do to deter theft, but he believed in making it difficult for someone to steal personal items.

Alex walked up the cobblestone drive, toward the mansion. The grounds, surrounding him as far as he could see, were immaculately kept. The splendor of the lawn, flowers, bushes and trees were out of a painting, truly a work of art, nature's way. The main house was an imposing stately manor. It was much more befitting of a President than any place Alex had seen. As he approached, he could not help but notice all of the chimneys, counting 28 by the time he reached the front door.

Alex walked past the front door, stepping into the foyer, with its gray slate floor. A desk was to his left with a pretty woman seated behind. Her mid length blond hair was pulled back, off of her face. She was dressed in a blue blazer with a white shirt, looking more like a prep student than a volunteer. She had a nametag, imprinted with INTERN, at the top. Her picture was underneath, followed by her name, Samantha Hayes.

"Good afternoon, sir, and welcome to Dumbarton Oaks," came the cheerful greeting. She flashed Alex a bright smile.

Alex returned the smile. "Hi, I'm here to see the exhibit set up on the United Nations. Can you tell me where that's located?"

"Yes sir." Samantha said handing him the pamphlet from the desk. "The main exhibit is here, in the mansion. If you follow this hallway down to the next and turn right, you'll find yourself in the main library. On the way, you'll see photos and various documents on the historical passage of the United Nations."

"Okay."

"If you want to see further studies and writings, the Garden Library has additional material. That building is easy to get to from the mansion's library. You just return to the hallway and continue heading away from the library, follow it to the back door. Go outside and the first building on the left is the Garden Library. If you pass the stone wall, you've gone too far."

"Thanks. What time does everything close?"

"The out buildings, including the Garden Library, close at four and the mansion closes at 4:30. If you have any questions, other volunteers and interns can help you. If you'd like a tour, there are two more scheduled today."

"When?"

"At 3:00 and 3:30. We leave from here. I'm scheduled to give the next one."

Alex thought about it. "How many people usually go?"

"It depends," Samantha said as she looked at her watch, then at Alex. "Today has been really slow. The last tour didn't go, and if no one else comes, then the 3:00 won't go either. If you're the only one here, you get the personal tour. It's easier to go into more rooms without having to keep an eye on people."

"I think I'll take you up on your offer. Do you think we can get started a little early?"

"I'll call for the replacement." She picked up the phone on a table to the side of the desk. Alex turned away and headed toward a painting on the opposite wall. It was of Mr. and Mrs. Robert Woods Bliss, who owned the property and allowed the mansion to be used for establishing the groundwork for the United Nations. They were in their twilight years when the portrait was painted, but they eschewed wealth and power.

"Sir," Samantha interrupted him from his fixture on the painting. He turned and walked toward her. "It won't be a problem. Jimmy is on his way now and should be here in a few. We can get started then."

"Sounds fine," Alex said as he continued toward her desk, taking the brochure, folding it and placing it in his coat pocket. He waited the few minutes by Samantha's desk, shifting from one foot to the other, uncomfortable in their silence. Footsteps on the slate floor could be heard approaching. The pace was upbeat, almost skipping. Sam turned in her chair as the steps came close, while rising in one swift and effortless movement.

"S-Sam, I-I'm here t-to relieve you. G-Go ahead and get s-started," Jimmy said.

"Thanks Jimmy. I'll see you later." She pushed her chair toward Jimmy, giving it a twirl.

"Right this way, sir, please," Samantha gestured with her right hand toward the hallway, the direction from which Jimmy had come.

"You can call me Alex."

"I'm Samantha, but everyone calls me Sam," she said smiling. "We're going to head down to the library. Is there anything which you're

103

most interested in here at Dumbarton?"

"I'm somewhat curious about the history of the United Nations," Alex replied.

"I'll guide the tour to that."

"That would be great." Alex looked at her as she preceded him down the hall. He guessed she was five foot four. Her hair was pulled back in a loose ponytail. She was trim and in great shape. People would notice her when she walked past.

"As we proceed down the hall here, you will notice a historical perspective on the U.N. There are numerous photos and documents which show the process by which the United Nations was created and how the United States approved of it."

The first photograph was a picture of Franklin Delano Roosevelt. Alex read the inscription underneath:

We have learned we cannot live alone, at peace; our own well-being depends on the well-being of other nations far away. We have learned we must live as man, not as ostriches, nor as dogs in the manger.

We have learned to be citizens of the world, members of the human community.

- January 20, 1945 -

The next several photos were of Dumbarton Oaks, showing how it looked over fifty years ago. Its appearance had changed little, except for the cars surrounding the grounds and the clothes people wore. Men and women, alike, wore hats. Those men who did not, slicked their hair back.

Next came two congressional resolutions. Each was marked above, The Fulbright Resolution, then the Connally Resolution. Between them were the words:

These Resolutions, the Fulbright Resolution, passed in the House

of Representatives on September 21, 1943 and the Connally Resolution, passed in the U.S. Senate on November 5, 1943, established the foundation upon which the United Nations would be created. All nations became closer, when much of the World was in turmoil. Great people recognized the truth we are all citizens of the World.

The sponsor of each Resolution was pictured next to their respective legislation. J. William Fulbright looked firm and unfeeling. His features were pointed, hair receding, with round spec glasses, much like FDR. He had a quote written beneath.

The United Nations, to a just and lasting peace among all the nations of the world. We, as a world, have grown to understand what it takes to attain a true and everlasting peace.

Thomas Connally, U.S. Senator, Texas. He was a distinguished and powerful looking man and was pictured toward the end of his political career in a white summer suit, with a black string tie. Even in his late seventies, he had a full head of hair, and looked in peak physical condition. He stated:

President Roosevelt carried on the vision for nations, united, to create an international organization for an everlasting peace. This body, to which all national sovereigns will serve, is an outlet to greatly reduce world tension, while alleviating international conflicts.

The panels that followed contained numerous photographs of the legislation being signed, pictures of people with the President and assorted foreign dignitaries.

Toward the middle of the hallway wall were gold letters, above a dozen assorted pictures.

DUMBARTON OAKS CONFERENCE
August 21 - October 7, 1944

The Basis For The United Nations

The next panel had photos of San Francisco. Many notable people were present. Centered was a picture of President Truman giving the keynote welcome on April 25, 1945.

A copy of the United Nations Charter was hung. All representatives present had signed it. Inscribed above the Charter:

To reaffirm faith in fundamental human rights, in the dignity and worth of the human person, in the equal rights of men and women and nations large and small.

"How can you make all nations equal?" Alex, looking back to Sam, asked. "All you accomplish is a weakening of the strong and a rising of the weak, creating mediocrity."

"I never thought of it that way," she said.

"Look at what it then goes onto say," Alex continued. "**The creation of a World Court, by which all nations must abide by**. As they say on television, 'Don't take the law into your own hands, take em to court, the World's Court."

Sam laughed. He felt brightened by her presence.

"**To promote social progress and better standards of life in larger freedom, and for these ends to practice tolerance and live together in peace with one another as good neighbors**," Alex read.

"Better have a good fence," She added.

Alex reciprocated with a smile.

"**To unite our strength to maintain international peace and security**," Sam continued to read from where Alex left off.

"Talk about forced compliance. I guess the meek will inherit the Earth after all,"

Sam nodded in agreement.

"**To ensure, by the acceptance of principles and the**

institution of methods, that armed force shall not be used, save in the common interest. I guess it must be utopia."

"It sounds that way to me," Sam added. "Especially saying **to employ international machinery for the promotion of the economic and social advancement of all peoples.**"

They continued down the hall. Toward the end of the wall, before the library, was the resultant U.N. Charter passed by the United States Senate on July 28, 1945. This statement was directly below.

On July 28, 1945, the United States voted to adopt the U.N. Charter establishing the United Nations in a format similar to that proposed in San Francisco. The Senate ratified it by a vote of 89 to 2.

Many other nations soon followed with the Charter going into effect on October 24, 1945, thereby ensuring stability in all countries throughout the World.

"You know, I never realized it before, but all of our political leaders lined up, ratifying a monumental piece of political machinery," Alex said. "There didn't seem to be much questioning by the World which was establishing a single political body."

"I never looked at those words quite in that light. You're right. It's like lemmings into the sea."

Right next to the doors to the library was information regarding the two dissenters.

The first picture was of Senator Robert S. Wheeler. Senator Wheeler, from Missouri, was a staunch opponent to the United Nations.

We must not become a world supergovernment. Each nation must be responsible for its own destiny, independent from others. Not subjecting themselves to the control and direction of others, even their neighbors.

After the Senate passed the Resolution, affirming the United

Nation's charter, Senator Wheeler ended his life on August 5, 1945.

The next photograph was Senator Andrew Westcott. Alex immediately recognized the image as a man he never knew, but had seen pictures of while growing up. Alex's Dad never talked about his grandfather, except saying he died when his father was eighteen years old. Alex never pressed for information, either, since he never was comfortable discussing something his Dad did not want to talk about. Alex remembered his father telling him his family stayed in D.C. after Senator Westcott's death. Remaining in Colorado would have been too stressful for the family. Below the picture of his Grandfather was this inscription.

The United States would weaken in stature if we, as a nation of sovereigns, are forced to submit to other nation's demands. Let us leave international affairs to those countries within whose boarders they occur. Strong walls make for better neighbors.

Senator Westcott was a populist Senator from Colorado. He was in his second term when he died in a plane crash on his way back to Colorado for the summer, on July 29, 1945. His last vote cast in the Senate was on July 24, 1945, voting against the United Nations.

Alex felt as though he was hit full force by a blow to the stomach. All of the breath left his lungs. He gasped, felt his knees buckle, and then he took two steps back.

"Alex, are you all right?" Sam's voice brought him back to reality.

"What?" he said, not taking his eyes off of his Grandfather.

"What's the problem? It as if you've seen a ghost."

"Actually, I have."

"What?" Sam seemed confused.

"I just came across something I didn't expect," Alex began to explain. "I've lived all of my life here, but my Grandfather was from Colorado. He was a Senator, who died when my dad was young."

"Just like Senator Westcott."

"That was my Grandfather."

"Really?"

"Yes, really."

"Did you know him?"

"I knew of him, but not much."

"You've got to be kidding. That's unreal."

"Yes, I guess it is. I really didn't expect this. I never realized he was opposed to the United Nations. I never had so much as an inkling what he did, nor an interest for what he stood for. My Dad really downplayed him. He didn't talk about him much. All I've seen were some photos. Nothing more."

"You know, now that you mention it, I do see a family resemblance." Sam alternated her gaze from the photo of Andrew to Alex. "You have his strong jaw, the same dark hair and eyes. Your smile is alike, too."

Alex smiled. "I suppose we do resemble each other."

"Why the sudden interest in the United Nations?"

"First a few questions for you Sam," Alex said as he fell back in line with his legal posture. "Why are you interning here at Dumbarton?"

"Sometimes," Sam hesitated, "you find yourself with limited opportunities. I graduated from Florida State several years ago where I majored in Poly Sci. I quickly realized I couldn't do much with that degree, besides wait on tables."

"True," Alex injected.

"Which is what I did for a little while."

"That would get old quickly."

"It did. My parents weren't too pleased with me. They forced me to attend various seminars, to see if anything appealed to me. Then I applied for graduate school. I was accepted to Georgetown's Master Business Program last fall."

"Good school. It's where I went to law school."

"Really?"

"Yes. Is this part of your master's program?"

"Not really. You see, I developed an interest for the political implications of various factors being introduced into our country. This keeps me in tune with our country's history. Remember, to know where you are going, you first must know where you have been. Plus, it gets me off of campus."

"Do you know a lot about the U.N.?"

"Not much more than what I studied while in college and here. There are several instructional courses I had to take before I could work here. The programs deal both with the history of the mansion and grounds and the United Nations," she paused. "Alex, let me ask you this," there was a slight pause. "Why are you so interested in the U.N.? Are you going to school later in life?"

"That hurt," Alex laughed. "Do I seem old?"

"You're not the normal college aged student."

"Some people I knew were discussing the U.N. I just wanted to get a better understanding. So, here I am."

"Shall we continue?"

"That would be fine," he said as he followed Sam into the Library.

The Senate of the United States advised and consented to the UN Charter on July 28, 1945, by a vote of 89 to 2. Other nations quickly added their assents, and the Charter went into effect on October 24, 1945.

CHAPTER EIGHT
OCTOBER 7TH

Alex downshifted around the corner. It was 5:20. Traffic was not heavy, but the tour took longer than expected. Sam was helpful and more knowledgeable than she implied, giving a complete tour of the mansion. Even taking him into rooms not accessed in quite some time. He turned up the radio. He loved to crank up the volume whenever he drove. It put him in a good mood, cleared his head. Alex was singing along to REO's *Roll with the Changes.*

"What happened next?" Garrett took a sip of scotch.

"He seemed harmless, that's all," she replied.

"What makes you so sure." Garrett's face was red, his nose ruddy from drinking.

"I've seen these people before. Professionals who harmlessly stumble into something. If it goes beyond their grasp, then they seem to lose interest after awhile, especially when other traumatic events come into their lives. The new event transposes them by diverting their attention. You'll never have to worry about anything again."

"What can be done to. . ." he paused, looking for the right word, "effectuate this?"

"Many things can cause the deviation and loss of interest."

"List some things. I want to have a sense of what you're talking about." He pushed himself deeper into his chair, closing his eyes while he swirled his drink.

"Loss of job, transfer, illness, injury, marriage, financial problems, marital problems, travel. Any of those could be tactics used to knock someone down. But," she paused.

Garrett opened his eyes and looked squarely at her. "But what."

"You have to be careful about one thing."

"Go on," he scowled.

"You can't push too far or it'll backfire. If there comes a point in a person's life where too much happens, they'll get a fuck this attitude and then the trouble begins."

Pulling the MG into the driveway, up next to their Explorer, Alex turned off the motor. He slowly pushed himself out of the car, then opened the garage door that led into the laundry room. The dryer was tumbling. With four people, two of them young boys, Laurel was constantly washing clothes.

"Honey, I'm home," he called from the kitchen.

"I'm upstairs, just finishing packing. I'll be right down," came Laurel's reply. "Why don't you get me a glass of wine?"

"No problem." Alex walked to the refrigerator and opened it. He searched around on the bottom shelf and found a Miller Lite, removing it. He shut the door and opened the beer, taking a long guzzle. He could feel a cold sensation follow his throat down to his stomach. Alex searched for the wine, and then called in the direction of the stairs, "I can't find any." He could hear Laurel coming downstairs. Alex walked over to the foyer from the kitchen, beer in hand. He looked up the stairs, which headed straight back to the second floor. His wife was burdened with two weekend bags with a jacket bag. "Need any help?" Alex smiled.

"If you don't mind, you could grab this one." She tossed one of

112

the bags toward him in a lively manner.

Grabbing the bag with his left hand, he tried not to spill the beer clutched in his right. The heaviness took him by surprise. "What do you have in here? Lead?"

"No. Just some stuff to tide us over. I brought you a change of clothes for tonight. I thought I'd get you to wear something I liked, for a change," Laurel said as she came down a few more steps, stopping two steps up from the foyer. Alex prevented her from moving down further, then he gave her a kiss on the cheek.

"That just won't do, Alex. Let's set the tone." She tossed aside her bags, then jumped up for Alex to catch her. He caught her legs with his left arm, as Laurel placed her arms around his neck and kissed him. Her force, added to the weight of the bag in his left arm, caused Alex to stumble backwards, first toward the front door, then, with the weight shifting, toward the living room. A fall was inevitable. Their momentum carried them in the direction of the sofa. They both fell on the couch, in one heap, laughing like kids. Not much beer spilled. Alex placed the can on the end table, as foam continued to bubble over the lip.

They kissed passionately for several minutes. Alex caressed Laurel's hair and face. "I love you Laurel."

"I'm looking so forward to spending this weekend with you," she said. "I can't believe you arranged this." Laurel pushed her hand back through his hair. She closed her eyes, committing the moment to memory, believing forever was the moment.

"Speaking of which, we should get going. It may take forty-five minutes to get there. Plus we still must get ready for dinner."

"When?" Laurel asked.

Alex replied, "At 8:00."

"You're right. Take the bags," Laurel said. "I'll be out after I straighten up."

They smiled and kissed, then untangled themselves from one another. They got up off of the couch, Alex picked up the bags and headed to the garage.

Garrett Baird was annoyed. "Now what do I owe this visit to?" His back was to Thomas Henry as he poured himself a glass of scotch, not bothering to offer Henry one.

"It may be a little more complicated than we all thought," Thomas Henry replied. "Do y'all mind if I have a glass?" He moved closer to the bar Garrett had set up in his library.

"You're the hired help, and this is my time."

"And?"

"You didn't hear me offer," intoned Garrett.

"So?" Henry was annoyed.

"So, the answer is No!"

He backed away and looked at Garrett as he lit his Cuban cigar, puffing several times to get it going, looking as though he was ready to explode. "It's what we all suspected. Richard Wheeler has been moving Lawton toward the policy of us first, cutting trade."

"Those are potentially, if not positively, protectionist measures," Garrett said, moving toward Henry.

"They are," he said in agreement.

"Get to Wheeler."

"We'll try, but that's easier said than done," drawled Henry.

"I don't care." Garrett slammed his fist on the counter, knocking the ice tongs to the floor.

"Y'all don't see, but he's protected more than most of the administrative staff. It's going take some time."

"That's what I pay you for." Garrett blew the smoke toward Henry, creating a blue haze between them.

Thomas Henry coughed. "Oh. One more thing which may interest y'all," he paused, wanting to raise the blood pressure of the short fat man.

"What?" Garrett downed the scotch in one gulp.

"Braxton screwed up." Henry smiled. "Your savior found some information."

"Take care of it."

"It's gonna cost."

"God damn it! Don't you ever question money!" Garrett shouted, his face red with frustration. "Done!"

Straightening his tie in the mirror, he buttoned his double-breasted jacket, then adjusted his cuffs so they would show below his jacket sleeves. "Laurel, we're going to be late for dinner. Aren't you ready yet?" he asked through the closed bathroom door. "Do you want me to call for a later time?"

"I'll be right out Dear." There was a pause. "I had to wait for you to get ready first, you know,"

He looked around the spacious room. The carpet was a plush burgundy. Three walls were dark cherry wood, while one had striped paper covering it. The bed was king sized, its headboard pushed against one wall, across from the entertainment center. Nightstands framed each side while a lamp topped both. Alex touched the sheets, smoothing and straightening them after the passion they experienced once they got to their hotel room. Double French windows overlooked the Mall, toward the Smithsonian. The view was much prettier during the day, than at night.

The bathroom door clicked. Laurel was standing in the

doorframe of the bathroom wearing a black dress, thigh high. She looked stunning. Alex observed from the bathroom mirror, briefly, before Laurel turned off the light, her dress, open in back, was cut low.

"How do I look?" Laurel purred as more of a statement than a question looking for a response.

"You look incredible. Why don't we get room service and call it a night."

"What? Waste this outfit on just you? I thought you'd want others to know what a beautiful wife you have," she laughed modestly.

"Who's to say the outfit would be wasted? We still have tomorrow. As for tonight, you're all mine." Alex walked up to his wife and placed his hands at her hips, keeping a distance between them so he could take in her glow.

"I suppose women are regressing to chattel. When we married, I don't recall me becoming your property was one of the vows," she quipped.

"That's because you wanted to marry me for my name. Being a Westcott is much better than being a Hardy."

"That's not true."

"Laurel." Alex looked at his wife.

She never forgave her parents. Her mother always favored the name Laurel, never associating it with anything different. "It may have been a reason, but only a small one. Besides my name gave me character."

"It wasn't from small kids, though," Alex added.

"Right. It was their parents who teased me."

Alex looked at her and smiled. "Is this new?"

"It's nothing new." Laurel looked down at her dress.

"I haven't seen it before."

"I haven't had the opportunity until today," said Laurel.

"Did I tell you how great you look?" he said.

"Really?"

"God yes. If I didn't know better, I'd say you were twenty years old."

"You're laying it on a little thick," she replied.

"Not only that, but I'd swear you never gave birth." Alex caressed her back, feeling her skin.

"Thank you. You know there is no one else I'd rather be with tonight."

"It goes with the territory," he said.

Laurel handed him a bracelet. "Would you please put this on me. I was having some trouble with the clasp."

He took it, placing it around her slender wrist and worked the clasp closed. "There you are, Honey. Shall we?" Alex looked at her as he headed toward the door.

She smiled back. "Let's."

She grabbed her purse from the chair by the closet, as Alex opened the door leading to the hall. Laurel proceeded him out, then he closed the door behind, turning the handle and pushing the door to make sure it was locked. It was a quick jaunt, less than five minutes, from the hotel room to the restaurant. Alex busily admired his wife, holding her hand in the elevator and while they walked.

"If only every day could be like this," Laurel sighed as they neared the restaurant.

"It would definitely be of a short duration. After all, the cost adds up."

"Must you be so practical?" Laurel looked into his eyes as she continued. "I'm only going to ask one thing of you tonight."

117

"What?" he replied.

"All I want you to think about is me. . . us, nothing else. Not costs, work or the kids, tonight is our night."

"Do you have reservations?" The Maître d', an older man, distinguished in appearance, asked. His gray hair was slicked from his forehead back. The black tuxedo he wore was impeccable.

"Do I have reservations? Where do you want me to start?" Alex replied.

"Sir?

"Alex, tell him. Remember," Laurel sternly reminded him.

"Okay. Two for Westcott, at Eight."

The Maître 'd glanced at the guest registry page, to the 8:00 pm listings. He placed a check next to their name.

"Your table is ready Mr. and Mrs. Westcott. Please follow me."

The Maitre d' took them past the front of the restaurant, where the dimly lit bar was located. Like the hotel itself, the bar was decorated in dark wood paneling. A pianist, at a grand piano in the far corner at the opposite end of the bar, was playing a song.

"Laurel," Alex whispered as he hummed. "What's the name of this? It sounds so familiar."

"Vivaldi's Seasons," she answered. "We had it played at our wedding."

"I was just testing."

"You seem to do that a lot." Her eyes sparkled.

"Your table Mr. Westcott," the Maitre d' informed them. He pulled out Laurel's chair, waited for her to sit, pushing it forward as she did. Alex waited for his wife to be seated, then he sat down, across from her, pulling his chair forward. There was a tall opaque candle illuminating the table. The diffused light the candle cast on Laurel was very flattering. He looked at his wife. His vision of her was briefly interrupted by the menu placed in front of him, along with the wine list.

"The wine steward will be by momentarily. I expect your dining with the Willard will be most pleasurable. If I can be of further service, please let me or our staff know." The Maitre d' turned on his heels and walked back toward the front of the restaurant.

Opening the listings, Alex glanced at the various wines. "Laurel, Dear, what do you feel like tonight?"

"Besides you?"

He stumbled an embarrassed laugh. "I was thinking Cabernet or Merlot, but your suggestion sounds better."

"Cabernet sounds fine with me," she replied.

"Fair enough. We could go with Opus One, or Conn Valley. Both are great."

"Why don't you choose? You know what I like Alex. I trust your judgment."

"Pick a number between one and ten," he instructed.

"Nine."

"Opus One it is. Thanks Honey, and remember, this is your selection."

"I'll take my chances."

"By the way, where is the steward?" Alex asked.

"Careful," Laurel replied.

"Why? You know how I like great service. I want everything to get started quickly, with the wine, that is." From his wife's reaction, Alex gauged something was amiss. "He's right behind me, isn't he?" Laurel nodded a discreet yes.

"Excuse me sir, I am Chris, your wine steward. Have you

decided on your wine selection for this evening?" The voice was close and definitely female. Alex sank a little in his chair.

"Yes, Chris, we have. We'll have number 287. The 2008 Opus One - Cabernet Sauvignon." He continued to look straight at Laurel, each smiling at his discomfort.

"Very nice selection, Sir. May I take the wine list, or would you like to hold onto that?"

"By all means. We'll stick with the Opus tonight." Alex closed the wine list, and handed it to Chris. She took it and placed it under her arm.

"I have to go to the wine cellar to select your wine, so I'll be back shortly." She walked toward the kitchen area, disappearing from sight.

"Why didn't you tell me she was so close?"

"I tried," Laurel replied.

"Not very much," he said.

"I wanted to see you squirm a little. Besides, how was I to know what your next question would be?"

"I hope she didn't catch me assuming she was a man," said Alex.

"She did. She sort of smiled at that. I would have her sample the wine before you drink it, just to be on the safe side."

"You would like that wouldn't you," Alex laughed. "I'm worth much more dead than alive."

"It's not something I have to worry much about Dear. Your family has that bitter stock in them, outliving everyone. It's how your genes obtain their vengeance. You have those genes. What worries me is that Jeremy has inherited them."

"You really think I'm like that? I'm shocked. Besides, who else is?"

"Where do you want me to start? How about your Aunt Mary. She has to be in her late eighties by now."

"85."

"She always brings up people she dislikes, and how they are now dead."

"Well," Alex hemmed.

"True," Laurel pointed.

"Well, when you get to that age, most people are dead," he responded.

"Yes, but she takes great pleasure in that fact. The only things which keep her going are her daughter-in-laws, who are still alive."

"Okay, okay, I may admit to her, but who else?"

"Next we could turn to your Uncle George, or your Aunt Donna."

"I'm going to have to concede this argument if you bring them into it. I'll agree there are some people in my family who live long. . ."

"Bitter end," she added.

Alex continued, ". . . but I want to make it extremely clear I am not like them."

"At times you are."

"So?"

"Well, you have potential, so you better be careful and watch your step, or you'll be old and cantankerous," Laurel said. "By the way, how many of your relatives have been stoned for witchcraft?"

"If any were witches, how could they be caught?"

"What about your grandmother."

"She was never stoned. And I would never call her a witch."

"What would you say, then," Laurel asked.

"I always believed my grandmother had supernatural powers and she passed them on to me," he winked.

"William Weylyn?"

"Yes. What can I do for you?"

"I'm here on special assignment for Internals. . ." He flashed his badge. ". . . from Texas, an I need to ask y'all a few questions."

"Regarding?" Sniper asked matter of fact.

"Y'all have been accessing certain information an I've been assigned to investigate why."

"What type of information?"

"Y'all accessed something regarding a New World Order."

"So." He glared at the swarthy young man.

"What's it for?" asked Henry.

"Curiosity."

"It killed the cat."

Annoyed, Sniper said, "I'm no cat and I don't appreciate you coming in here and telling me what I can or can't access."

"Listen. Perhaps I didn't make myself clear."

"Oh, I heard you, I just don't understand you. It must be that accent," Sniper replied.

"Perhaps y'all understand this," he paused. "Y'all don't have a choice in this matter. I'm with Internals, an I have all the authority I need. If y'all don't like it, then let's call in your supervisor an then I'm sure y'all be singing a different tune."

"You should be so lucky." Laurel looked away for a moment then back at him. "Do you remember our first date?"

"How could I forget? There I was, a lost soul, starting my senior year in college, when you appeared at a party, out of place," he said.

"I was only a freshman."

"Right then, I thought to myself, I've got to get to know this knock out, but how? Sniper set it so he went out with your roommate and he played up how I needed a date, so he suggested you. Your roommate, what was her. . . ."

"Anna."

"Yes, Anna. We double dated and went to dinner in Georgetown."

"The Tombs," Laurel said.

"Right by where they shot the staircase scene for the Exorcist. Sniper and Anna took off after dinner, leaving us alone to fend for ourselves. We had a few more beers, then went for a walk."

"All part of the plan," Laurel added.

"Obviously you have heard this story before. Shall I continue?"

"By all means," she said.

"As we went by the Exorcist stairs, I had you walk first, telling you all about them, trying to get you to look down. Just as you peered over the edge, Sniper and Anna came running up screaming." Alex laughed.

"You don't have to laugh every time you relive this story. Wipe those tears," Laurel said as she laughed along.

"All of a sudden, you turned in shock and came running toward me. I thought you would leap into my arms. There I was, arms outstretched, waiting, when what happens? You go right past me, running down the street. It took me five or six blocks to catch up to you."

"I should have known right then and there you were bad news."

"That didn't stop you from seeing me again."

Laurel looked at him. "To this day, I don't know what possessed me to go out with you a second time."

"Other than my charm and boyish good looks? It had to be the security you felt with me. After that, you wouldn't let go of me the rest of the night."

"How could I? I was still scared. The Tombs restaurant was deep in Georgetown University territory. We at GW did not venture there too often."

"In fact, you kissed me, for the first time, that night. I knew right then and there I would marry you," Alex said.

"You did not." Laurel moved her eyes down to the table

"Sure did. I called you the next day to see if you had a good time and when we could get together again."

"You were just in it for the three date scrump expectation, and then you'd decide if you wanted to see me again."

"Laurel, I'm deeply hurt you'd think that."

"Sir, the 2008 Opus One - Cabernet Sauvignon." Chris wiped the bottle, placing it in front of Alex for his inspection. "Shall I open it?"

"Yes. That'll be fine."

She took the bottle from the table and, in the same motion, took the corkscrew from her jacket side pocket, flipping it open. She cut the tin from the top of the bottle, wiped the glass lip, then placed the pointed tip of the corkscrew into the cork. She twisted the device deep into the cork, until the metal pry bar was even with the top of the bottle. In one movement, the cork was released with a slight popping sound. Chris placed a glass decanter on the table, next to the candle, and poured the wine into it, looking for sediment. Seeing none, she placed a sip of wine into Alex's glass.

He took the glass, holding the stem with his forefinger and thumb, and swirled the wine around a few times. He held the glass to the light of the candle, to look at the color of the wine and for any signs of sediment. The wine was a deep burgundy, without detection of impurity. Alex placed the opening of the glass under his nose, breathing in the bouquet. It had a sweet smell. He took a sip, swished it about his mouth, and then swallowed.

"Smooth. Dry. Hint of nutmeg. Very good. Please pour."

Chris took the bottle over to Laurel, walking around to her right and poured her glass one third full. She then walked to Alex's right, filling his glass and set the bottle on the table, between them, just off to one side, and left them alone.

Alex took his glass and held it up toward Laurel. She did likewise.

"I'd like to propose a toast. One that I've been practicing for weeks." Alex looked at his wife, the sparkle in her eyes, and the smile upon her face. "Laurel, you are the love of my heart, you make me laugh until I cry, thank you for saying yes."

"Alex, I love you."

"Here, here," he said as they clinked their glasses.

Delegates of fifty nations attended the grand conference at San Francisco which opened on April 25, 1945. President Truman gave the welcoming address. The ensuing UN Charter, which was signed on June 26, 1945, established a General Assembly of all member nations to meet periodically, each nation with a single vote, together with a Security Council of eleven members in Continuous session.

CHAPTER NINE
OCTOBER 15TH

It was just past noon when the Escalade pulled up next to the Lincoln Continental, away from where other cars were parked in the Capitol Centre parking lot. The portly man opened the door of the Lincoln and went to the passenger side of the Escalade, where the window was rolled down.

"Aren't you worried about someone seeing us together?" Garrett asked.

"No. This is the safest area to meet right now. There aren't too many people around and no one will suspect a thing." The parking lot was quiet. Occasionally a car would pull in, drive past them and park close to the stadium.

"What about Alex Westcott?"

"That's okay. He doesn't know what kind of car I drive. It could be one of many. Why don't you come in, the door's open."

Garrett placed his chubby hands on the handle and pulled the door open. On the second try, he propelled himself into the car. "Quite a height for an old man like me."

"It should give you some incentive to get in shape." The reply was curt. "I'm here, like you said, what do you want?"

"Take a good look at this picture." Garrett handed a photo. "I want you to find out as much as you can about him, then let me know."

"What's in it for me?"

Garrett Baird reached into his pocket and pulled out a cigar. He licked it from end to end, then clipped an opening.

"I don't think that would be a good idea."

"Why not?" Garrett said.

"While I like your company, and I don't believe anyone would recognize me with you, the people I'm around do know that I don't smoke, at least not cigars, and then suspicions would arise."

He put the cigar to his lips and bit down. "I imagine you don't mind if I chew on this then."

"Knock yourself out," came the response. "Again, what's in it for me?"

Reaching into his breast pocket, Garrett pulled out a thick envelope and tossed it onto the console between them. It made a thud as it landed. "There's Ten Thousand."

"What for?"

"Consider it a talking fee. I'm not asking you to do anything for this. It's yours, just for meeting me here today. Think of it as a token of my appreciation." Garrett looked at him for a response.

"I couldn't." He pushed the envelope back toward Garrett.

"It's yours. You know what I want. See what you can do to help me out and there'll be plenty more where that came from."

"What if I can't come up with anything?"

"Oh, I'm sure you'll be able to," Garrett said.

"Why's that?"

"Money doesn't sing or dance, son, but it sure does talk. And right now, it's talking a thousand miles a minute in your head."

The United States has a special relationship with the United Nations. There would have been no U.N. founding conference in 1945 in San Francisco without U.S. leadership. The U.N. Charter adopted there reflects the principles of U.S. constitutional democracy, and the U.S. always has been and remains the U.N.'s most generous supporter. Since the U.N.'s founding, the U.S. has contributed some $17 billion to the various U.N. bodies and agencies.

CHAPTER TEN
OCTOBER 16TH

"I want a trace on Weylyn and I wanted it yesterday. We've been shotgun shy too long."

"Garrett, I have everything under control," Thomas Henry tried to reassure him. "I'm a professional an I know what I'm doing."

"Listen. I don't want some hard dick feebie subverting my plans. I have others to answer to, just like you answer to me."

"Don't we all."

Garrett Baird, slumped low in his driver's seat, pushed far from the steering wheel and looking worse for wear. Henry set up the meeting at the dusty, desolate parking lot near National Airport. Thomas Henry was standing outside, resting his arms on the roof of the Lincoln. His head was bent toward the window as he talked to Garrett.

"I'll get on it when I get back," Henry replied. "My plane leaves in forty minutes to the west coast. I have some personal matters to attend to before I can handle this."

"This isn't going as smoothly as I thought. I may have to resort to other methods." The odor of alcohol permeated from Garrett's car.

"Do what y'all have to an I'll do what is required." Thomas looked at the fat old man. "I need the receipts now."

Garrett reached up to the visor pulling down two receipts. "Here you go, everything is set."

"Not everything. Remember, things take time." Henry glanced at the money transfers and placed them in his pocket. "See y'all in a few days." He turned to head to the airport.

"Your parents are here. I heard a car door slam," Laurel said. It was 2:30 on Sunday afternoon, the time his parents were expected. "You know how they're prompt."

"Yea, I know. Dad hates to be late for anything. Mom just goes along with him now. I guess she has merged into him."

"Hey everyone, we're here!" Jack Westcott called out as he and Mary came in through the front doorway. Laurel walked from the kitchen to the foyer to greet them. Alex followed.

"Hi Mom," Laurel said as she kissed her on the cheek. "You look nice today."

"I should," Mary Westcott said. "Your father made me get up early to go to church this morning. Every now and then he gets into a religious mode that lasts for a few months. Then he'll disagree with something the Minister says and we'll not go until the next major holiday. It's all a cycle with him."

"You know that's not true Mare." Jack affectionately referred to his wife. Whenever he was upset, the long form would be used, Mary Margaret. They had been married for close to forty-five years.

"Dad, how've you been? Have you recovered from the boys last weekend?" Alex firmly shook his father's hand. It was a stoic gesture his Dad liked. Jack Westcott did not outwardly express his emotions.

"Laurel - How are you Dear?" Mary asked.

"Just fine Mom, Dad." She greeted her father-in-law with a kiss. "Why don't you all go into the family room and relax, while I finish up in the kitchen."

"That would be fine. Where are those two terrors? I promised I would bring them both a gift." Jack held up a shopping bag in his left hand.

"I'll take that from you and put it in the den until the boys get here." Laurel took the bag from her father-in-law.

"Dad, they're at a party. They'll be home in a little bit. Come on inside and get comfortable. The Skins are playing the Cowboys." Alex motioned for his dad to join him in the family room.

"What's the score?"

"It was tied at seven at the end of the first quarter."

"Jack, why don't you spend some time with Alex, and watch the game. I'll help Laurel with dinner."

"I believe I will, Mare. Let me know if you gals need any help."

"Hey Mom, will you grab me a Miller Lite from the fridge?"

"Do you have any other kind, Alex?" Jack inquired.

"Bud and Sam Adams."

"Would you like a beer too, Jack?"

"I'll have a Sam Adams, Dear," he replied.

"I'll be right back." Mary went to the kitchen with Laurel. Alex and his father proceeded to the family room, sitting down on a couch across from the television.

"Is that a new TV?" his dad asked.

"Yes. We got it last month," replied Alex.

"What size is it? Fifty inches?"

"Sixty-five. It's a smart TV," Alex explained as he turned on the set. The screen lit up, vivid in color. He turned the channel to the Skins' game.

"It's a nice picture. Almost like you're at the game. Must have cost a pretty penny."

"Not too bad. I got a good deal from a corporate client filing for bankruptcy. Everyone in the firm was putting in orders. The office seemed like a retail store for a while, with boxes piled everywhere. It was hectic, like Crazy Marvin's."

"You could have placed an order for me," Jack said.

"Next time Dad. I promise."

"Speaking of which, how's the job?"

Mary came back into the family room with a beer for each. "Here you are. If I can be of further service, come to the kitchen and help yourself." She turned and left them alone.

It had been some time since Alex had a discussion with his father. His father seemed older than he recalled, both in appearance and tone of speech. "Work's okay. That's why they call it work, not fun. Firm politics can be a little trying. I'm satisfied the senior partners are relying upon me to handle more high profile litigation. But, as with anything, there are a few people in the firm who wouldn't mind seeing me fall."

"I don't believe that son. It's only people showing their insecurities."

"How's that? You've been retired for six years now."

"Five." Jack Westcott corrected.

"Five. Plus, being a lobbyist wouldn't be very political, especially when you work for yourself."

"Alex," Jack said sternly. "I'm talking about human nature here. Nothing more. When someone says they wish they weren't at their present stage in life, and are upset you are, what does it mean?"

"What?"

"It shows you those people aren't happy with life's current station. They were happier sometime prior and they don't believe their lives will get any better in the future. They may feel you get in the way of their success. In actuality, it's a great misconception. Many people have it. We must be responsible for our own successes and our own failures. Managing success can be just as difficult, if not more so, than handling failure."

"You only fail when you fail to try." Alex interjected some of his own philosophy.

"True."

"So when attorneys denigrate my ideas, they wish they thought of them and they're upset I was able to have the foresight."

"For the most part."

"What about dealing with personal tragedy. That's something you have no control over, yet it could be responsible for one's failures," Alex said.

"Well, everyone reacts to personal tragedy differently. If you dwell on it for too long, it'll destroy you," Jack Westcott explained.

"Is that what you did when your father died."

"It was a long time ago, I was very young," Jack said in a halting monotone, caught off guard by the comment. "To be honest, I don't remember what I did to get through that time. I grieved, accepted the loss, apportioned the blame, and then went on with my life. You don't forget, but by all means, you don't make it a cross to bear. You've got to go on with your own life, or you will be destroyed. It's a matter of survival, self-preservation"

"Go on, dad," Alex said.

"Why the sudden interest?"

"I don't know, just curious."

"This hasn't been a topic of conversation before," Jack said.

"It's just something's come up and I want your perspective. That's all."

"I'll go over all of this with you, I haven't given it much thought, though."

Alex nodded in agreement. "So what happened?"

Jack looked at his son. "Are you asking how did he die?"

"Yes."

"Your grandfather was in the middle of his second term in the Senate. He had been in Congress for as long as I could remember. I was born after he was elected to the House and was about eight or nine when he was elected to the Senate. He was quite a well-liked man, handsome and a great orator. Those were winning combinations back then." Jack put the beer to his lips and took a quick sip. "It was the summer recess in Forty Five. He was flying back to Colorado to meet with his constituents."

"Would he do that a lot?"

"He usually did on a regular basis, however, this time he was in a hurry to get back," Jack explained

Alex asked, "Why?"

"He wanted to explain his position on the United Nations. He was getting a lot of bad press for voting against the formation of the U.N. All of the papers in Colorado came out against him. He was concerned about not being able to explain his reasons for his vote."

"Why the travel?"

"Remember, back then, communication was not as advanced or sophisticated as it is now." Jack hesitated a few seconds, glanced at the

133

television, took a preoccupied drink, and then continued. "My mother, brother and I were at the summer home, back in Colorado, waiting for him. We drove out there in the middle of June, after I finished my studies. I was spending time with friends, just enjoying the summer. I was enrolled for the Fall term, at Harvard, so I was, you know, having fun. It really had been a fantastic summer. Dad called on the day he left. He spoke to my mother and told her he looked forward to getting out of Washington during the dog days. He wanted a break from the piranhas. I distinctly remember Mom saying a driver would meet him at the airport, so we didn't have to." Jack looked down. In a soft voice he added, "As the plane flew, it experienced mechanical problems. It crashed in a cornfield in Iowa. All fifteen people aboard were killed. We found out about it through the news agencies, which came to our house, asking questions. My mother never forgave the media for interfering in her privacy in our time of grief."

"Why did you leave Colorado?"

"After the funeral, my mother didn't want to be under the restrictions and glare which would result from living there. We were living in a small, closely knit community. People would watch our moves. I would always be Andrew Westcott's boy. It was better. Also, we had our main home in Georgetown, where I spent most of my time growing up."

"Was it easier in D.C.?" asked Alex.

Jack looked at the television. "In Washington, people didn't remember my father as being one of the only two legislators who voted against ratification of the United Nations. They thought of him as a person who died a tragic death. He became idolized for a brief time. Then, people forgot. Living in a large city gave us the comfort to be ourselves. Anonymity"

"What about Grandma, how did she take it?"

"Things were rough on her, no question about it, but she was strong. She had her public side. Whenever she was outside, she was capable, very, very capable. Right after his death, though, when she was behind closed doors, she would become withdrawn. Moving back to Georgetown allowed her to be with her circle of friends. She continued with and became even more involved in community activities. Dad's death made her stronger." Jack hesitated. "As for me, I live by the philosophy life will throw you many obstacles. Go over, around, under or though them to survive. No one can do it for you. It probably developed from this incident. You must realize Alex, I haven't had a terrible life. When all is said and done, I am proud of all I accomplished."

"What did you do after his death, after reality hit?"

"I started college a year late, which was the best thing I could have done. It gave me time to get my thoughts together. Instead of Harvard, I went to Georgetown, to be closer to my mother and brother. I met Mary. We had you, then your brother. You had your two sons and now here we are. Life is a continuum."

"Why was he such a staunch opponent of the U.N.?"

"Let me preface my statement with - Growing up as Andrew Westcott's son was not easy. He was a very intense man. Topics at the dinner table, when he was around, which was rarely, always comprised current events and pending legislation. The U.N., as Dad saw it, was an evil force. How did he refer to it?" Jack searched for the phrase, closing his eyes briefly. "If the United Nations is ratified, individuals will never be satisfied. His belief was there was an underlying movement taking place for a one world government. If that occurred, he felt, we would all lose our individuality. Government would dictate to the world's population all it could do. It was much like Orwell's *1984*. He did not want other countries to police us. In the same breath he would say we had no right to tell other countries what to do, especially if it didn't directly affect us."

"So he was more of a laissez faire politician."

"No. I wouldn't use that term to describe him. He saw the

creation of the U.N. as lessening the direct influence of the individual for self determination. States within the United States, he believed, were to be a thing of the past. He believed the U.S. would be divided into various regions. Wealth was directed to remain with those who had it. Any newly acquired wealth was to be destroyed through taxation, audits. Most everyone else was to be moved up or down to allow for an average middle class existence," Jack explained.

"How could he believe that?"

"Provide everyone with a basic existence and they'll be content. He said an opiate was being created for the masses. Take care of their basic needs and you control them. People have always lived a clan existence. Forced compliance is welcomed. That's why the military does so well. There's a hierarchy in place. You know your job. You do what you are told. If you don't follow orders, you don't move up. If you ignore orders, you are punished. It is that principle the United Nations wanted to apply to all human life."

"It doesn't seem plausible," Alex replied.

"It's happening right now. Everyone looks to the government for more and more, while doing exactly what they are told to do."

Alex nodded as he mulled over what his father was saying.

Jack continued, "He also foresaw various countries being responsible for providing different commodities."

"Like what?"

"He said the U.S. would become service oriented. You know, manage money, stock markets and run the world's banking system, tying everything into the dollar. Poorer countries, where labor was plentiful, would provide cheap labor for mass produced items. Other nations would be agricultural, for feeding the world. Still others would provide their vast resources for everyone to use equally. It was to be utopia. By establishing this system of total world management, no one would be responsible for his own destiny."

"What would do the managing?"

"The United Nations was to become the ruling governmental body to determine every country's fate and fortune, to the point where there would be no more nations or ethnic diversity, not even in name. Gradually those words would be worked out of our language. Erase them, as if they never existed. The U.S., working in consortium with other select developed nations, was to control the new world government. My Dad wasn't optimistic that, once created, the world government could be managed for our own benefit."

"Why not?"

"Because there would be too many unpredictable events which could occur. Look at how the world has changed in the last fifty years. Who could have foreseen all of the turmoil? What if it was all of a bigger plan to force compliance or suffer the consequences of world intervention? Korea, Iraq, the Sudan, the Middle East and Bosnia are all areas where we have sought to force compliance with the big picture."

"Well then, what about his death?"

"What do you mean? I've told you how he died."

"Do you think it was plotted?"

"It's purely speculative. I guess I could say someone from the government killed him, that it was a conspiracy. That it was best to remove Andrew Westcott's voice of conscience from being heard because his view differed from so many others. Sometimes I wonder. But then again, maybe his belief would have destroyed his career. He was bucking a big national directive. To be honest, at first, I thought about a conspiracy. But I couldn't prove it. It didn't seem credible. If I had thought about something I couldn't prove, it would have destroyed me. I couldn't let that happen."

There was a pause in their conversation. All his Dad had explained settled in. Occasionally, Alex would hear the voices of the broadcasters commenting on the game. He was not focused on it.

137

"Son, why the sudden interest?"

Alex thought for a moment. "Dad, it started with a conversation I had with a Judge who mentioned the New World Order. He was very forceful in the presentation and pursuit of that agenda. He made inferences of it extending to both political parties, this force was apolitical. He said while social legislation may differ between Republicans and Democrats, each party has pushed for the strengthening of the political structure of the U.N."

"How's that your concern?"

"It's not, really, I guess. I never heard of the New World Order, so I started some research. Then I saw a link from the League of Nations to the United Nations, both being the same type of political organization. One failed, the other succeeded. Then there were two connections. One was FDR, who was in the Wilson Administration and saw the League fail. He then developed the U.N. The other connection was my Grandfather was one of two Senators opposed to the United Nations. Both died shortly after the vote in 1945. I found that rather peculiar."

"I would not get so worked up about the U.N. and this New Order thing."

"New World Order," Alex corrected him.

"There's nothing you can do about the New World Order if it does exist."

"What if Andrew Westcott was killed for trying to show people the truth? What if he had a true sense of what was occurring? Don't we owe it to him to speak out against something he was so opposed to?"

"That was his battle, not yours."

"I believe we owe it to him to investigate his beliefs. If he was right, we must let others know," Alex said.

"There are a lot of 'what ifs' there. You, as an attorney, should realize you can conjecture about anything. Just change the hypothetical situation and there's a different outcome."

"Things don't seem reasonable."

"Approach it this way Alex. First, remember it happened a long time ago."

"True."

"A lot of Andrew Westcott's beliefs have not held true."

"I'm not entirely in agreement."

"You're now involved in politics," Jack Westcott's voice was becoming strained at the shift in his argument with his son.

"Yes."

"You have a great job which tries your ability on a constant basis, it teaches you and it rewards you."

"True."

"You have a lovely wife and two beautiful children."

Alex nodded in agreement. His thoughts, however, went beyond this conversation. "Do you have any of the papers he wrote?"

"No. Your Grandmother threw most everything away. All she kept were some pictures. She didn't want to be saddled with all of his documents."

"I would like to look a little further."

"With all you have, don't give it up."

"What's wrong?" Alex asked.

"You never know which dangers lurk about. Don't be like your Grandfather. Self-preservation is better than destruction. My advice is don't get involved. It's not worth your time or effort. Even if this movement exists, it would be far too big for you to do anything about."

"Okay."

"I know that tone. Remember, your Grandfather voiced his opinion, and where did it get him? Politics are entirely impure and being involved in politics corrupts. Stay out of politics and stay away from the wild goose chase about this issue. Promise me you'll just let this die."

Alex did not know if he could. Politics and standing up for beliefs were his family's stock. He looked squarely at his father. "Sure Dad, I will."

We have too often ignored another major opportunity for the resolution of disputes: the international organizations created for this purpose, such as the United Nations.

The superpowers have turned to the United Nations as the best avenue through which peace might be pursued. The best hope for progress in and around Palestine lies in an international peace conference predicated upon United Nations and sponsored by the five permanent members of the Security Council.

Jimmy Carter
40th President

CHAPTER ELEVEN
OCTOBER 17TH

BEEEEEP - "Mr. Westcott, it's 4:30, time for your meeting."

He put down the complaint he was reading, swung his chair around, and faced the credenza, away from his desk. "Thanks Maura. I'll be leaving shortly," he said in the direction of the speakerphone. "Have you finished the brief for Ameritrend yet? I want to add something."

"It's almost ready. If you'd like to make changes, just pull it up from the file server. I'll have it finished tomorrow."

Alex pushed the button on his phone, forwarding all of his calls. He had to leave for the mid-month office meeting. The Partners of the firm would get together on the first and fifteenth of every month, or on the Monday following if it fell on a weekend, at four thirty. They would discuss current cases, who was handling what, inner-office procedures, new and old, along with the firm's agenda. The firm's founders believed these bi-monthly meetings created cohesion among its members, plus, it enabled them to keep an eye on their employees.

Before Alex was a partner, he wished he could be a part of the firm's internal workings, deciding and charting direction. He felt the firm moved too slowly, it was unresponsive and it should rely on today's technology. By the time he became a partner and started to attend the meetings, twice a month, he discovered they were extremely dull. All that was accomplished was whatever the senior partners wanted. The four main partners were in actual control of the firm. They had most stock interest and would maintain it for the rest of their lives. It frustrated him. He knew it was more difficult to be at the helm, having the assorted headaches that go with it. Alex also realized he had good ideas, wanted them implemented, but could not. There was something to be said for security, though.

He grabbed the agenda from the credenza, which had been delivered to each partner, along with his notes for the meeting and his legal line pad. Alex headed toward the main conference room. The firm had four conference rooms and one library. The main conference room could accommodate the fifteen members of the firm who would be in attendance. It was on the same floor as his office, toward the receptionist's desk. Three of the four walls were glass, one offered a view of Connecticut Avenue and several buildings across the street. One wall was the multimedia center, which had a large screen television built into it, with several VCR's, tape decks, assorted copying devices, a pull down screen for slides and projections. It allowed attorneys a place to take video deposition and to put together any presentation that might be needed for trial. Alex was pushing the firm to construct a mock courtroom. The next big advantage, he foresaw, for attorneys was to have mock trials of cases in progress, those certain to go to trial. Complete with jurors, randomly selected people, who could give them insight into their case's strengths and weaknesses. Alex knew if they did, the firm would be on the forefront for litigation in the twenty-first century. It was an item he would talk about today, under new business.

"Hey, wait up," Quinn Colton said as he hurried toward him.

Alex cringed as he heard Quinn's voice. In work places of any type, there are individuals whom you would rather not see, associate with or talk to. Alex felt this way about Quinn. Quinn had hired in four years prior to him. He did not make partner until two years after Alex. Alex believed Quinn was bitter. Quinn Colton's appearance was the opposite of his. He was shorter than Alex, overweight, slightly disheveled, with a nasal voice. Alex never understood it when people suffered from short man's complex, trying to compensate for their own lack of stature. For Quinn, it was stories of who he knew or how he was related to famous people, which made him feel important. His nickname, Percy Boy, was bestowed upon him by one of the partners.

"Alex, how've you been?"

"Fine Quinn. What's up?"

"Just plugging away like everyone. I saw on the agenda you're heading out to California on the Ameritrend Matter. Do you need any help?"

"Thanks for the offer, but I have everything under control."

"Hey, guess who I had dinner with on Friday." Quinn kept plugging. For him, talking seemed a necessity.

"Who?" Alex asked, humoring him.

"Richard Wheeler."

"I don't believe I've heard of him," he replied, not wanting to, but in actuality he could not recall the name as being anyone important.

"Dick Wheeler," Quinn responded, with a look of disbelief. "He's the President's top Advisor. What he says, President Lawton does. He has the man's ear. What he says into President Lawton's ear comes right out his mouth. You never can tell who's talking"

"How'd that happen - How did it work out so you had dinner?" Alex asked as they continued toward the conference room.

"My wife became friends with his wife while they were working as administrative liaisons for the Red Cross. Anyway, my wife tells me we have these dinner plans and the Wheelers are coming over to our home for dinner. She mentioned the name in the past, but I never put two and two together. Well they came over-"

"To your house?"

"Yes - and when Dick Wheeler steps in through the front door, I sort of stopped and did a double take. I looked at him and said, 'You look awfully familiar. Have we met before?' He laughed and said in a thick southern accent. . ." Quinn imitated a southern drawl, responding like Dick Wheeler. 'I don't believe we've met before, but the reason I look so familiar is probably from being on TV' Then, suddenly, it hit me. I said 'Aren't you the advisor to the President?' All Dick said was 'Yep.' And a hearty laugh followed."

"Quite a story. Did you ask him about the economy? About how inflation is getting out of control? Or how about high unemployment caused by governmental policies restricting new business opportunities?"

"He was my guest." Quinn emphasized the word my. "I didn't want to come off as being ungracious. Besides, my wife would have been miffed if I had acted that way. I figured if my wife maintained this friendship, then I could use it by influencing the current administration for our clients, for the firm's gain."

"Did Wheeler give you any insight into the administration?"

"Like what?"

"Did he talk about pending social legislation or any international expansion plans?"

"We talked about a lot of things. After all, they were at our house until one. They said it was the most fun they had in some time. They liked being away from the executives for a while."

"What do you remember most?" Alex was trying to press Quinn along.

"Dick did say he wasn't worried about the national numbers for inflation and unemployment. He told me the first year of the administration was spent organizing. This year they were going to concentrate on redoing the social legislation of the previous administration."

"What did he mean?"

"It seems the big push for social reform and legislation is over. Dick is of the belief that once those hurdles are removed, the economy will rebound and inflation will reduce and unemployment will decrease."

"Anything else?" Alex asked as they were about to head into the conference room.

"Yeah, he said the U.S. is going to move away from the control of the United Nations to more of a protectionist stance. Something about being tired of trying to protect the world with no benefits."

He opened the door for Quinn. From the outside, he observed most of the partners present, milling around, drinking coffee and sodas, waiting for the meeting to start. Bill Dougherty called the meeting of MacClennan, O'Brien, Dougherty & Ernest to order. All of the senior partners were in attendance. They alternated chairing the bimonthly meeting to free up time for one another. When the door closed behind them, Bill Dougherty looked around the room as if to count the number of people present. Twelve partners were there.

"All right, let's get this meeting started," Dougherty said in his Hamptonesque, blue blooded accent. He always seemed tight in his voice, posture and mannerism, like Thurston Howell. Even his clothes had a constricting look to them. His shirts always had white collars and cuffs, with the rest of the material being another color. It gave Bill Dougherty a locked-in look. The boarders prevented any color from running out, like a child who only colors within the lines, restricted in creativity. "Why doesn't everyone have a seat, so we can get started."

The partners sat down at chairs lined around the table. A few already staked out their seats, knowing it was best to have a view of the outside. It relieved boredom. Dougherty was seated at the end of the table, with the entertainment wall behind him. He believed people were more inclined to focus on him and what he had to say. A senior partner would sit to each side of the presiding partner.

Alex sat three quarters of the length of the table down from Mr. Dougherty, facing the windows. He placed his note pad in front of him. On the top, he had the meeting's agenda, followed by the Ameritrend case and then the information on the mock courtroom. The Ameritrend matter was one of the bigger cases the firm was handling. Attorney fees for all of Ameritrend's litigation, by year end, were projected to surpass Five Hundred Thousand Dollars.

Mr. Dougherty continued. "First we're going to review current case matters. As I was reviewing the agenda, I've moved Ameritrend from third to first. We should begin with that." Dougherty looked toward Alex, who straightened up in his seat, adjusting his tie as he acknowledged the glances. "We'll move TKM to second and Harris Industries to third. I would remind everyone it would behoove you to speak when spoken to and to enunciate loudly and clearly since we have gone to the electronic secretary," he said as he pointed out the microphones situated around the room. "Each microphone is voice activated. It'll pick out the closest and loudest voice to record. That should take some heat off of our firm's acronym."

Everyone laughed at the inside joke. The firm was sarcastically referred to as MODErnest because they were slow to change with the times. Money was slowly reinvested back into the company. The computer system, for one, was a recent phenomenon, along with the telephone system and the multimedia center. On the agenda was Alex's big push, the mock courtroom, which he believed would hone the skills of their litigation department.

"Without delay, I would ask Alex Westcott to give an update as to Ameritrend."

Alex stood. Some attorneys preferred to remain seated when

they talked, but Alex felt it was far more effective to stand when giving a presentation. It added an air of authority, gathering more respect. He moved the agenda from the top of his notes on Ameritrend. He glanced briefly at his paper, then looked toward Dougherty.

"Good afternoon." He pulled down his shirtsleeve cuffs, exposing them beneath his jacket. "I guess something like this happens when I get here last. A little test to see if I am prepared." A few of the attorneys laughed.

"I know we have a lot to accomplish so I'll keep this brief." Alex continued as he looked around the room at each of the attorneys present. "It really is amazing how cases turn and twist. This one is no exception. When I first handled Ameritrend, I took a purely defensive approach. I informed the client how much I thought it would cost to fully litigate their cases, along with what I would recommend to settle. The Board was understanding and said they wanted me to defend all of their current litigation regarding any patent infringement." Alex paused, looked down at his notes, and continued. "Since the last meeting, one case is progressing quite nicely in the D.C. Federal Court. We are gearing up for trial. We have started discovery, which has been burdensome, but the Plaintiff's attorneys have their work cut out. There are three other suits pending, in Texas, New York and California. All pertain to patent infringement, as an ancillary matter. I am scheduled to head out to San Francisco at the beginning of November to conduct discovery and depositions. There are a few motions scheduled, so I'll be spending some time there. The case is moving along as planned. If there are any questions. . . ." Alex gestured, looking around the room.

Dougherty looked up. "How long are you scheduled to be in California?"

"From five to ten days, depending on the scope and duration of discovery."

"Have you scheduled coverage for you here?"

"Not yet."

"I'd recommend you do it tres vite. The holidays are quickly approaching. Schedules, with vacation time, are in place. We cannot overlap. We must make sure there is coverage." Dougherty said stiff lipped, almost indignantly.

Quinn Colton raised his hand, as if in grade school. Quinn, for all he tried, liked to keep behind the scenes. He was good at the research aspect of things, but his public speaking and physical appearance lacked inspiration.

"Yes," Alex said.

"Mr. Dougherty." Quinn remained seated, his voice quivered. "I discussed this with Alex prior to the meeting and, if it is all right, I'll cover for him while he's out of town."

"I don't know if it's such a good idea," Alex responded. "Quinn already has a heavy case load as it is. I could get by with an associate during the time I'm not here."

"I think it's a fine offer Quinn," Mr. Dougherty said while looking through Alex. "We need someone with experience as back up. If you need some help while Alex is gone, then you can fall to the associates for support. Play it as it comes."

"But, I. . . I," stammered Alex, not wanting to be associated with Quinn during this, or any other, case.

"I won't hear anything about it. I want you two to get together after the meeting to sort through this matter."

"Yes sir, that would be fine." Alex did not hide his displeasure. He glanced at Quinn, who was grinning from ear to ear, just wanting to be one of the boys and he was attempting to do so through Alex.

"Are there any other questions?" Alex asked. No one moved.

"Thank you for the information on Ameritrend. I'm confident you and Quinn will work well together. We will hear from you again under new business. Now let's turn our attention to the TKM matter."

Alex drowned out the words being said. Everything became an undertone, as he was more absorbed in the commotion less than one hundred feet away, on the street below.

At first, toward the corner of the building across the street, he noticed a panhandler asking for money. It was not one he had seen before. Panhandlers mark their territory. No one else moves in. It was an unwritten, but obvious rule to life on the streets. The man looked grubby, unshowered, but not as weathered as others. He appeared unusual, sitting on a blue milk crate, his hat was on the ground in front, with a sign attached. It was too small to read.

Most ignored the man, looking the other way as they walked past. Some would hesitate for a few seconds, converse, then move on. Once in a while, someone would give him something, which he would readily accept.

Alex shifted his focus further down the street, where there seemed to be a group of three young people approaching the panhandler. Two appeared to be white and one looked Hispanic, with a dark complexion and jet black hair. They became more animated as they approached the corner. People reacted to them, not diverting their eyes, like deer being shined, stopping in their tracks until the ruffians passed by.

Once these punks approached the vagrant, they hassled him. One kicked away his hat, sending money in different directions. Another picked up the bills, while the third grabbed the man, picked him up and pushed him toward the wall. Alex could not believe what he was seeing. He looked to his left and right, but the other attorneys seemed oblivious to what was in the real world below. As he looked back to the skirmish, three unmarked cars pulled up. Six people sprang out, all sporting badges, including the bum. Alex heard his name called.

"And now onto new business. Alex will present his argument for a practice courtroom." Alex took a second, gathering his thoughts before proceeding. It was kind of exciting for him to witness all of the street commotion. Now he had to put forth a concise argument to have the firm invest in a room that would not have much use. He would need to use his power of persuasion to allow his idea to live to the next step in the firm's selection process. Anything that did not make it past this round could not be brought up again for six months. Alex took it all in stride. Nothing ventured was nothing gained.

"Distinguished members of this firm," began Alex. "Once again we have the opportunity to be at the forefront of civil litigation. We owe it to ourselves and our firm to continue to prepare for the future. We have done that in numerous ways. Our firm is fully computerized. We no longer waste endless hours in the library, researching and shepardizing cases, plus statutes and codes. We can now accomplish that through our own computers. We have CD-ROM, which allows interaction and research at the drop of a hat, or should I say, push of a button. We have access to the Internet and Lexus. How many of us balked at progress, when now we find it to be invaluable. The same goes for cellular phones, lap top computers, templates and forms and our telephone system. If we stopped to think about it, and I mean really think, where would we be without taking those steps?" Alex looked around the room, pausing for added emphasis. "I'll tell you where we'd be. We would have gone the way of Nunn Sachs or Barnes and Mitchell. We would be extinct. Oh how quickly the mighty fall. There are hundreds of firms who have shunned progress only to be rendered obsolete. There are hundreds more on the verge of dissipation because they are technophobic. They fear technology and being prepared." Alex looked about the room.

"Technology and being prepared go hand in hand. You cannot have one without the other. We have the technology. We go to the seminars. We experience law first hand. What more do we really need, you ask. Well, I'm glad you did. We need to further our preparation for the battle. Law is no longer about gentlemen getting together to work things out for their clients. It's no longer a closely knit fraternity where everyone knows one another. It's no longer about developing

150

friendships with fellow attorneys, knowing you will inevitably see them again. It's not trying to create a win-win situation. Law is Darwinism, Darwinism is law. Only the strongest survive. If you are like me, then you want to see MacClennan, O'Brien, Dougherty and Ernest still in existence when Spacely's Sprockets is formed. If you want this firm to be Mr. Spacely's attorneys, then I propose we look into the next legal elevation. I propose we establish a practice court room to enable every one of us to hone our craft." Alex let the idea sink in.

"A mock court room will benefit each and every one of us in the following five ways. First, it will better prepare us for trial. By preparing for a mock trial, we will have done most legwork for trial. That's an added perk. Second, It allows others to assess a case's strengths and weaknesses. Third, it shows what the opponent's strengths and weaknesses are. Fourth, we can impanel impartial people to sit as jurors and get their feedback. We can have cameras recording their deliberations, unobtrusive, but all seeing. An added insight. Finally, any motions, or objections which need to be raised, are fully contemplated, adding to the element of being fully prepared. Ready for the attack."

Several attorneys were nodding their heads in agreement, some had blank looks on their faces. Alex looked at his watch. It was approaching Six. Many were tired and wanted to get home. Outside was becoming dusk. He had to make it short and succinct.

"Remember one thing before we vote to put this through to the sub-committee for further investigation. The legal profession is about survival and tenacity. Those items must be learned and sharpened. By establishing this system for litigation, we will become the standard by which all are judged. Thank you for your time, attention and consideration." Alex sat down.

"Thank you. That was quite a dissertation. Since I am the presiding partner, I will abstain from the vote. I will now put it to the members for any questions." Dougherty looked around the room. No one responded.

"Seeing there are no questions, let's put this motion to investigate the proposed idea for a trial room to a voice vote. All those in favor say Aye."

Most present said "Aye."

"All opposed, same sign."

A few said "Aye."

"Motion carries, the matter will proceed to the next stage. That being the end of new business, this meeting is adjourned. Everyone have a good night. Be careful on your way home and we'll see you in the morning."

You just didn't want a surrender of the United States of America to go under American ideals. That's why you didn't care for the League [of Nations], which is now deceased.

Warren G. Harding
23rd President

CHAPTER TWELVE
OCTOBER 24TH

Alex proceeded on the winding roads to Garrett Baird's estate, outside of Falls Church, Virginia. He knew the area since he was born and raised in Leesburg, never venturing too far from the nest, living the upper middle class existence. As he drove along scenic roads, Alex took in the trees changing their hues, in a magnificent display of autumn colors.

He was in no rush to get to Garrett's since he was ahead of schedule. They were to meet and discuss his ability to raise additional funds for the Republican party. It was to be an informal setting, just the two of them.

It was 7:00 p.m. The news was on so he turned up the volume on the radio.

"You are listening to WDM Washington," a voice over indicated.

"I'm Chris Austin. Welcome to News on the World. The economy has suffered a setback, as the strength of the dollar has fallen dramatically against both the yen and the European mark. Both are at new lows. When questioned, President Lawton had this response,"

"It seems to be the market overcorrecting itself in response to the Federal Reserve tightening the monetary supply to get interest rates under control. I have confidence the dollar will make a strong comeback before the end of the month."

"Trouble in the Middle East does not seem to be ebbing. After the United Nations passed a Resolution to mediate the situation, Secretary of State Christopher Grover, was dispatched to Israel, Damascus and the Gaza Strip, in Palestine, to try some shuttle diplomacy, for the current Administration, circumventing the U.N. When asked what he hoped to accomplish, Mr. Grover replied:"

"I'm here on a diplomatic mission. Our objective is to put an end to the hostilities that have escalated in recent months. It's not an easy task. When there has been a conflict, which has sustained generations and generations of a nation's people, it will take time to resolve. At the present, if we can get all sides to sit down and begin negotiations, I will consider it very fruitful."

"The speaker of the House says he'll push the President on rejecting the Trade Agreement. Tennessee Republican, Walden Cassott has indicated the struggle won't end there. In a Washington Post interview, Cassott refers to the President as being 'brack brained' in understanding the American people, and to the White House as being a 'bunch of latrine lawyers who only know how to jibber jabber."

"From the FBI, crime statistics are on an increase over last year. According to the Bureau, this is the fifth straight year for a rise in criminal activity. The latest reports show an increase of five to thirty percent from those statistics of last year. The highest increase is in assaultive crimes, up thirty percent so far. The lowest is property thefts, up three percent. Civil Libertarian Howard Katz believes these numbers are misleading,"

"The downturn in crime may be due to the drying up of individual rights and liberties. Government has been limiting personal rights and increasing police powers. People respond by saying if I having nothing to hide, then why should I worry about the police questioning me. Be worried because it is an intrusion upon your inalienable right to privacy. The masses must be intimidated and brought back to reality. Our nation was founded upon the supposition that government is not a necessity. No one should be entrusted with too much power, and the police are no exception."

"This is News on the World Tonight. We'll be back after these messages."

He flipped the radio over to FM, as he approached the Falls Church turn off. He signaled to turn and now was only a few miles away. Around this part of the state, the homes were estates. Each had so much property, lending to an openness, one of being free, never worrying what the neighbors might see or hear.

"Garrett, we're running into problems," Thomas Henry said in his southern accent. He stood up from the chair across from Garrett, who was seated at his desk in the library. "I don't think y'all appreciate the magnitude of this situation."

Garrett was silent, leaning back in his chair. His belly hung over his belt, obscuring most of it from view. He chewed on his unlit cigar for a moment. "Go over it again. I want to be sure of the details before I decide."

"It's been confirmed the Feebie has been accessing information."

"His name?"

"Weylyn. William Weylyn. Friends call him Sniper."

"How long has he been with the Bureau?"

"Almost twelve years."

"He's tied in with Westcott?" Garrett continued to chew on his cigar.

Thomas Henry nodded in agreement. "That's why I had y'all arrange a meeting with him tonight. I want y'all to be fully apprised of the situation, so nothing comes as a surprise."

"What information do you have tying in Alex?"

"Background check on Weylyn shows they've been close friends for quite a number of years. When Feebie was accessing information, we were notified. He was extensively questioned. He indicated he was checking into this for a friend. We pushed an he told."

"I want the Agent transferred," Garrett demanded.

"Consider it done."

"Any more on Alex?"

"Yea. There's more. I was present when he had a discussion with Michael. He was pushing the envelope. He's pushed further," Thomas Henry said.

"How's that affect us?"

"He's looking. We know about the library access. He's been to the Wilson house, where a breach occurred."

"I remember."

"We've heard from another source he's been to Dumbarton."

"And?" Garrett asked while still chewing on his cigar. The end was soggy, almost paste in consistency.

"If Alex Westcott is persistent he could derail our plans. If he was outside of the loop, I'd pay no heed to it. However, he's running in the same circle."

"Why not make him part of this?"

Thomas Henry stopped. He looked out the library's bay window. "There's an old adage 'Don't let someone piss on your fire.' Either way he's gotta be stopped."

"When?" Garrett looked directly at Henry, biting down harder on his cigar.

"Tonight. I want you to do everything as I instruct, then once Westcott leaves, I'll take it from there."

Alex turned into the drive. The gate was open. No need to announce his presence through the intercom. Alex meandered his little car up the tree lined drive. Any worry one had would dissolve quickly as they approached this home. Alex neared the main entrance to the house. Two people were outside, exchanging words, shaking hands. One turned to leave in a navy blue Caprice. It was Thomas Henry. Alex found it strange Tom would be meeting with Garrett. He did not realize Henry had such close ties with the party in Virginia. Alex pulled to a stop next to Garrett. Thomas Henry drove by and acknowledged him, as Alex held up his hand in a sign of recognition. He turned off the engine, exited the MG and approached Garrett.

"Alex, how are you?" Garrett said as they shook hands. "I owe you my life."

Alex blushed. "I'm just fine. Thanks for inviting me over. I'm glad you're doing well."

"I won't keep you too long. However, with all that you've done and you being an up and coming star in the party, I felt we should get to know each other a little better." He gestured for them to enter the home.

The big wooden entry door was ornate in its design. The foyer had a dark marble floor. The interior walls were painted white in comparison. Any and all woodwork and trim was a light oak. The interior was more modern than the exterior would indicate.

"Let's go to the library to sit and talk," Garrett instructed.

"Sure," Alex said as he followed Garrett down a hall to the library. There were two French doors leading in. Entering before Garrett, Alex looked around the room. Books dominated, up fifteen feet to the ceiling. A bay window faced the front driveway. Right in front of him were two high backed chairs, facing toward the bay window, separated by a table. Toward the opposite end was an editor's table. Two chairs were on opposite sides. A ceiling lamp hung low, centered above the desk. Alex noticed the fireplace in the right corner of the room. Two short, overstuffed leather chairs were nestled close.

"Would you like anything to drink? How about joining me in a scotch on the rocks." Garrett said more of a directive than a question to answer.

Alex nodded in agreement.

Garrett turned to his right, gliding in a portly manner over to the dry bar behind them, settled inside of the doors. He grabbed two baccarat highball glasses, and then opened the icemaker, filling each glass one third full. Garrett set the glasses down on the bar and reached for the bottle of Glenmorangie. It was the only bottle on the bar. He filled the glasses to the rim, then handed one to Alex. "Here you go son."

Alex took the glass, immediately sipping from it so none would spill. The scotch warmed him immediately. The room was masculine in nature. Alex felt comfortable. This room was dark. The fireplace was lighted, giving off a feeling of warmth.

"Please sit down." Garrett gestured toward the high backed chairs.

Alex sat down. He noticed his head was nowhere near the top of the chair. "I feel like King Louie, ready to be coronated. This chair engulfs me."

Garrett laughed. "It does indeed. These are chairs fit for a king. I hope the scotch is to your liking."

Alex took a longer sip. "Smooth."

"Yes it is." Garrett studied Alex. "There are a few things I want to discuss with you."

Alex left feeling more secure in his rising position within the Republican party. Garrett had given him a strong sense of security, telling him he could receive political backing to run for elective office.

Must be an infantryman before you can be an officer, was imposed upon Alex this evening. The conversation turned to the New World Order with no prompting on Alex's part, which made him feel it was agreeable to have someone share the same beliefs. There was no arguing, just a sense of agreement.

Alex drove away from the manor, down toward the Old Falls Church Highway, taking the same route home. He was tired and figured it would be easier to navigate the winding drive. A gentle mist enveloped the area, adding to the sense of autumn, and the coming winter.

He glanced at the dimly lit clock in his MG. It was a little after 9:00 p.m. He had not phoned Laurel, as promised. That was something he needed to do since she worried about him. As he reached for the car phone, on the passenger seat, another vehicle approached quickly from behind with its beams on high.

"Who's this ass?" Alex said as the car approached faster, tailgating, forcing him to increase his speed, but his tires were losing traction as he rounded the curves. As he downshifted, he felt a sharp jarring as his car was struck hard. Metal impacted upon metal, almost sending his MG off of the high embankment.

"Jesus Christ!" Alex shouted. "What the fuck is your problem." He could not panic. The other car was closely following him, even speeding up, trying to hit him again. He could not risk going for the phone. He had to concentrate on the road ahead.

Without missing a beat, Alex slammed the gas pedal to the floor as he approached a straight-a-way, distancing himself from the other vehicle. The MG was no match for the other car. It quickly caught up, getting along side. Alex shot a glance as the vehicle swerved into his driver's side door.

"Where's a cop when you need one?" Alex maneuvered the MG around the next corner.

The cars proceeded along a steep incline. Trees lined the road toward the top of the bluff, then down to the ravine. Alex rode his breaks trying to determine the year and model of the other car.

"God, that car looks familiar." He was shouting as he felt the car jar him with greater impact than before. The force threw him up against the steering wheel. The little MG swerved hard to the left, then even harder to the right, forcing the passenger side against the guardrail, then back onto the road.

Alex tried to look at the license plate of the other car, but found it impossible to read from the rear view mirror. Plus the plastic rear window distorted everything.

"Oh my God," Alex uttered under his breath.

The sedan slammed hard into the MG. He could do nothing to control his car from heading off the embankment, down into the ravine. There was no guardrail to prevent him from going over. Alex kept steering the car as it went over. It felt as though he were flying, until the front end of the car dug into the wet ground. Then the rear of the car hit hard, sending the front of the car up high into the air, with the rear soon following. The muddy descent slowed him, but seemed to take forever. The snaps of branches, trees and field grass could be heard as he continued downward. The car's headlights gave bits and pieces of information as he continued. Trees guided him toward the bottom as he glanced off of one, only to be hurtled into another. It was a giant pin ball game, only he was the ball. He saw a cluster of large trees and swerved around them. Then came the large oak. There was no way he would miss.

"Oh fuck!" The impact of metal twisting against wood, glass breaking, rivets popping could be heard, followed by complete silence.

He opened his eyes, slowly, not knowing if he had been knocked unconscious, or how long he had been in the car.

"Holy shit." Alex's voice, in the silent night, surprised him. It

160

seemed so loud. He was pinned in the car. The steering wheel was jammed against his chest. He could breath all right, so he knew no ribs were broken. He placed his hands on the steering wheel, close to his chest. He manipulated each finger.

"Everything's okay there. Now for the legs and feet." Alex moved his legs, feet and toes. They were not caught in anything. "That's a good sign."

He put his hands on the steering wheel and pushed. It did not budge. Alex was banged and bruised. He had cuts on his face from the windshield crashing in. He wiped the blood from his brow, but some headed down his cheek, into his mouth, tasting warm, salty sweet.

Alex reached under the seat, for the release bar. He moved his seat back four inches. He then reached with his left hand down to the side corner of the seat and released it to tilt back. "That'll give me some breathing room," Alex laughed, trying to keep his sense of humor."

He tried to open the driver's side door. It would not move. He released the latches to the top of the convertible. First the driver's side, then passenger's, flipping the top back as he did so. The mist had become heavier, almost to the point of rain.

Alex reached over to the passenger's seat. He fumbled in the darkness for the phone. Without the moon, it made seeing difficult. Alex could tell the MG was totaled. It was a miracle he survived the fall, let alone with only minor injuries. He found the phone under the driver's seat. His heart raced, excited and relieved. He edged his way out of the car and, once out, leaned against the trunk. He strained to look up toward the direction from which he came.

Alex looked at his watch, holding it close to his eyes. It was 9:20. He knew he had not lost consciousness.

He flipped open the phone and dialed 911.

"Police emergency, how may I help you?" came a woman's voice.

"There's been, I've been in an accident," Alex said haltingly, trying to catch his breath.

"Where are you calling from, sir?"

"I'm not quite sure. It's somewhere off of the Old Falls Church Highway."

"Is anyone injured?" Emergency asked.

"No, no, everything seems to be okay." Alex told her.

"How many vehicles were involved."

"Two, I think."

"Is the other vehicle present?"

"No. Not here with me. It probably took off," he replied.

"Okay."

"Hey, how much longer?" Alex grew impatient.

"We are tracing your telephone call right now with cell transferors which are in the vicinity. Emergency vehicles should be on the scene within five minutes."

"I'm down the embankment. Not on the main road. Please tell them."

"Okay, sir. They'll be there shortly. We have your location on computer. Would you like me to remain on the phone with you until the authorities arrive?"

Alex thought about it. "No. I'll be all right."

"Good night."

"Bye," said Alex. He then dialed home.

"Hello."

"Hi Honey. Sorry I didn't call earlier, but something came up."

"Alex where are you?"

162

"Well, there's been an accident."

"Are you all right? You don't sound well." Laurel's worried voice carried through to him.

"Don't worry Dear. I'm fine. The MG is totaled, but I can walk away. So I'm fine." Alex tried to reassure her. "You know what pilots say."

"What?"

"Any landing you walk away from is a good one," he replied.

"Were any other cars involved?" Laurel asked.

"One other car. He may have left."

"Are you all right?"

"Yes. I'm fine."

"Do you need to be picked up?" she asked.

"I see some flashing lights up the road, so I got to go. If I need a lift, I'll call, otherwise I'll tell you about it when I get home."

"I love you. Be careful, Alex."

"Bye." Alex closed the receiver and put the phone in his jacket. He walked toward the spotlight shining down, some 300 feet away. He picked, pulled, slipped and stumbled his way up the ravine. Once at the top, flashing lights combined with the heavy mist made everything seem surreal. It looked like a UFO landing site. Three police cars, lights flashing, blocked the road, directing the few approaching cars around their field of investigation. There was one fire vehicle and a paramedic unit. The flashing yellow lights of a wrecker were seen in the distance.

Alex climbed onto the shoulder of the road. He glanced behind him seeing for the first time the path his car had taken. He realized how lucky he was nothing more serious happened to him. Without the car phone, or if he was seriously injured, he would not have been found for days.

"Sir, my name is Deputy Ellis. I'm with the sheriff's department. You look kinda of tagged. Why don't you come with me to the paramedic's van, so they can get a look at those cuts on your forehead." The Deputy grabbed Alex by his right elbow, directing him to one of the sets of flashing lights. Everything seemed unreal. Alex felt he was dreaming.

"Now go on and get up there."

He positioned Alex next to the bumper of the paramedic unit. Both of the back doors were open, outward. Alex was trembling from the cold and excitement of the accident.

"I think he's on the verge of shock," one of the paramedics yelled to his partner. Alex was grabbed by both arms and forced down in a seat in back.

"Let's get his vitals."

"Roger," said the young paramedic.

"Sir. We will remove your jacket and take your blood pressure. We'll look at those cuts, then make sure nothing's broken."

Alex nodded in agreement, comprehending most of what was being said.

"I doubt he broke anything," Deputy Ellis chimed in, sticking his head into the paramedic unit. "He was able to climb the steep embankment pretty fast."

"Thanks officer. We've seen people do some remarkable things once the betas kick in. We'll look at him. You should be able to ask him questions before we transport," the paramedic said, motioning for the Deputy to leave as they attended to Alex.

The paramedic took out the pressure sleeve, placed it around Alex's upper arm, increasing pressure. Alex could feel his heart beat in his facial cuts, as pressure increased. The medic then released the restriction, which sounded like a punctured tire loosing air.

"One forty over ninety."

"It's a little high. Check his pulse."

"Eighty-five."

"Good." He turned his attention to Alex. "What's your name sir?"

"Alex. Alex Westcott," came the reply in a voice stronger and more under control, now that he had a chance to collect his thoughts.

"Well Mr. Westcott, your blood pressure is elevated, but it does not pose a problem. We're going to get you cleaned up, see what those cuts look like and make sure you have no serious injuries."

"Sounds fine," Alex told him.

"After we finish, that Deputy will want to talk to you. We'll let him and then we'll transport you to the hospital, where the doctors can look at you."

Alex closed his eyes as a cold, wet gauze material was applied to his face. It had an antiseptic odor about it. He cringed, slightly, from the stinging, as the solution hit his wounds.

"You don't look too worse for wear, Mr. Westcott. You'll need a few stitches here and there, though. It will not take away from your looks."

"I guess it will give me some more character, not that there's anything wrong with that," Alex chuckled.

"We're just going to close up the cuts temporarily, with some butterflies."

The paramedics spent close to an hour cleaning him up.

"You're set for the time being. It looks as if the Deputy is approaching. Probably just wants to check on our work so when he needs our services he'll be reassured."

"Do you have any pain in any of your extremities?" the

165

paramedic asked.

"Not really. I feel more banged up than anything." Alex replied.

"You had quite a tumble down the hill. When we got here, we didn't know if we would have to make that climb down. You saved us a lot of aggravation by coming up to us."

"Glad I could be of service."

"In all seriousness, Mr. Westcott, you should realize you're quite lucky to be so unscathed. Also, you are in good condition, which probably contributed to your run of luck tonight."

Alex sat up and looked out of the van. Deputy Ellis was standing outside of the open door, clipboard in hand, looking at him.

"Are you boys all done now?" The Deputy asked.

"For now. We've radioed ahead to the hospital to let them know we are on our way, so Officer, I'd appreciate it if you could keep the hen party short."

"I'll see what I can do," Deputy Ellis retorted. He shifted, glancing away from Alex before he started in on his questioning.

"I'm told your name is Alex Westcott."

"Yes officer," Alex replied.

"Mr. Westcott you are quite fortunate. You suffered quite a drop and have come out like this. Why don't we start." Deputy Ellis said with a slight Virginian drawl.

"That would be fine."

"Where were you tonight."

"I had a meeting at a house near here. I was just going home."

"Where was the meeting?"

"It was at Garrett Baird's home."

"Garrett Baird's?

"Yes."

"How long were you there?"

"From seven thirty till nine."

"Did you have anything to drink?"

Alex thought about his response. He had two scotch on the rocks, at Garrett's request. It was not something he would ordinarily do, but based upon the circumstances, Alex did not believe he had a choice. When the General says jump, you ask 'How high?' Now it was a problem. "Why?" Alex asked.

"Mr. Westcott. There has been a single vehicular accident. The lone occupant of that vehicle suffered injuries. An automobile was totaled in the interim. Based upon that, and the fact I detect an odor of intoxicants from your person, I am now conducting an investigation which could have criminal implications."

"I did have a couple of drinks while I was with Mr. Baird." Alex said, not wanting to imply he had a lot to drink, hoping to downplay the role of alcohol.

"Only two? What were they?"

"Scotch."

"That's quite a powerful drink there."

"Officer, I don't mean to step over your investigation, but there is more to the story than the fact I had a couple of drinks tonight and was in a car accident."

"Such as?"

"Such as the fact my car was forced off of the road." Alex looked at him. "This car followed me, hit me a few times and before I knew it I was heading down the embankment."

"Did you get a description of this other car?" the Deputy

sarcastically asked.

"It was a dark colored sedan."

"Did you get the make, model, or year?"

"It was too dark. I couldn't tell."

"How about a license plate number? Either from the front or rear?"

"No." Alex could sense this conversation was futile, but he had to get across the point another car ran him off. "The back window of my car is made of plastic. Over the years it's become more discolored, worse to see out of, so I couldn't tell."

"Were you able to see the driver?"

"I got a glimpse of a man with dark hair, but I couldn't see any defining characteristics."

"Mr. Westcott, why don't we just settle this once and for all and have you take a preliminary breath test. If you pass the test, then there is no need to worry about anything else. If you don't pass, then we'll issue an appearance ticket, and go from there."

"Well, I. . . ."

"Deputy Ellis, Deputy," a voice from the shadows called out. It was difficult to see who due to the lighting from the surrounding emergency equipment. The shadow he cast forward, toward the Paramedic unit, hid his face.

"What is it Luthy?" Ellis shouted back.

"I've been doing some walking back to the main point of impact, where the MG went down, and I found a license plate."

"Whose is it?"

"I don't know."

"What's that supposed to mean Luthy? I don't have all night to play some guessing game with you. What's up?"

"Deputy Ellis, here's the plate." Luthy handed over a battered Maryland license plate.

"So," responded Ellis handing the plate back.

Alex caught the license plate number. TMW 994, black lettering with a white face. He recognized it as a Maryland plate. To commit the plate to memory he devised a rhyme. The Merry Whore, was all he could come up with, then he added had Nine Hundred and Ninety Four. After a few repetitions, 'The Merry Whore had Nine Hundred and Ninety Four, The Merry Whore had Nine Hundred and Ninety Four,' it was committed to memory.

"Well, I ran the plate numbers with dispatch and it came back as an unregistered vehicle."

"Unregistered?" Ellis hesitated. "Don't you mean expired."

"No. Unregistered. This car has no existence." Luthy explained. "It could have been driven by a ghost."

"Maybe Mr. Westcott's story has some truth to it." Ellis glanced back at Alex. "Why don't you look into it a little further Luthy?"

"Yes sir." Luthy turned and left Ellis and Alex alone in the rear of the Paramedic unit.

"Now Mr. Westcott, even if your story is true, drinking and driving is against the law if your blood alcohol is above a certain level.

"I know, .08," Alex said.

"What's your occupation?"

"I'm an attorney. So you can dispose of the explanation. I'll take your test."

Deputy Ellis held out a little tube, about the size of a pen extending into a box about the size of a cigarette pack.

"Blow into this," he instructed Alex.

Alex blew, hoping his blood alcohol level was not over the limit. It would be difficult enough to explain what happened, but then to be arrested for drunk driving, no one would believe someone ran him off the road. Another pink elephant story.

".06."

"What happens now?" Alex asked.

"I'm going to broom this one. I'll reference it in my report, as to your level. You won't have to take a regular breathalyzer to determine whether charges should be brought."

"Thank you Deputy."

"Mr. Westcott."

"Yes Deputy?" Alex looked at him more out of being grateful than interested.

"Remember this. Just because your level was .06 doesn't mean I couldn't write you up for drunk driving. All it means is I am giving you a break. A big break."

"I realize that Deputy. Thank you."

"Boys, this one is ready for transport," Deputy Ellis yelled to the Paramedics. "I'll get the doors back here."

"Okay," came the response.

As Deputy Ellis closed the doors, he leaned in. "Remember, you got your break tonight. We'll tow your car down to Stone's, south of Falls Church." He shut the back doors and knocked on the side of the unit, signaling he was finished.

There must be, not a balance of power, but a community of power; not organized rivalries, but an organized common peace.

Woodrow Wilson
21st President

CHAPTER THIRTEEN
OCTOBER 25TH

Alex awoke late. It was 2:30 a.m. before he got home from the hospital. He received twelve stitches over two cuts. 'Facial cuts are bleeders,' the doctor told him as he was wheeled into the emergency room. Physicians performed tests on him, to make sure there was nothing else wrong. The hospital staff gave him a clean bill of health, told him to rest and then sent him on his way.

Laurel phoned Maura in the morning, before Alex got up. She told her Alex had been in a car accident, but he was fine and would be into work late. He took a cab to the office, less tossing about than in the subway, he figured. Plus they now were a one-car family and Laurel needed it to run the boys around.

He glanced at his watch as he opened the firm doors leading into the lobby. It was five of eleven.

"Hello Mr. Westcott. How are you feeling this morning?"

"Just fine Sarah, except for a little stiffness," Alex told her as he quickened his pace past, heading down the hall toward his office.

As he approached his secretary's desk, Maura was working on dictation, her back was turned to him. "Good morning Maura, how are you today?" Alex asked in an upbeat tone.

She turned and faced him, giving him the once over. Looking closely at his face, down, then back up. "I should be asking you," she replied.

"I'll tell you, last night was quite an experience. It's not one I'd want to go through regularly, but I'm fine," he said as Maura continued to look at his face where the stitches were visible. "By the way, I don't mean to interrupt your staring, but do I have any messages?"

"A few phone calls, nothing urgent." Maura expressed her opinion what she considered important. "Judge Connally - he wants to get together after work on Friday. Andy Vassily - some request for production of documents. Copy Services wants to know if you wanted to submit documents to them for transcribing. That's it."

"Thanks Maura. I'll be in my office. Please hold all of my calls, except the usual ones. Tell anyone who calls I'm in a conference."

"Yes Mr. Westcott. Oh, I almost forgot, this message came by overnight mail."

"Who's it from?"

"I don't know. I didn't open it and there is no return."

Alex took the package, then walked into his office and turned off the lights. He surmised Maura must have been in there earlier. He closed the door behind him to drown out any noise, with keeping the curious at bay. He tossed the envelope on his desk. His first order of business was to call Sniper and have him run a check on the license plate the officer found near the scene of the accident. Alex flipped through his rolodex for Sniper's name. He found it and dialed up the FBI's Washington D.C. office.

"Federal Bureau of Investigations, how may I direct your call?" A pleasant woman's voice inquired.

"Yes. I'd like to speak with William Weylyn, please."

"May I tell Mr. Weylyn who is calling?"

"Tell him it's Alex Westcott."

"Yes sir, Mr. Westcott."

While on hold, waiting for the transfer, Alex looked at the message from Judge Connally. He wanted to get together for drinks in Georgetown on Friday. Alex knew it would be a madhouse, it was the weekend of Halloween. There is no bigger party than Halloween in Georgetown, with the possible exception of Mardi Gras in New Orleans. He remembered Mardi Gras, twenty years ago, with Sniper. Talk about wild times, he thought. The headache he now had was about what he suffered the day after in New Orleans. Alex looked around his office, taking in all of the work piled on top of and next to his desk, which remained undone.

"How are you? To what do I owe a phone call from you during working hours?"

"Fine Snipe, a little whammed up, but no more worse for wear."

"Why? What happened? Is hockey becoming a little rough for you? You're getting a little old and out of shape to play."

Alex laughed. "I wish it were just a hockey injury. The abuse is expected in the hit and run aspect of the game, but, I was in a car accident last night."

"I know how you drive Alex, so I can tell you it won't be your last one. What happened?"

"I was coming back from a meeting in Falls Church. As I was driving along the highway, a car pulled up alongside of mine and rammed into my little MG."

"You've got to be joking. What did you do, gesture to him you thought his IQ was one?"

"No. Nothing like that. At least not this time."

"Then what happened?" Sniper asked.

"Well, I found myself hurtling down a steep embankment. I kept driving, as best as I could, until the car came to rest against a tree, down a ravine."

"Whoa. That'll tighten the old sphincter. What happened to you? You're still kickin', so that's a good sign."

"Yea. Just a few stitches to accompany the ones I got from hanging with you. Nothing major. The usual bumps and bruises."

"Did they catch who ran you off?"

"No. And that's where I need your help," Alex said.

"I'm not in municipal traffic control," Sniper cracked.

"I know. Apparently a license plate came off the other car. When the locals tried to run it, it came back as unregistered or non-existent," Alex explained.

"What's the plate number?"

"The Merry Whore had Nine Hundred and Ninety Four."

"Quite the nursery rhyme, Alex. Please translate it or I'll send you back to the hospital for a CAT scan and further observations."

"It's how I remembered the plate. It wasn't as if I could ask the officer for paper and a pen. The plate number is T M W Nine Nine Four, from Maryland."

"I'll run it for you and call you once I get the information," Sniper said. "It shouldn't be too difficult. And don't worry about the charge. It's on the government."

"You're too kind. I owe you one buddy."

"You owe me more than one Alex."

"And Snipe."

"Yes?"

"Do me one more favor."

"Sure. What?"

"Make sure you get back to me soon. I know how you can get

side tracked."

"No problem," replied Sniper.

Hanging up the phone Alex realized, with his head pounding, he would accomplish little today. He decided to give Morris Braxton a call to see how his trip to California was, and to work into his schedule another review of Woodrow Wilson's personal writings. Alex opened his rolodex, flipping it to the B's. He passed Barris, Bentice, then Braxton. "There it is," Alex said as he dialed the telephone number.

"Woodrow Wilson Foundation, may I help you?"

"Morris Braxton, please."

There was a slight hesitation. "I'm sorry, but Mr. Braxton is not here," came the hesitant reply.

"I'm a friend of his," Alex started to explain, knowing the more pleasant one was, the more receptive receptionists and secretaries were. "So do you know how I can reach him?"

"Please hold sir. I will connect you to the Director."

He recounted that Morris should have been back from his trip out West by now. After a long period of time, a woman's voice came on the other end.

"Kathleen Korte, how may I help you?"

"Ms. Korte, I'm trying to reach Morris Braxton," Alex explained all over again, spinning his wheels over a simple phone call. "He's an old college friend of mine."

"Sir, can I have your name please."

"Sure. It's Alex Westcott."

"Mr. Westcott, I'm sorry to tell you," she paused, "but Morris Braxton is no longer with us."

"That's too bad," said Alex. "Do you know how I can reach him?"

"Maybe I wasn't clear enough Mr. Westcott." She paused for a moment, and then continued. "There was an accident and Mr. Braxton passed away."

"What? How, how did it happen?" he stammered.

"Morris was in California on some business for the Foundation. While there, he was taking some time off touring Route One. He lost control of his car and crashed into another car coming in the other direction. He was killed instantly. The coroner said he may have suffered a heart attack prior to the accident, but the autopsy was inconclusive."

"God, just incredible. I just can't believe that happened." Alex rubbed his forehead, letting out a slight groan as he touched his stitches, forgetting they were there.

"We are all saddened by the loss," she replied to Alex's moan.

"When did it happen?"

"October eleventh," Kathleen Korte responded without allowing him to finish his sentence. "The first week of his trip. The funeral was one week ago in Morris' hometown of Lafayette. Any contributions can be made in Morris' name for the Woodrow Wilson Foundation."

"Thank you for the information." Alex said slowly, as if reading a script.

"I'm sorry I had to provide you with the unfortunate news. His death was untimely"

"Yes it was. Thank you again." Alex hung up the phone. His head was reeling. Alex slumped in his chair. "Boy is that a shocker." He was the first person Alex went to school with who had passed away. Alex sat in silence, not thinking about anything. His mind went blank, as if he fell into an abyss. He was brought back to reality when some people walked by his closed office door, talking and laughing. It was 12:40 p.m.

Sniper turned his chair back to the computer terminal. He stared at the screen, thinking about how he would request the information from the FBI's data bank. After the last inquiry, he was reprimanded for unauthorized use of FBI information. It was the first time, during his tenure with the Bureau, that he had been reprimanded.

"It's all or nothing." Sniper typed in the license plate number.

TMW 994 MD

The screen flicked. ALPHA ZULU

"Oh shit."

ACCESS INFORMATION DENIED/NO AUTHORIZATION

"Now I've done it."

The computer terminal shut down. The screen went blank.

"I'm a dead man." Sniper watched his computer seize. "They'll probably send me to Peoria for this one." He picked up the sports section from the corner of his desk and waited for the Department Director.

"I guess I'll make a few more phone calls, wait till Sniper calls back with any information, then head home and call it a day." Alex ran through the series. He picked up the message from Judge Connally and dialed his number.

"Judge Connally's chambers."

"Marion, this is Alex Westcott. How are you?"

"I'm fine Mr. Westcott, how you?" came a heartfelt response.

"Just fine Marion. Why are you working during lunch? Don't you have a union which prevents that from happening?" Alex joked.

"I'm tying up some loose ends for the Judge. We had a trial

scheduled for this week which settled yesterday, after the jury was selected. So now we have some free time," Marion explained. "I'll put your call through. Judge Connally said to place your call through."

"Thanks Marion." She switched the phone over to the Judge. There were several clicks.

"Judge Connally's chambers."

"Marion, it's Alex. The call didn't go through."

"I'm sorry Mr. Westcott. You'd think I'd have this system down by now. I'll try again. Please hold." Marion transferred the call.

"Alex, how are you today?" Judge Connally asked.

"Fine." Alex had his eyes closed. "I'm looking forward to our next game on Sunday. It'll be my last one for several weeks though."

"Why?"

"I'm heading to California for discovery purposes. I leave on the third or fourth of November."

"Where in California?"

"San Francisco."

"That'll be fun. San Francisco is a great city. Have you been there before?"

"No."

"You'll love the diversity, not to mention the food. You can eat in a different restaurant every day, all of your life, and still never have to go to the same one twice," Judge Connally said. "Plus the climate. November can be warm. I always thought the city should play baseball during the fall and winter and football in the spring and summer. The seasons are backwards. You also have to go to Napa and tour the wineries. I could go on and on."

"I'm looking forward to it. Too bad it's for business. Laurel will be home with the boys."

"It's a romantic city."

"So I hear. I wanted Laurel to go, but she'd rather take care of the boys, than wait for me all day, while I work. She also feels we take advantage of my parents enough as it is, and didn't want to impose."

"Well, that's too bad. I suppose you're returning my call."

"Yes Judge."

"I was calling to see if you'd like to spend some time with me on Friday night, after work. This week opened up, plus my wife is out of town, so I figured we could go to Georgetown for a few."

"I don't think it'll be a problem, but I'll have to check. My question is whether you know what we'll be in for since it's Halloween weekend. It'll be wild."

"It will be fun. I promise you. Live a little Alex. Remember, I'm older than you and if I can do it, so can you. You're never too old to let loose."

"I suppose you're right Judge. I look forward to it."

"Then we'll plan on it."

"Why don't we meet at Houston's at Six. If something comes up, you call me or I'll call you," Alex said. His eyes were still shut, his head throbbing. He hoped it would clear soon.

"Okay, Alex. It's in my book. Make sure you do the same. And write it in pen, not pencil."

"I will. See you on Friday." Alex hung up the receiver, shifting his weight to the back of his chair, forcing it to recline to a forty-five degree angle. He brought his feet up to the corner of the desk, straight out. It was quiet. He enjoyed the solitude, knowing and dreading the fact it would be momentary.

"BEEEEEP." The sound jarred Alex back. He was not asleep, but, he was not in active thought either. It was somewhere in-between where dreams appear drug induced, hallucinogenic. Everything was psychotropic.

"Yes Maura," Alex said after reaching back to his credenza and pressing the speaker.

"Mr. Weylyn is on line two. He said you were expecting his phone call. Would you like me to take a message?"

"No. I'll take the call," Alex said "Thanks." He picked up the receiver, shifted his legs on the corner of the desk to keep them from cramping, then pressed line 02.

"Hey Snipe, what do you know?"

"Well, I ran the plate for you and discovered some information."

"Go ahead Snipe, but talk up, I can hardly hear you. Where are you calling from?"

"I'm calling from Union Station."

"Why?"

"I'm on my way to National Airport. I have to make a quick trip to Cleveland on a bank case," Sniper explained. "As I was leaving, I realized I hadn't called you back yet, and it is almost one thirty, so I remembered to give you a ring."

"Much appreciated."

"You're quite welcome. But I. . . ." Sniper's voice was drowned out by the sound of a train.

"Sorry Snipe. I didn't hear what you were saying. There was too much noise."

"I ran the plate, but it had an Alpha Zulu classification. I couldn't get access."

"What does that mean? Put it in terms I can understand."

"How much do you appreciate your family and your life?"

"What? Are you yanking my chain here Sniper?"

"No. I could not be more serious than I am right now."

Sniper's tone was unlike any Alex ever heard in all the years he had known him. Through the good and bad, even the arguments they had, he never experienced this tone before.

"You need to be careful. Whatever it is you are involved with, forget about it and concentrate on work and your family."

"I'm not involved with anything," Alex said in a pleading manner.

"Think, Alex. Tell me what you are working on. I'll scope it to see what I can find."

"Well, at work, I have the Ameritrend Chem Company account I've been working on." Alex strained to think of anything else happening which was out of the norm. "There really isn't anything all too important. That's my main priority right now."

"What about any other clients?"

"Most other cases I work on, I'm not the lead attorney. I don't think I'd be the one anyone would be gunning for."

"Where did the accident occur?"

"Near Falls Church, after I met with Garrett Baird.

"Who is he?"

"Garrett's the ace of the Republican party in Virginia. He lives in Falls Church, where we met."

"Anything happen?"

"No, not that I can remember. There was one person there before me. He was leaving around the same time I arrived."

"Who's that?"

"Thomas Henry." Alex said as he could hear the sound of a train pulling into the station.

"What did you say? I couldn't hear."

"Thomas Henry." Alex talked louder into the phone, to make sure Sniper heard him. As he yelled, it made his head pound all that much more.

"Okay. Anything else out of the ordinary? Anything you can think of," Sniper prodded.

"Some discussions I've had with Michael Connally."

"Judge Connally?" Sniper inquired. "The same one we played hockey with a few weeks ago?"

"Yes."

"The meeting dealt with what?"

"Just what we talked about a few weeks ago." Alex hesitated, and then said. "The New World Order."

"Oh, yea, I remember."

"But, to be perfectly honest with you, I can't see anything which would make me the target of something."

"Alex, based upon the Alpha Zulu classification, I would like to look into this matter a little further, to see if something turns up. Let me take this information you've given me and see what I can find out."

"When do you think you'll have something?" Alex asked.

"I should have something in a week or two. I'll have to do this on the side. Keep it quiet. Maybe it's nothing, but I just want to make sure."

"I'm leaving next week for California. Do you think you'll have something by then?"

"Maybe. When I find something, I'll let you know."

"Snipe," Alex paused.

182

"Yes Alex?"

"How many times have you seen this classification appear?"

"Once."

"What was that about?"

"I can't get into it. Be careful. That's all I can tell you."

"Is there anything else I should do?" Alex inquired.

"You should consider buying a gun to protect yourself. Keep it away from the boys, and don't tell Laurel," Sniper instructed, knowing she objected to any type of weapons in or near the house.

"Think I'm in trouble?"

"Stay away from anything if it doesn't involve work."

"I'll try."

"I'll see you later. . . ." Sniper's voice was drowned out as another train pulled into the station.

"Bye." Alex slowly hung up the phone. His head was throbbing. He could feel each beat of his heart pulsate in his stitches. "God, I hope this goes away." He picked up the overnight envelope, grabbed the pull tab and opened the letter. He took it out and read it. There were only four words, scrawled in black crayon.

NEXT TIME YOU'RE DEAD

When Kansas and Colorado have a quarrel over water in the Arkansas River they don't call in the National Guard in each state and go to war over it. They bring a suit in the United States Supreme Court and abide by the decision. There isn't a reason in the world why we cannot do that internationally.

Harry S. Truman
35th President

CHAPTER FOURTEEN
OCTOBER 28TH

He walked into Houston's, in the heart of Georgetown, at half past six, running late. Traffic was heavy, chaotic. It was a combination of being Friday and Halloween. Many were excited the weekend was here, time to unwind. Others approached this as a holiday. All Saints Eve, a day when one's true inner soul is exposed. What better place to experience it than a city where even politicians are likened to gumps and yahoos. Only now one dressed as oneself, without worrying about societal constraints.

As he headed to the bar, Alex noticed several people were already on their way to celebrating Halloween dressed in various costumes. The number of outfits would progress throughout the evening, with greater numbers each day until Monday, the official day of festivities.

Taking an obligatory glance around the bar, he did not see Judge Connally. It was crowded, loud and smoky, which made finding someone difficult. He waded through, bouncing from one person to the next. Occasionally he would get to an open area, catch his breath, rub his eyes, then move on. He worked his way around the bar, excusing himself as he passed, not focusing on faces, only trying to tune into the Judge.

He wound up back near the entrance. There was no sign of Michael Connally. He hoped he remembered to meet him here tonight. Alex knew he should have called and reminded the Judge, but he had been too busy.

"No use waiting." Alex worked his way past those sitting at bar stools. He then tried to get one of the bartender's attention, reaching into his pants pocket, pulling out a twenty, holding it up, trying to let the barkeeper know he wanted a drink.

A short stocky bartender came up to him. "What can I get you?" he asked in an abrupt New England accent, barking to be heard above the din.

"Bud Light," Alex replied.

The bartender reached into a cooler below the counter directly in front of Alex, grabbed a bottle, flipped the top off and placed it in front of him in one swift, effortless motion.

"Need a glass?" came the short howl.

"No thanks."

"$4.75," he barked again.

Alex gave him $20.00 and waited for change. The bartender placed $15.00 on the counter, along with a quarter. Alex left $1.25. He turned around, working his way out of the crowded main bar. He took a few sips of beer, waiting for the Judge, when he felt a hand on his shoulder. He turned. "Judge." Alex greeted him with a handshake. "I was wondering where you were. You're lucky I was running late or I would have imposed the twenty minute rule."

"Alex - Sorry I'm late, but traffic was a bitch. Much more problematic than I remember. I hope you weren't waiting long. What's the twenty minute rule?"

"You can tell someone is old when they don't know that."

"So what's the rule?" Michael Connally asked again.

"Whenever anyone is later than twenty minutes for a meeting or a date, then the date is called and the person waiting is free to stay or leave. It saves the hassle of waiting around wondering where the other person is. You just find out the next day."

"Sounds like a good policy to have. Everything changes so quickly. When I was younger, we never had to worry about rules or anything. Maybe I should impose that in my court."

"So long as you don't tell anyone where you learned it," chided Alex.

Judge Connally paused. "Not to change the subject, but are you ready for another beer? I know I am. This one's on me since I was late."

Alex looked at his half full beer. "Sure, why not. I'll be finished by the time you get back."

"Right."

"Have fun working your way up." By the time he finished his sentence, Judge Connally disappeared through the hazy smoke, moving behind a group of people, toward the bar. Alex looked around. It was more crowded than when he first arrived. He took a sip of beer, much as he took in his surroundings, long, slow and deliberate. Most times, Alex liked crowds. They energized him.

People were talking, laughing, consorting. He felt a gentle touch on his shoulder. It trailed down his back, caressing him. Then it was gone. Alex turned to his right. A striking young woman was standing next to him. Her face was familiar, but he could not recall from where.

"Alex, how are you." She smiled at him.

"Fine," he replied, surprised by the attention, while still trying to place how he knew her.

"What happened to you?" She looked at his forehead. "You look a little banged up."

"You mean this." He moved his hand toward his stitches.

"Yes."

"I was in a car accident a few days ago."

"Is everything all right?"

"Sure. The car's totaled. But at least the swelling has gone down.

I don't look like a tusker anymore, which is a plus," Alex said.

"What's that?"

"A tusker."

She stared blankly. "A what?"

"I don't have to say 'I'm not an animal, I am a human being'." Alex did his best sarcastic English impression, making both of them laugh.

"Now I get it. So the MG was totaled?"

"How did you know I drove an MG?" Alex asked before he thought.

"You don't remember me, do you?"

"Sure I do. I just can't recall your name for the life of me. It must be from all of the beer," he said

"I'll give you a clue." She paused.

"Fair enough."

"Dumbarton." She smiled again. "That should do it."

"Samantha - Sam Hale?"

"Close. Hayes. I won't hold it against you," Sam said softly. "My car was near yours when you walked me out after the tour. I saw you drive away. That's too bad - it looked royal."

"Royal?"

"Cool, awesome," Sam explained.

"Oh yea, I guess we're even."

"Okay," Sam said.

Alex paused. "Is it my imagination, or do you look different from what I remember?"

"I got my hair cut, plus this outfit is not something I wear to work or school."

"You can say that again." Alex looked at her youthful appearance. Her hair was cut above shoulder length, giving her a more mature, professional look. Her outfit showed what great shape she was in. "Oh to be young again," Alex said.

"What?"

"I said time flies," he backtracked.

"What did you mean by that."

"Nothing Sam. Just a slip."

"Freudian."

Alex smiled. "So what brings you out on a night like tonight."

"Perhaps that question should be posed to you. After all, you're the married father of two rambunctious boys."

"Touché. You really know how to hurt a man."

"Keep that in mind." Her smile seemed to radiate from her.

Alex returned the greeting.

"So what do you think of my new look?" Sam looked demurely at him with her deep blue eyes.

"I think you look great." Alex hesitated. "So what are you doing here?"

"I'm meeting some friends. We're making a night of it. They should be here shortly. How about you? What brings you out tonight?"

"I'm here with a friend of mine. His wife's out of town, so we decided to get together."

"Is your wife out of town too?"

"No, but she gave me the green light to go out."

"It's good to see you can get out on occasion."

"Yea, but only once in a while. I'm sure you'll experience it soon enough."

"Think so?" She touched Alex on his sleeve, moving her hand slowly up his arm.

"Without a doubt." Sam was flirtatious and it made him feel young. Alex did not notice or care the bar was becoming louder. More people arrived, many more were costumed. He was now oblivious to the smoke enveloping the room. The push of the crowd forced Sam closer. Her body pressed against his. He could feel the warmth of her breath, as her breasts pressed against his chest. Alex, detecting a hint of her perfume, inhaled deeper. He wanted to breath her in, committing her scent to memory.

"It's kind of strange, but. . . ." Sam hesitated. "I don't think I should tell you this." She looked down and away from him.

"What Sam? You can't just say something, and then stop. You've opened the lid."

"Like toothpaste from the tube," she added.

"Don't change the subject. You were saying."

"It's somewhat embarrassing. I shouldn't have brought it up."

"Too late. Come on, don't be shy. You're among friends." Alex egged her on. "I told you quite a bit about me. Now you can tell me a little something about you."

"Okay. If you must know. It's kind of strange, but I dreamt about you the other night."

Alex was surprised by her admission. "Maybe I'm the one who should be embarrassed."

"I feel as if I know you," Sam continued as she looked up into Alex's eyes. "Intimately."

Alex, somewhat flustered, said, "I hope I didn't disappoint you."

Sam smiled. "I woke up and asked myself 'Was that Alex?' Then I thought about it and it definitely was you." She grabbed his elbow, gently squeezing it.

"I don't know what to say. Really, I'm quite flattered you'd think of me that way." Alex looked down, finding himself turned on, yet embarrassed by the attention.

"I hope I didn't take you by surprise, but I feel like I've known you for quite some time. I even had a premonition I'd run into you tonight."

It was a good thing Laurel was not here, he thought. He would not be able explain this situation. He looked at Sam. She smiled, which seemed to enter him. Do not be a fool Alex, he said to himself, over and over, while looking silently at her.

"Alex, who's this lovely woman?" Judge Connally asked as he positioned himself between them, handing Alex a beer.

"Judge Connally, this is Samantha Hayes."

"Samantha. Nice to make your acquaintance." He held out his hand, took hers, then half bent over it.

Sam smiled. Alex felt the room become silent. It was a strange feeling for him to have, making him feel uncomfortable, guilty of the fact he found himself physically attracted to someone other than Laurel.

"So how do you know this man?" Judge Connally asked in a voice loud enough to be heard above the racket.

"We've met before. I guess you could say we're getting re-acquainted," Sam replied, shifting her weight, moving from one side of the Judge closer into Alex. She positioned herself near to Alex's ear and whispered "He makes me feel uneasy."

He felt her breath swirl around inside his ear, taking great pleasure in it. "Me too," Alex whispered back, smelling her perfume and hair as he did. He liked the closeness too much, he thought, as he inched a little further away.

"Are you two talking code here, or can I be included?" The Judge said in a stage whisper, mimicking them.

"Sure Judge. I was telling Sam I'm leaving next week for

California, on business. But since it was dealing with a matter connected to a case before you, I thought I'd keep it quiet. You know how it is these days, people talk about any conduct being improper," Alex said to keep him at bay. "Just trying to keep appearances above board, so there is no hint of impropriety."

"Where are you going? I didn't hear you," Sam asked.

"San Francisco."

"Great city," The Judge replied. "You must make it to Napa and tour the wineries. The last time I was there they had a special train which dined us while we took care of the wine part along the route. The countryside in northern California is truly remarkable, crisp, pristine. It makes me want to go back, just thinking about it."

"Yes. Me too. I love it there," Sam said eagerly. "I spent one summer there when I was in undergrad, just hanging around. I loved it." She smiled. "I've been back there at least once a year since. I wouldn't miss going if my life depended upon it. When are you leaving?"

"November 4th. . . out of National. I want to get settled out there over the weekend. I have some hearings and depositions the following week, but it'll give me some free time to venture out and catch the sights. I'm looking forward to it."

"I'd love to join you," Sam said soft enough for Alex to hear, causing him to blush. "But since I can't, let me give you my phone number, so if you have any questions on what to see or do before you leave, then call and I'll give you some suggestions." Sam reached into her purse, fished around, pulling out a pen. "Do you have anything to write on?"

Alex took a sip of beer, feeling its coldness travel within. He looked around, then picked up a discarded bar napkin from a table behind him. "Here," he said as he handed it to her.

"Thanks." She wrote down her telephone number. "Don't lose this," she instructed him as she placed it inside his jacket breast pocket. Sam glanced past Alex toward the entrance. "It looks like some of my friends are here. I'll let you two have your fun for the night."

"Do you have to leave us so soon?" Connally asked.

"I'm afraid so Judge Connally. My friends are just using Houston's as a meeting spot before we go out. Maybe we'll hook up later. Georgetown isn't all that big, you know," Sam replied. "It was nice meeting you."

"The pleasure was all mine," Michael Connally responded, grinning.

Sam leaned so close to Alex, he could smell her perfume again. She spoke softly. "I enjoyed seeing you again. I'd like to see you again." She kissed Alex gently on his cheek. "And I have a feeling I will."

"Be careful and have fun tonight." Was all Alex could think of saying as he watched her walk off to greet her friends.

"She sure was attractive and sweet," Judge Connally said, forcing Alex back to reality. "And she has a great figure."

"She certainly does."

"She wants you," Judge Connally told him.

"Yea, sure," replied Alex.

"No, really. I know the look. I've been there before. She flirted with you. Whispering in your ear, touching your arm, kissing you good-bye."

"Judge, there are several reasons why I can't. First, I'm happily married. Next, I don't have the time. Finally, I'm too old. I'm old enough to be her oldest brother or young uncle."

"Don't flatter yourself. You're almost old enough to be her father, Alex."

"Besides, we're just acquaintances."

"All the better. Affairs of the heart are rather tempting. It rejuvenates relationships. Besides, an affair with this girl." Michael Connally gestured in the direction of Sam. "Would be short lived. Don't fool yourself Alex. It'd be a novelty for both of you. It probably wouldn't be anything more than some good sex for you, and an experience with an older man for her. If it became anything, serious, then it was meant to happen."

"Have you ever?" Alex started to ask since the topic had been broached, but he was not sure how to finish the question.

"Me? Sure. Several times," he said without hesitation. "The first time was when Annie and I were having a difficult time early in our marriage. Annie had a problem adjusting to married life, so she went home to her parents."

"What happened next?"

"I was approached by a young DA, who worked with me. We knew full well what we were getting ourselves involved with. Our relationship lasted several months."

"And?" Alex prodded.

"It was pleasurable. Even working late nights were more enjoyable. Eventually, she transferred departments, upwardly, and I reconciled with Annie. There was no harm. We were consenting adults. It was a mature relationship. It ended that way too."

"How can you say it was a mature and consenting relationship," Alex countered.

"Why?"

Alex continued "It was a breach of the covenant of marriage, not to mention Annie did not consent to it. It was wrong. That's an issue I always have thought of in black and white, right and wrong." The Judge was handsome, in his late forties. "Temptation must come regularly for you, especially with your position of influence."

"Not as often as you may think," Michael Connally replied.

"You can't always give into your temptations, desires or addictions. When you do, they'll destroy you."

"Alex, a onetime fling isn't giving into one's addictions or calling you an addict. It makes you appreciate life on the straight and narrow that much more. It just depends how you look at it."

"It's only a manner of justification you're using Judge. It doesn't make it right." Alex paused.

"Let he who is without sin cast the first stone," Judge Connally said sternly. "Many people would say thinking about something is just as terrible as the actual sin."

"No one knows what one thinks. It's like a crime. You can't get arrested if you think about killing someone. If you act on it, then it's a crime. The same is true with an affair."

"I'm not here to argue with you Alex. We're here to have some fun. All I was trying to say was I felt Sam was very attractive. She was captivated by you and if the opportunity existed to bed her, she would be difficult to pass up. I wouldn't. Now, before we argue any more, let's go get two more."

We must recognize that every nation determines its policies in terms of its own interests.

John F. Kennedy
37ᵗʰ President

CHAPTER FIFTEEN
NOVEMBER 4TH

Sniper looked at the message from his Department Director and immediately knew he would be transferred. It was only a matter of where. There was a knock on his partially closed door.

"Weylyn, mind if I come in?"

Sniper remained seated, his feet were perched upon his desk. "You know my door is always open for you, boss. What's up? I got your message." Taylor sat down in the chair across from him.

"It seems the powers that be are concerned with some of the extracurricular investigative work you've been involved with. You know, using FBI computers and resources to answer friends' questions. It's against policy."

"I've been in this field for quite some time now. I'm not a greenhorn but, I also know this is the first time I've ever been called on the carpet for this when it's done all of the time by every agent here." Sniper looked at Taylor. "I'll even wager you've done this, maybe even worse trash. Why use me as a scapegoat?"

"Weylyn." Taylor leaned into him. "We've been over this before. What you've been asking about can't be accessed by you. It's not your detail. But for your track record, you'd be like dried shit, blowing in the wind. Now you're going back into the field."

"Shit." Sniper slammed his fist on his desk, then kicked his feet to the floor. He stood up and leaned over his desk toward his superior. "I've done grunt work before. I know it inside and out. I'm ready to command, you know it and I do."

"It doesn't matter what I do or don't know. I have superiors, just like me to you. Take the mustard, handle this with dignity and I'll make sure you're back in eighteen months, no longer."

"It's not like I have a choice," Sniper said.

"We always have choices and you had yours in Old Town"

"You know what I mean. So where?"

"It's not too bad. I swung Miami," Taylor informed him.

"Not refugee and drug detail."

"Yes, a little R and D. Try not to get too much sun. You're starting to wrinkle. And Weylyn. . . ."

"Yes?"

"If you fuck up, you're gone."

Alex handed his suitcase, with his plane ticket, to the baggage handler, outside of the doors to American Airlines at Washington's National Airport. "San Francisco - The Four Thirty flight." Alex told him as he glanced at the clock above his head. 4:10. Good, Alex thought, just enough time. He turned from the porter and walked to the driver's side of the car. Laurel was patiently waiting for him. By the time he got home from work, she had everything packed. All he had to do was toss the suitcase in the Explorer, grab his briefcase and then off they went. It was advantageous to have the airport close to their house, along with a partner who was on top of his schedule, filling the voids his personality left as he sailed through life. Laurel was his ballast, keeping him on a true course.

"Laurel - Thanks for getting everything ready. I don't know what I'd do without you. I know how I can be."

"No more so than usual. Come on, hurry up. That officer has motioned several times to move. I don't want him to come over and give me a ticket."

"It's all right. After all, you know a good attorney. I'm sure he'd cut you a deal with his fees."

"You think so, do you? What would I have to do?" Laurel laughed.

"Depends on what you want to have happen to the ticket."

"I want it to do what you're doing." Her eyes smiled.

"Go to San Francisco?"

"No, no. Just go away."

"Are you sure you don't want to join me? There's still time." Alex placed his hand into the car, around Laurel's shoulders. Leaning in, he kissed her.

"I'd love to, but you know I despise going when you have business to attend. You forget about me. You know I hate to be neglected. It forces me to shop."

"It's settled then. You can stay. Our budget could use a reprieve from your shopping excursions." Alex laughed.

"Mine?" Laurel asked in disbelief. "Coming from a man who thinks of money as water, so when he has extra money in his pocket, he feels forced to spend it."

"I think you mean compelled."

"Compelled is right. Besides, I need to be with the boys. They have some school projects which need tending to." Laurel smiled a tired grin.

Alex knew the signal well. Laurel used the time he was gone to revive herself. She enjoyed her space to read, rearrange and create. She was most creative, artistically, when her husband was not around.

Laurel embraced Alex. They kissed quickly.

"I can't wait to get back."

"Me too."

"Give my love to the boys and tell them I'll bring them back something if they've been good."

"You want me to use it as leverage, right?" Laurel asked.

"Only as needed. It's a powerful force which could backfire if it fell into the wrong hands."

"They're getting to be pretty perceptive. Soon they'll realize they get gifts no matter how bad they've been."

He smiled at his wife. "Let me grab my briefcase and let you get out of here."

Alex opened the back passenger door and removed the briefcase from behind Laurel's seat. This was not his usual briefcase. It was twice the size. It belonged to the firm for attorneys to use. He had various documents in it, with his lap top computer, and a personal laser printer. It was his office away from work. It was what he needed to accomplish things in San Francisco. He would have this weekend to get the case in order.

"Bye Laurel." Alex's gesture was part wave, part salute.

"Have a safe flight." Laurel motioned gracefully, with a wave of her fingers. She turned her attention to the traffic, working her way out of the entanglement of cars and people heading to and from the airport.

Alex went to the porter to get his plane ticket.

"Here you are sir. You're leaving from gate A 7. I've written it for you on your ticket sleeve."

"Thanks." Alex took the ticket and handed the porter five dollars.

He walked past the sliding glass doors, inside, to the baggage x-ray, placed his briefcase on the conveyor, and walked through the metal detector. Before he could pick up his briefcase from the other side of the conveyor, the guard asked. "May we look inside?" It was more of a demand than a question.

"Sure," said Alex. "Here, let me help you."

"It won't be necessary." The guard opened his briefcase. The lap top computer was taken out, flipped open, then closed and placed back inside the briefcase. "All set."

"Thank you." He hurried to Gate A-7, where he handed his ticket to the agent by the gate. Most everyone was already on the plane. No one was standing in line. A mother and her child were pressed up against the window, looking out toward the plane, waiving. The agent jabbed at the computer keyboard. "You're pre-checked Mr. Westcott. Thank you for flying American Airlines."

He walked down the ramp to board the Boeing 767.

"Hello." The flight attendant greeted him in a non-specific, repetitive manner, as she glanced at his ticket.

"Hi," Alex replied as he headed toward his seat. He stopped at his row and opened up the overhead bin and placed his briefcase inside. He took the seat next to the window. The isle seat was not occupied. He could stretch out during the flight, not having to make small talk for five hours with someone, he thought, not needing, nor did he like specifics from strangers.

Alex picked up the In-Flight magazine to find out what movies were being shown during the flight. As he was leafing through the magazine, he noticed one person rush on board, hurrying down the aisle toward him. Alex glanced at her. She seemed attractive, from a casual observance, but he paid little attention to her until she sat down next to him.

"Hi."

Alex thought he recognized the accent. He looked over.

"What are you doing here?" he asked in a halting tone.

"Funny you should ask. I was wondering the same thing about you."

Alex shot a glance over the back of his seat, wondering if anyone he knew was on the flight. "No seriously," was all he could think of saying.

"To tell you the truth, I had some hesitation about. . . you know. . . doing this. I wondered whether this was too forward, but then I thought, 'You only live once.' If you want to experience life, instead of it experiencing you, then do it before it's too late. That's why I'm here."

"How's that?"

"It's simple." Sam touched his arm. "It's like when you drive down the road and see older people in sports cars going the speed limit. It's not what the car was designed for. Those people should not be driving cars like that. Someone young, with flowing hair, who appreciates the scorch and fleeting vitality of youth, should be behind the wheel."

Alex smiled, laughing inwardly. How often had he thought of the same analogy. Now he was the old person driving the sports car. "Don't let life get in the way of your dreams."

"Exactly. And now, even if I wanted to stop everything, I couldn't. There's no turning back now."

"Why?"

"We're moving away from the gate."

Alex took in his surroundings. There was a video playing on the television monitors throughout, showing the safety features of the 767. They were showing how to fasten and unfasten a seat belt.

"If you have to show someone how to put on or take off a seat belt, then they shouldn't be allowed to fly."

Sam laughed. "Are you angry with me?" she asked innocently. "For being here?"

"I guess if I am, I have five hours to get over it." Alex looked ahead, shook his head and smiled. He wondered how he got himself into this. Never had any woman come onto him like Samantha Hayes. "I suppose we'll have the chance to get to know one another."

"Good afternoon ladies and gentlemen, I'm Captain Smith. We have been cleared for takeoff. Flight attendants, please prepare the cabin for departure."

The engines whined, full throttle forward. The brakes were released, forcing Alex and Sam back into their seats as the plane began its ascent. Sam reached over and placed her hand over Alex's. His breath became shallow, his mouth was dry, his heart beat faster. Alex cupped his fingers around Sam's. Her hand was soft, delicate. Alex fidgeted. Sam's other hand rubbed his arm, as the plane became airborne.

"I've got the situation under control, as asked."

Garrett looked at the tap indicator, next to his phone. Privacy was a must for him. He was not someone who had a lot of trust in others. He was a product of his times. Garrett looked at the tape recorder attached to his phone. Every event was transcribed and placed on disc, which covered him at both ends. He was a control freak. If tasks were delegated, his chest would tighten up. He would unbutton the top button of his shirt and loosen the tie which he was wearing. Anything that constrained him was magnified tenfold. "Give me details." Garrett sunk into his chair, in the comfort of his library.

"I've worked it so Weylyn was reassigned to Miami. He'll be leaving in a few weeks. Y'all not have to worry about him no more." Thomas Henry explained.

"Good, good. What else do I have to be concerned about?"

"Y'all have to make your decision about controlling Lawton. I've gotta know how y'all want me to proceed."

"Any news on the DC one front?"

"DC one is under close surveillance."

"And?" Garrett asked.

"Soon as there's a crack in the armor, I should be able to rectify and stabilize the situation."

"You're earning my trust more each day Thomas. What's next?"

"I'm off to California to attend to some loose ends."

"When can I expect you back?"

"Before the end of the week."

"So Sam." She looked at him and smiled. Her smile always seemed to weaken him. "How'd you know I'd be on this flight?"

"You told me you were heading out to San Francisco today, that part was easy. I called your office and told them I was with the airline and I needed to confirm your flight. I was told your flight number."

"You certainly took some chances, Sam."

"Such as?"

"What if my wife was traveling with me? What would you have done then?"

"I gave a lot of consideration to me being here. I'm not out to put you on the spot or to show up and say hi to your wife, and tell her my name is Samantha. Please. To prevent a confrontation, I called the airline to reserve the seat next to yours. I told them we were with the same company and I needed that seat."

"And."

"Well, they told me the seat was not taken. I figured no one from your office or your wife was going with you. I assumed it was safe."

"We all know about assuming."

"Don't even say the ass part. I don't find it amusing."

"I won't, but you got the gist."

"I think it's all in your mind. But to prevent a scene, I waited until I saw you here. I watched to make sure you were traveling alone. That's why I was the last one on board. No one was waiting for you. You weren't walking to the gate with anyone. Plus, if by some freak chance someone here knew you, you wouldn't have to admit you met me before. Traveling always forces you to sit with people you don't know. It's a communal, nomad existence."

"I think of planes as glorified buses."

"Alex," Sam said in feigned shock. "Don't let the pilot hear you. This road is much higher."

"Maybe you should forget about grad school and go into investigative work. I have a friend in the FBI. You know, someone on the inside to get you in the door."

"No interest. I like what I'm doing now. Besides, I am interested in you, not any further investigations."

"I'm flattered, but why me?"

"Why not." Sam's reply was softened by her smile.

She looked especially young today, Alex thought, as he looked at her slender body. He wondered why he was being tested. "Seriously." Alex tried to sound strict. In a voice barely above a whisper, he continued. "I'm married. I have children. I'm old enough to know this isn't right."

"Don't you want to say you're old enough to be my father."

"That never crossed my mind. I'm not that old."

"Sometimes you seem uptight, especially if you're out of your element."

"You may have a point there, but I would never admit it." Alex continued back to his original thought. "I couldn't commit to a relationship outside of my marriage. You know, the usual reasons along those lines, adultery, and the negative stuff about an older married man and a young single woman. Don't you read about the negative impact those trysts have in Cosmo. I'm sure Ann Landers would tell you to run, not walk, but run away from the married man and find yourself a nice single guy. Something like this goes nowhere. People end up destroying themselves and others in the process."

"I'm attracted to you for many reasons. You're ruggedly handsome. You're extremely intelligent. When I met you at Dumbarton, I realized you were a person I wanted to know. When I saw you in Georgetown last week, it was for a reason. A real chemistry exists. It's not my imagination. I've been dreaming about us, and fate brought us together. Face it - it's a force beyond our control.

"I think most of this fate was initiated by you and American Express," Alex interrupted. "God just doesn't give you a plane ticket and say here, go have some fun."

Sam laughed. "You aren't listening to me. I did call and get the information, but it was only one call. I didn't hire a private detective. No one was sitting next to you on this flight. Your wife wasn't going with you, nor is anyone from your firm here. Now was the opportunity to see if we fit inwardly, not externally. I'm not asking for a commitment, I'm only trying to see if we are meant to be, on a soul level. It's rare to feel this strongly, so I had to do something."

Alex paused, then asked, "How long do you plan on staying?'

"Til' Tuesday. I have to be in class and back at work on Wednesday." Sam paused, looked directly at Alex, then said forcefully, as if to punctuate her statement. "I'm not here to coerce you to do something you don't want to do. Nor am I holding an apple for you to bite, tempting you in the Garden of Eden. It's not my intention to break up your marriage. I've never been one to lay it in the line, and I don't intend on starting now. Also, I'm not into a fatal attraction type thing. I'm not someone to worry about. If you don't want me to be around you in San Francisco, I can arrange it so you won't even see me. It's a large city, you know, and I have a lot of friends there."

"Do you own any guns?" Alex and Sam laughed.

"No, I don't. And something else Mr. Westcott, I want it to be clear to you I'm not looking for a quick grunge. If I only wanted sex, I wouldn't have to fly across the country for it."

"I don't doubt that for one second."

"I see you as someone I would like to be friends with. To have fun with and enjoy each other's company, as adults. I was hoping you were mature enough to want the same thing."

"Let's see how I handle it, okay?" he said. "This request is new for me. I've never been friends with a woman before without there being a physical attraction, inward or outwardly. Maybe you're right and we'll become friends. There will be a few bridges to cross along the way, though."

"Sure. I know. I couldn't ask for anything more."

After several minutes of silence, Alex turned to Sam. "While flattered, I do find your actions somewhat upsetting."

"Why?" she asked.

"It goes along with a conversation I had with Michael Connally." Alex paused.

"What?"

"Nothing," he replied.

Sam looked at him. "Come on. you opened the box. Remember at the bar? You made me tell you something I didn't want to."

"Okay, but it's sort of stupid."

"I'll be the judge of that," Sam replied.

Well, I was thinking about the last time someone came onto me with such force."

"When was that?"

"I was 12 or 13, beginning to discover girls," Alex answered.

"The last time?" Sam asked in disbelief.

"Okay, it wasn't adult behavior but something similar. Are you sure you want me to tell you this?"

"Yes, I'm sorry. I'll be good." Sam rubbed his arm.

"Her name was Maggie. She would constantly follow me around, always wanting and willing to do anything I wanted."

"Did you like her?"

"Sure, I enjoyed her company. I mean she was a tomboy. We did kid things, like ride bikes, fish, even played catch. It was the summer before I started junior high. Once school started, however, my outlook changed," Alex said.

"How?"

"My friends teased me for having a girlfriend."

"And not spending time with them, I bet," she said.

"Yes. So, at first, I wouldn't talk to Maggie. Still, she would show up at my house. I would see her in school. She would ask me to do things, but I ignored her."

"How sad," Sam said.

"When I look back upon it, I do feel bad. Even though I did all those things - I mean I was rotten, she still pursued me. Maggie told me there was something special about me."

"I would have to agree. So what happened to her?"

"Finally, to end it, I told her she wasn't a real girl, that she had no friends and that I wasn't one either. She started to cry, running away as she did. She moved away the following year, leaving me to wonder what happened to her." Alex looked down. "I never felt so bad in my life."

"Do you still think about Maggie?"

"On occasion. More about the incident, you know, replaying it over in my mind. I promised I would never act like that again."

"Have you kept your promise?" she asked.

"I have, for the most part. I learned that first friendships show understanding and teach forgiveness. Reflecting upon them show where one is in life. They are very extraordinary."

After a few moments, Alex asked, "Where do you plan on staying?"

"I wasn't able to find out where you were staying. . ."

Alex interrupted, "Maybe you aren't as good at detective work as I presupposed."

". . . I thought," Sam continued undeterred, "I'd ask if it would be all right for me to stay in the same hotel. Not in the same room, but close enough to see each other while I'm there.

"I don't see a problem. Find out if they have one available," Alex said. "We can see how this friendship thing progresses."

"Where we staying, then?" Sam asked.

"The Fairmont."

"That'll do just fine. I like it there."

"Can you afford it?"

"Money has never been a problem for my family. I'd prefer to keep financial matters on an equal basis," she replied.

"Fair enough."

Sam removed the aerophone imbedded in the seat in front of her.

"What are you doing?"

"Calling the hotel to check in. That's all right, isn't it?"

"Sure. It's not like I've had a say in anything so far, so why not."

"If you don't want me to, just say so Alex. After all, you are old enough to decide your own."

"Yes I am." Alex lightheartedly emphasized all three words, which caused him to nervously laugh.

What has happened to the dreams of the United Nations? What has happened to the spirit which created the United Nations? The answer is clear: Governments got in the way of the dreams of the people.

Ronald Reagan
41st President

CHAPTER SIXTEEN
NOVEMBER 7TH

"Aren't you going to answer the phone?"

"No. I can't bring myself to, not yet."

"Laurel." Sniper had his arm around her. He pushed her hair away from her face. "I think you need to get your act together. Make up your mind what you want to do. Personally, I find this all hard to believe."

"Why?" She looked at him, her eyes swollen and red. "All of the signs are there."

"Like what?"

"I have her number. She's out of town. They're staying at the same hotel. I called his room and she answered. She sounded like she just woke up. What more do you need. Photos?"

Sniper laughed. "No, no. It's only that I've known you and Alex for such a long time. I've never seen him unhappy. He's never complained about being married and he never has mentioned an affair or even that he's been tempted. He's not like you."

"Meaning?"

"You're much more sensitive, Laurel. Your need for companionship, to be his equal, while important to you, mean nothing to Alex. He doesn't even know your needs exist because he's blind to them."

"You really think so?"

I do. His concerns are with providing for his family, taking care of his job, and having an occasional night out. He knows you don't care for some of his beliefs, so he gives you space, but you don't want it."

"It's all so difficult. I don't know what I'm going to do. I've got the boys to consider. They're so young. I don't know what to tell them. I don't know. I'm just spinning. I feel like I'm in a haze."

"Do you want some advice?"

"Yes." Laurel pressed her head into his shoulder.

Sniper spoke gently. "You've already decided."

"Really?"

"Yes, really. You know what you want to do. Now, you need to get away for a while. Take the boys down to your parents for a couple of weeks. That will give you time to sort through your thoughts."

"What about right now? Should I confront him?"

"I suppose it's inevitable. I would wait until he gets back in town before you do. Talk to him like nothing is wrong while he is there. Once he gets back, ask him about what you know, then decide what to do."

"William, I don't know what I would do without you right now."

"It's a good thing I was in town," Sniper said.

"How much longer are you going to be here?"

"I'm winding things up here before I move to Miami. Probably before the week's up."

"With you down in Florida, if I were to need you. . . ."

"I'm close by." He kissed Laurel on the cheek.

"Oh William." She nestled in closer. "Your comfort is making this much easier." She ran her hand down his back, as he directed her down on the couch. They kissed passionately as Laurel's hands searched to unbuckle his belt. Sniper's hands moved to her legs, slowly feeling her body as they went upward.

There was a knock on the door separating the suites from one another. Alex hung up the phone after leaving a message for Laurel on their answering machine. He went to the door and opened it.

"Sam - How was your day?" Alex kissed her on her cheek. She walked into his suite, leaving the adjoining door open.

"I had a great time shopping. I met an old friend for lunch, and now I'm looking forward to taking you to dinner. Remember, tonight is my last night, so we should make it special, memorable."

"You're right. Besides, I never turn down a free meal, especially when someone as attractive as you is treating. Here, sit down." Alex gestured to the couch centered in his suite. "I had room service send up a bottle of wine. Let's start the night right."

"You didn't have to."

"It's the least I can do to repay your company."

Sam sat down on the sofa and crossed her legs. Alex noticed the soft sound her skin made as she did this. A soft swoosh - slow and sensual. She was attractive in her short black dress. He opened up the bottle of wine, poured two glasses, handing her one and sat down next to her.

"So Sam, where are you taking me?"

"I thought we'd go to the Fog City Diner."

"Sounds great. I've never been there."

"I know. There are many places here you haven't been to. I only hope I've been a good tour guide."

"You're the best personal tour guide I've ever had."

"I'm the only personal guide," Sam bantered back, "you've ever had."

"See. How can I complain if I have no one to compare you to?"

"So Mr. Westcott," she addressed him formally to make herself appear much younger, "you seem charged. How was your day?"

"Interesting Miss Hayes."

"Why? Were you able to leave the miserable constraints of the office and take advantage of this beautiful weather we've been having? It had to be in the eighties."

"Let me start by saying I'm pleased you took it upon yourself to come to California with me. I've had a lot of fun. Yesterday's tour of Napa Valley was terrific."

"It was, wasn't it," Sam said. "I don't think I can recall the last time I sampled so much great wine in such a short period."

"I hope that won't slow you down tonight." Alex looked into her deep blue eyes, feeling a deep attraction.

"Not a chance. This city switches me on."

"Me too. I've had a great time." Alex paused.

"What's wrong?"

"Nothing." Alex picked up his glass of Cabernet with his forefinger and thumb, clasping the stem at the base of the chalice. "I don't think I've ever developed a real friendship with a woman before, especially when sex hasn't been a part of it."

"And even then I'm sure sex hasn't turned all of your relationships with women into friendships."

Alex laughed, nodding his head in agreement. "To friends. You never know how you will meet. May we always walk side by side, with never a cross word, while not losing sight of our friendship."

"Here, here," Sam said, extending her glass toward his.

"I respect you Alex, for keeping your relationship with Laurel first. She's fortunate to be married to you. I hope she realizes what she has."

"She does, but I don't think she'd understand this. I'm sure Laurel would suspect something happened if she knew you were here with me." Alex smiled slightly. "Hell, I'm not sure I understand. You're intelligent, beautiful and fun."

"So what did you do today. Were you able to make it to the University?" Sam asked.

"As a matter of fact, I went to USF after my depositions were finished. They had a complete history of the United Nations, along with the League. The material was extensive."

"Anything new?"

"A lot. Do you want to hear about it?"

"Go on, Alex."

"Are you sure?"

"Tell me. I love to hear you talk about the New World Order. I find the history behind it fascinating, even though I'm still not convinced about it. You're reaching."

"Well Miss Skeptic. Let me run something by you. Let's see if I can build a stronger foundation. How does a conspiracy implicating the office of the Presidency of the United States sound?"

"In what way?"

"The Presidency being used to fulfill a prophecy."

"That's pretty strong."

"Try to punch some holes in it."

"Okay," Sam said eagerly. She looked into Alex's eyes as he

talked.

They were now connected on another plane, each digging deeper into the other. "It goes along these lines. The United States foreign policy changed drastically under the administration of Woodrow Wilson during World War One."

"The person you claim started the New World Order," Sam added.

"You're a quick learner. I haven't concluded whether Wilson started it, was forced to go along, or developed it from an ongoing organization. What is known about President Wilson is this - he rose from obscurity in an exceedingly quick manner. He was non-political. He became governor of New Jersey in 1910, followed by President of the United States two years later."

"He did nothing before?"

"Not really. He was President of Princeton, but his professional career was going nowhere. Some scholars would even argue he never had a career. If he did, it wasn't on any track, fast or slow. He never knew what he wanted to be in life. He was highly educated, yet struggled through menial employment. His assent to power was quicker than Hitler's or Mussolini's."

"Incredible."

"Save that for later. Wait until I tell you about the deaths and misfortune associated with the Presidency and the New World Order."

"Wilson didn't die in office."

"True, however, if you look at his administration, he was elected President with big money behind him. Those bankers and industrialists included the likes of the Carnegie, Mellon, Hearst, Rockefeller and Ford, to name a few. Those tycoons made a fortune during the industrial revolution of the United States. They saw unlimited potential and wanted to expand their scope of power. They wanted to create a global environment for trade. President Wilson rebuked them, at first."

"How?"

"Wilson denounced cronyism. The U.S. would not get involved in World War One. He was perceived as a pacifist and probably was. He was protectionist in his speeches and attitude toward the world. Then his wife died. Wilson's bio said she had a disease."

"What kind?"

"Brights, some sort of kidney disease. She languished for a while, then died. All of a sudden Wilson's philosophy changed. He brought the U.S. into the war for two years. With our help, the tide turned, and we won. After that, we exerted our dominance and control over the rest of the world." Alex looked at his glass of wine, picked it up from the table, holding the stem, took a sip, savoring its flavor.

He continued. "Wilson, while riding a wave of popularity, came up with the League of Nations. He said its purpose created a body, which would allow a dialogue to occur between nations. The League was created to permit several dominant nations, the U.S. included, to make decisions on behalf of other countries. Those decisions would directly affect them, without giving those sovereigns any say how their country should be run." Alex took another sip of wine. "The forces that be, the industrialists, directed him to vigorously campaign for the League."

"Why?"

"Money. Plus it was believed the League would open up new markets for them. He campaigned hard, but his health failed. There was a counterinsurgency to his League of Nations. In 1920, he was not capable of running for a third term. He was too ill. He suffered several strokes, which left his speech impaired. The campaign of 1920 rolls around, which proved to be a disaster for those involved in the New World Order or Worldists. The Worldists put forth the slate of James Cox for President and Franklin Delano Roosevelt as Vice President. FDR, remember, was the Under-Secretary to the Navy during Wilson's administration."

"I didn't realize Roosevelt was politically active so early. Is that how FDR got his idea for the U.N.?"

"Hold on Sam. You're a quarter century too early. More happens before then."

"What's next?"

"In 1920, a politician from Ohio campaigns vigorously for the Presidency. Name?"

"Ah, Harding. Warren G. Harding." Sam smiled

"Yes. Harding was a Republican Senator from Ohio. His family had money from the newspaper industry. His platform was Anti-League, Pro-U.S., and protectionist."

"But his Presidency was marked by scandals. I remember something about a tea pot." Sam interjected.

"Tea Pot Dome. True, but then again, scandals have been present in every administration. No President's been able to control what his Secretary of State, Interior, Defense, etcetera's, does. Harding was not an exception. He had no control over corrupt appointments. His policy on foreign affairs became one of keeping the US isolated from the rest of the World during his re-election campaign. While out west campaigning, explaining his reasons to oppose the League of Nations, President Harding died. Someone wrote a book claiming he was murdered. No one knows." Alex collected his thoughts. "Calvin Coolidge took the helm as President and served until 1928. He refused to seek an additional term for unknown reasons. Many were surprised he didn't."

"Nothing happened to him?"

"Right. Other than the fact he was called Silent Cal. He never really took a stance on anything, which probably saved his life. Herbert Hoover became the next President. He was a one termer. His reign was short lived due to the depression. Worldists were desperate to get one of their own back in power. The industrialists had the strength and control to create, survive and flourish financially during a depression. It destroyed Hoover. He lived longer than any other President, dying in 1964. Still, no one heard a word, or sought his advice between 1933 and his death, thirty-one years later. Incredible, huh?"

"Keep going," Sam said.

"We all know the next President."

"Franklin Delano Roosevelt."

"Right. He continued building upon the foundation for the New World Order where Wilson left off. He was all the Worldists could ask for and more. FDR came from an extremely wealthy family. He was one of them, plus he had an advantage over Wilson. He saw where Wilson failed in the execution of the Worldist's plan."

"Did the Protectionists try to get him?"

"Yes. There were still forces opposed to the New World Order. Few people remember the assassination attempt made on FDR's life."

"Really?"

"Yes. In Miami. The Mayor of Chicago was killed and FDR escaped, narrowly. Remember, FDR's main objective was to not allow history to repeat itself. In retrospect, FDR modernized the League. He made a few changes to strengthen the United Nations. Control of the U.N. was placed within the U.S., New York City, not Geneva, Switzerland. That move would allow us complete access, oversight and control. FDR executed fulfillment of the Worldist's prophecy perfectly during World War Two. The superpowers, the Soviet Union, the U.S., Britain and China, formed a coalition to decide the fate of the entire world. However, before the U.N. was finalized, signed, sealed and delivered, something unexpected happened."

"FDR died," Sam stated.

"Yes. Then what?" Alex prompted

"Truman took over."

"Now imagine what the Worldists were thinking at this point. They had on their hands, as President, someone they considered to be an uneducated country bumpkin from the plains of Missouri taking over control of the Executive Branch."

"I don't imagine he would have had an industrialist view of the World," Sam said.

"Clearly, he did not," Alex replied. "This man did not have so much as an inkling of what his predecessor was involved with. The Worldists, playing it safe, believed they had to force Truman in line. So before Truman carries out signing the U.N. Charter, there's an assassination attempt on his life. It happened right outside of Blair House, across from the White House. Truman was there during the transition. Two extremists are involved. One was killed, along with a cop. The other was wounded and sent to jail. Truman fell in line with the Worldist's view. He supported the United Nations, goes to San Francisco and gave the opening key note speech, endorsing it."

"Then what?"

"The Senate ratifies the Charter, effectively giving Worldists control. There are only two Senators who oppose ratification, one being my grandfather. They both die shortly afterwards. How about that."

"What about since ratification?" Sam asked. "How could these Worldists continue with their control and dominance, without anyone knowing?"

"Back to Truman." Alex pushed his hand through his hair, brushing it back, as he looked at Sam. "Remember the next conflict? Korea."

She nodded in agreement, her hair softly fell from her face.

"Truman used the United Nations to obtain approval to send

U.S. troops to Korea. It was the first time the U.N. was used to exert its control elsewhere in the World. He circumvented Congress to accomplish a Worldist, or should I say Superpower mandate. That conflict ended in a draw. The United States has never seemed to exert enough military dominance to win any foreign civil war conflict we became involved with. Look to Korea, Vietnam, Nicaragua, El Salvador or Lebanon. It seems that unless we know who our enemy is, we don't win. I'm not crossing over things, am I?"

"No."

"Anyway, after Truman left, Eisenhower took over. Ike was a Worldist. He even used the U.N. to fight the battle of the Cold War, which escalated during his tenure. In his eight years in office there was relatively little military world conflict. It was a rebuilding time after World War Two. Communism had to go. It blocked the Worldist's objective of a united global economy. Communism goes counter to trade. Eisenhower had Nixon debate Khrushchev in the U.N. The objectives of the Worldists were being accomplished." Alex looked down, then out the window. The sun was setting. "What time is dinner set for?"

"Eight thirty." She filled their glasses with wine.

"1960," Alex continued. "It was a close Presidential election. Kennedy won. Worldists were worried about his close ties to the Catholic Church. The Cold War continued to intensify. No one knew how he would react globally. He circumvented the United Nations and Congress to accomplish certain goals he believed were in the best interest of the United States. First you had the Bay of Pigs, the U.S. sponsored invasion of Cuba. Vietnam was heightening and he increased troops."

"The airlift to Berlin," added Sam.

"All events went ahead without approval from the United Nations. Kennedy was a live wire, uncontrolled. Then he was assassinated. Lyndon Baines Johnson took over, but he kept the policies already in place. He had to continue those policies because he couldn't stop the process. Personally, LBJ was not concerned internationally. He turned his direction to the 'Great Society', our new internal social legislation, which caused a centrist view that big government was good. It added to the Worldists line. Again, he surprised everyone by deciding not to run for the Presidency. Then it was Nixon's turn."

"1968. Worldists didn't want another Kennedy. Robert was assassinated. Nixon won and began the peace process with Vietnam. He opened the door to trade with China and the Soviet Union. He stepped beyond the Worldists objective. He became too friendly with the enemy, Communism. It's no use trading with them. They had no money or currency. A disparity in trade was created. Nixon was destroyed through Watergate."

"Much like Harding through Tea Pot Dome?"

"You have a point there." Alex smiled as he mulled it over before starting in again. "Ford takes over. Two assassination attempts were made on his life. There was little time for him to do anything - however if he were killed, his vice-president would have succeeded him."

"Rockefeller," Sam said, "from the industrialists."

"Ford dumped Rockefeller as his running mate and then lost the election to Carter. Carter used the U.N. to accomplish a lot of his foreign objectives, including peace talks in the Middle East with Israel and Egypt. The U.S. suffered with high inflation."

"Carter loses and Reagan takes over."

Finally, I'm born."

Alex laughed. "It's about time Sam. You did learn a lot in school. Well, Reagan had always denounced the United Nations as a waste of time and money. He thought of it as a do nothing organization. He's then wounded in an assassination attempt during his first few months in office. His philosophy changed and the U.N. became his chief ally. He used the U.N. to permit the U.S. to attack various Latin American countries, and to allow us entry into Lebanon. Reagan forced the Soviet

Union to crumble through the use of media and outspending them through military growth, even dreaming up the Star Wars defense system. It almost bankrupt our country. Just look at our deficit. Fighting the Cold War caused most of it. Worldists lucked out in that the Soviet economy collapsed before ours. Then comes George Bush, a consummate Worldist advocate. His father was a Senator from Connecticut. His family had a lot of money, and he parlayed it into even more."

"Wasn't he also Ambassador to the U.N.?" she asked.

"Yes, and as President he used the U.N. as a means to attack Iraq. He was the embodiment of being a Worldist, much along the same lines as FDR."

"Quite a scenario you put together, but I have two questions. First, how can something of this nature be accomplished, and second, the current administration. What's its position?"

"The wine's empty Sam. It's time to go."

"Nice tap dance."

Alex laughed. "You're right. I told you I just started this theory today while at USF."

"How?"

"It was just like a story unfolding before my eyes."

"And."

"If it were only one person, then it would seem like much of a story, but this transcends our modern history."

"How's it accomplished?" pressed Sam.

"I'll venture a guess for you. The more I think about it, the more plausible it seems. Governmental agencies were created to allow the continuance and growth of the Worldist and New World Order. It's a form of auto-pilot. The system takes care of itself. Something like this had to have certain measures in place to make sure the Worldist conviction survived from Presidency to Presidency. Each new administration could screw up a Worldists perspective of how the world should be. I've considered how that could be accomplished and look to the steps Wilson took. FDR, upon seeing the failure of Wilson, created more safeguards."

"Go on."

"Wilson created the Federal Reserve as a means of controlling the economy. Look at how influential it is today. The Federal Reserve Chairman sets interest rates and establishes the monetary supply controlling the course of inflation."

"That's true."

"Then Wilson created personal income tax as a means to divest wealth and exert government control. Let's see what agencies FDR created. How about the IRS, the FBI was strengthened and the CIA was formed. Those creations of both Wilson and FDR ensured continued support. Without Wilson's failure, FDR would not have created them. They could keep this manner of thought alive in their training of agents, by having the masses fear the agencies themselves. It's forced compliance. Plus each agency is distrustful of the other. No one will share its information. As to the current administration, it seems closed in its world vision. From the articles I've read, the President is isolationistic in his beliefs."

"Do you really think it's possible?"

After a few moments, Alex said, "I guess I need to work on that. I definitely see a pattern. I have to say this again, the Presidential conspiracy really struck me out of nowhere when I was reviewing the U.N. material. It seems like anything negative happening to a President coincides with his position against the U.N. Enough of that."

"Okay."

"Let's go to dinner. It's your last night and your treat."

"I am starved." Sam said.

"Me too, besides the wine is gone. Ready?"

"Let me get my purse and jacket, and then we can head out."

"I have to make a quick call - then I'll be right over," Alex told her.

Our ultimate goal is a World without war. A World made safe for diversity in which all good men, goods and ideas can freely move across every border and every boundary.

Lyndon Baines Johnson
38th President

CHAPTER SEVENTEEN
NOVEMBER 12TH

He took an early morning taxi from National Airport back to his home in Old Town Alexandria, not having slept much on the red eye from San Francisco. He looked forward to getting some rest and spending time with his family. It was a successful week in California. The Ameritrend matter looked more and more promising in each venue. Alex opened the front door, put his suitcase and briefcase down on the floor of the foyer, and quietly proceeded up the stairs to the bedroom. Everything was so quiet, except for the first two stairs whose creaking boards chattered beneath him.

He opened the bedroom door. Laurel was standing next to their bed. The lights were off. Her expression was difficult to see. Everything appeared to be a varying shade of gray. She was dressed. One suitcase was on each side.

"Good morning Honey. Where are you off to?" Alex jokingly said as he approached her. Laurel stepped back. Alex stopped his forward motion. He could sense something was wrong, only he did not know what. "Is everything all right?"

Laurel cried. It was quiet, at first, then her tears grew in intensity. Alex drew closer. Various thoughts went through his mind. He tried to place his arm around her, to assure her, but she pushed him away. Her hands were clenched into fists as she pressed them into his chest. Her strength and force caught him by surprise.

"Stay away from me you bastard!" Laurel blurted as she slapped his face. "You're a goddamned son of a bitch! The sight of you nauseates me." She tried to hit him again, but Alex grabbed her to prevent her from striking him.

Words were her strength. The sting of the slap, coupled with her comments, startled him. Alex could feel his brow perspire. A rush of heat came over his entire body. Perspiration seemed to explode out of every pore. His cheek stung even more. "Laurel. What's wrong." Alex said directly.

"You know goddamn fucking well what's wrong. Don't pretend you don't," Laurel sobbed. She brought her hands up to her face.

"Laurel, I have no idea what you are talking about."

"Don't lie to me again." Laurel's voice grew louder. Her eyes were red and puffy. Her cheeks were raw from her tears that drenched them.

"Where are the boys?" Alex asked in a concerned hushed tone.

"Don't worry Alex, they aren't here," she replied sarcastically. "They spent the night with some friends."

"Okay, okay." Alex tried to calm her down. "Now tell me what's wrong. I can't read your mind."

The silence between them was tense. Laurel spoke. "So how long have you been seeing her?"

"What are you talking about?" Alex asked incredulously. "I haven't been seeing anyone."

"You've lied to me long enough Alex. I just hope you can be upfront with me now. About Samantha." Laurel said her name with disgust, looking directly at him to gauge his reaction. "Trailer trash."

Alex was taken aback. "What are you talking about?" He said as a diversion to allow himself more time to think of a response that would not upset her further.

"Don't try your time tactics with me. I've been married to you too long not to know how you react to situations. Samantha Hayes. Does her name ring a bell? Because it should. I know all about her." Laurel placed her right hand against her hip, her head hung down, heavy in weight.

"How?" Alex stammered, shocked by the sudden confrontation. After a successful week, he was supposed to be crawling into bed with his wife, not arguing over what he considered a non-issue.

"I found her name and number on a napkin you left in your suit coat pocket."

"So?"

"I was curious, so I called her number."

"Why?"

"I guess you could say it got the best of me."

"And."

"Her answering machine said she was out of town for the weekend." Laurel paused, placing the back of her hand up to her nose and mouth. She whispered, "I wanted to trust you. I've always trusted you, but now I was suspicious. So I called the Fairmont. You had adjoining rooms." Laurel glared at him.

"It's not what you think."

"Why bother. It would have been cheaper to stay in one room. All for a piece of ass. And now, here you are in my house, in my bedroom, wanting to get into my bed, pretending nothing happened. Pretending you didn't fuck her. Why bother? Why bother being here at all."

"It's not what you think."

"I'm not naive. I'm sure it was a coincidence I found her number in your jacket, and she was out of town and, as luck would have it, was in the same hotel, on the same floor, in adjoining rooms. I suppose you're going to tell me she was attending a Shriners convention. Or maybe you'll go with a more logical explanation and say you hired her as a new employee, and she was just helping you out, but you didn't want to tell me because you thought I would make a scene."

"I'm not going to pretend. But first, I want you to give it a rest so we can talk. Here, sit down." Alex motioned for both to sit on their bed. Alex sat down first. Laurel haltingly sat down, at arm's length from her husband "Where do you want me to start?"

"The beginning." Laurel's voice trembled.

"There's really nothing to tell." Alex felt her jerkily move away. "I mean nothing happened between me and Sam."

"So it's Sam," Laurel said rhetorically. "How special!"

"Laurel, she is just a friend. Nothing more," Alex explained. "She came out to San Francisco without me knowing about it. It wasn't something I planned. I wasn't interested in her."

"How can you be so cavalier about it. What do you take me for?"

"What do you want from me?"

"I was expecting you would be man enough to own up to what you've done." Laurel leered. "I guess I was wrong. You're not the man I married. You've destroyed the security we had. You've destroyed the sanctity of our marriage."

Alex looked at her. "I don't believe you're doing this. You're making this hard on both of us." He wiped his brow with the back of his hand.

"You know what the hard part is? It's the destruction you've caused. I felt more secure in our relationship as time went on. I found you more attractive and exciting after fifteen years of marriage, than when we were first married. And now, well you've ruined that for us."

"Laurel, please. You're being melodramatic."

"You can shove your melodrama."

"Honestly Laurel, listen to what I'm saying," Alex told her softly. "Nothing happened between Sam and me. I wouldn't think of destroying our relationship by sleeping with someone else. I cherish what we have, our home, our relationship, our children. I would do nothing to jeopardize our family. That is the God's honest truth."

"Who is she?"

"Sam?"

"Yes. Who is she?" Laurel looked at her husband. Her voice was controlled, exhausted from the ordeal.

"Sam is," Alex hesitated. "She's working on her graduate degree from Georgetown. She comes from a wealthy family - she paid her way to California - I met her when I went to Dumbarton Oaks. She was very helpful. What more can I tell you." Alex looked at his wife. Her eyes were still puffy. Every now and then she would rub her runny nose with the back of her hand. Occasionally, she would breathe deeply, swallowing harshly as she did. "I didn't have anything to do with this. I didn't pay for anything." Alex tried to explain.

"What difference does it make who paid. Like it will make me feel better knowing you're the hired stud."

"I didn't mean it like that. What I'm trying to say is if I was involved, then I would have been involved, but I wasn't." Alex's voice grew louder. "I didn't sleep with her."

"Why did you go to Dumbarton?" Laurel asked.

"Dumbarton Oaks is where they developed the U.N. Charter," Alex started to explain.

She sighed. "Not again, Alex. What is your preoccupation with this U.N. thing? I thought you weren't going to delve deeper. You've got yourself on a wild goose chase about something that doesn't exist. You might as well search for the fountain of youth. It may be easier to find."

"I'm just explaining how I met Sam."

"Alex. We've gone over your New World scenario. It is just air."

"Come on honey."

Laurel was exasperated. "Listen to yourself. This is what you've told me. You met this girl. . . "

"Girl?"

"I'll call her a girl because if she's still in school she isn't a woman yet. She's young, has lots of money and has taken an active interest in my husband, which he's returned in kind. I'll guess she's attractive, too."

Alex looked at his wife, but did not respond.

"Well?" Laurel asked. "You are not standing on firm ground, so don't skirt my questions. All I am asking is for you to be honest with me. Is she?"

"Sure. I suppose you want me to say if I wasn't married to you, then I'd be with her, but that's not true. I've been faithful to you. I've always been and always will be. I love you," he emphasized. "You're the mother of my children. Up to this point, we seemed to be handling this thing called life just fine."

"Why didn't you mention you knew her before I found out?"

"I didn't think it was a big deal. She's a friend."

"A friend? And if I had a male friend and the situation was reversed, how would you feel?"

"I would believe whatever you told me. I've never had any reason to doubt you, why would I?"

"Why didn't you tell me about her while you were in California. If she was just a friend and you had no idea she would be there with you, then you should have been upfront and told me what was going

229

on."

"There was nothing to tell. Nothing was going on." Alex felt he was being pressed back to defensive. He was ready to auger in. Now was the time to try damage control. "Laurel, we had separate rooms. Everything was on the level. I didn't have time to explain a situation I found myself in thousands of miles away from you. It would've made matters worse. I found myself busy, very busy. I was working most of the time. I didn't see Sam much. I was going to tell you about everything once I got home, when I got some rest. Besides, we didn't even come back together. She left Tuesday."

"Why wait to explain the situation if she was not with you?" Laurel said coldly. "Alex, I feel you've been unfaithful to me."

"But I. . ."

"You've hurt me deeply. I've had some time to think about everything and to be honest I don't think I'll ever be able to forget what has happened. Only time will tell if I can forgive."

"Please try." Alex was losing. "Nothing happened."

"Even if nothing happened, as you claim, I believe affairs of the heart and mind are just as offensive and intrusive, if not more so, than sex."

"What?" Alex was bewildered. "You're not being logical here Laurel. You should take some time and think about what you are saying."

"You've committed the adultery, Alex," she sighed. "Don't act this way toward me. I've thought about a lot of things. I've had time. A lot of time." She paused. "You've deliberately brought another woman into our lives. Two people were at our marriage ceremony, not three. I've agonized over whether this was the first time."

"I didn't do anything!"

"How many other times have you used work to have affairs?

230

This has made me wonder and question every early morning, each late night, all the evenings spent in the firm's condo, every trip away from home. I can't worry about you. It will eat me up. It almost has."

"So what happens now?" Alex said quietly, realizing Laurel had already decided.

"I've thought about what we should do. I realized it wasn't about us anymore." Laurel looked at him. She still appeared gray in the darkened room. "I think we need to spend some time apart, so we can sort through our relationship. We have to find out if we should be together, if we are meant to be."

"Meant to be?" Alex repeated.

"Yes. Spending time apart will let us see if we should continue in our marriage or get a divorce. It won't be easy, but it's for the best. If we have the strength to survive, then we will. If we don't, then it's better for us to go our separate ways."

"Seems you've made up your mind."

"I have, it's done."

"What about the boys? They're too young to be subjected to us breaking up. They won't understand what's happening."

"Children are resilient. It's for the best. It'll give us time to think," Laurel said in a tired voice.

"Do you want me to move out? It'll be less disruptive to everyone. You know, your schedule, your studio, the children's school. The boys can stay in their own home during any adjustment which needs to take place."

"That won't be necessary. There's too much of us here." Laurel emphasized us. "I've had difficulty in dealing with it as it is. I need to get away so I arranged for the boys and me to stay with my parents. I can spend some time with them, think about us. We'll see how it goes. It's best if you stay here."

"How can you? Your parents are all you ever complained about," Alex argued.

"That's just not true," responded Laurel.

"Bullshit!" Alex paused. "You've told me story after story of how they neglected you as a child. How they were too busy and ignored you, plus the form of mental abuse they put you through. Why would you want to run to them now?"

"I'm not running to them. I need some support and I am not getting it from you. My parents are there for me. They always have been and they always will be. Besides, I'm not little anymore. Our relationship has changed greatly since I was a teenager!"

"There's nothing I can say?" asked Alex.

"Or do," Laurel replied.

"For how long?"

"Two weeks."

"What about Jeremy and Christian's school work?"

"It's been arranged with their teachers. I talked it over with them on Thursday. No one has any clue as to the reason. Just a convenient trip during the school year. It happens all the time."

"I want to talk to them on a regular basis."

"Sure."

"You can't take my boys away from me. You know how I need to see them." Alex looked down, then turned his head to look out the bedroom window..

"I know it'll be hard on them, so I'll have them call you every few days. I don't want you calling. After all, why should you make this any different from any other time."

"Laurel, you're not being fair," Alex said.

"Being fair has nothing to do with my decision. I told you it's about me, not us anymore."

"Do your parents know?"

"I told them things were rocky between us. I said with your upcoming trial, you were under too much stress, and I needed to get away. They asked me to come stay with them for a couple of weeks. They suggested it. I felt it would be a good move. Besides, they haven't seen the kids in some time. They're looking forward to it."

"When are you leaving?"

"One."

"One?" Alex's voice rose. "Today?"

"Yes."

"I have to see them before they leave."

"You will."

"Promise me one thing."

"What?"

"Promise me that no matter what happens between us you won't keep them from me."

"I won't. Why don't you pick them up this morning."

"Okay."

"Remember. Jeremy and Christian are looking forward to Florida and Disney World."

Alex hesitated. He reached over and placed his hand on Laurel's back. She did not move away. He rubbed her shoulder. Laurel sat still, not reacting to his touch. "How about the airport. Can I take you?"

"No. I've made arrangements."

Alex paused. "Laurel, I love you, very much, more than you will ever know. I want you to understand that. I need you to realize that no matter what happens, no matter how you feel toward me, I love you. You were and are the love of my heart. There is no one else but you."

"You've caused me so much pain and anguish, it's going to take time for us to figure out what is best for everyone. I just need some time."

We shall have World Government whether or not we like it.
The only question is whether World Government will be
achieved by conquest or consent.

James B. Warbury
February 17, 1950

CHAPTER EIGHTEEN
DECEMBER 1ST

It was a bitterly cold December morning in the Nation's Capitol. The setting was appropriate for preparing one for Christmas and New Year's festivities. The damp chill went straight to the bone. On his way into work, Alex had to walk around and over many people huddling for heat. He referred to those less fortunate, those who survived life on the harsh streets, in a tongue in cheek reference to what most politicians referred to themselves and the political institutions located within this city, as grate people. For most grifters, the only means of survival were on top of the vents which spewed dry hot air. That was all they could afford to do to get them through the cold winter months. The heat had to be dry. Steam, due to the dampness, would subject them to greater illnesses and, perhaps, death.

Alex's personal affairs were in a state of chaos. His whole life had pulled apart at the seams when he returned from San Francisco and the possibility of putting the pieces back together was dismal. His parents and Laurel's family knew they had officially separated. She was with the boys in Florida where they were enrolled in school. He would talk with them every few days, but it was not enough. "

This was the first year, ever, he had spent Thanksgiving alone. He had offers to spend the holiday with his parents and assorted friends, but he had no heart to without his own family. Sam offered to help out by inviting him out on several occasions. She even suggested going to his house to be with him. Alex felt it would be better to talk on the phone, so as not to ruin any chance he had to reconcile with his wife. Laurel still did not believe him and she told him there was no trust between them. Alex delved into his practice with a vengeance. He did it to occupy his time, especially now.

"God I am trying," he would say on occasion to anyone who would ask how he was handling the separation. Most family and friends would not even broach the subject with him. Those who did would tell him either everything would be all right or things always work out for the best. Alex was growing tired of hearing the same advice over and over. He was also surprised and angered by those who knew of the separation but could not approach him. It was as though they were fearful his misfortune would rub off on them and they wanted no part of that.

His first appointment with a psychiatrist was the Friday right after Thanksgiving. He was at his lowest. He could not shake his feeling of hopelessness and despondence. What the hell, he thought, it was worth a try. He had always talked down the profession, believing only those people who were mentally weak would need counseling. But even escaping into work did not ease his pain.

His first visit went surprisingly well. Alex made it clear to the doctor he did not want to be medicated. They talked for two hours. Much concerned his childhood and parents. He recognized that having a better understanding of himself would aid in his recovery, but it would take some time. In the first session he realized he could not fault Laurel for what happened and that he was not entirely free from blame. It would take time and patience for many of the issues to be resolved.

"Christian?"

"Yeah?"

"Are ya up?" Jeremy asked his brother.

"Yeah. Are you alright?"

"I don't know. Talkin to dad last night got me thinking."

"About what?"

"About being home, playin out back, being with my friends."

"About mom an dad together?" Christian asked.

"Specially that. I miss him."

"Me too."

"I dreamt about all of us together."

"Where?"

"At home. Everyone is happy. Like old times. I get so sad when I wake up and dad's not here."

"Jeremy. . ."

"Yes?"

"Promise me that you won't leave me."

"We're brothers. Where I go you go, no matter what anyone says."

"Do ya think mom and Dad will get back together?"

"Honestly?"

"Yeah."

"No." Jeremy cried softly, turning his head into his pillow to muffle the noise.

"Jeremy, I'm scared."

He did not reply to his younger brother.

———————————

Alex was working at his desk. Thinking about Ameritrend, interspersed with his personal situation, vacillating between the two, when there was a knock on his office door.

"Come in."

"Hey Alex. How are you doing today?"

"Fine Quinn. What can I do for you?" Alex did not look up.

"We were supposed to get together this morning, you know, to go over the Ameritrend file." Quinn Colton looked at Alex's blank expression. "We scheduled it last week."

"Oh sure. I forgot to write it down." He tried to recall the meeting but could not. "I believe now is as good of a time as any. Shut the door, come in and sit down."

"Please let me know if I can be of any help. I heard you and Laurel separated and, while things always have a way of working out for the best, I know this time can be rough. If you need anything, just let me know." Quinn closed the office door and sat in one of the two chairs directly across from Alex, who was seated behind his desk.

"Thanks Quinn. Thanks for the offer." Alex looked down and wondered how gossip spreads so quickly. He only told Maura and Mr. Dougherty. "I wanted to thank you for handling the file while I was gone."

"Sure, it wasn't that bad," Quinn paused. "Alex. Are you feeling okay? You look tired."

"I'm fine. I'm trying to get used to the life of a bachelor. It's been years since I was one. I'm not a great cook. Housekeeping is a chore. Doing laundry is not a treat. It's a good thing there are cleaners around or I'd really be in trouble."

"I'm sure it'll stabilize soon," Quinn said, then added, "Maybe you should get a maid, or a housekeeper of some type. It would save you a lot of time. You could even get a geisha girl."

"I'm not into the mail order thing. I'm just going through a life change. I'm not the first person to go through this and I won't be the last." Alex felt on edge. He knew it was time to change topics. "Anyway, enough about me. How are the Wheeler's. Have you gotten any new insight into President Lawton and his staff, after all Dick Wheeler is the chief advisor."

"I'm still working the angle. If I can land some government contracts, we'll be all set for a while."

"At least until a change in administrations," Alex injected.

"It's better for us if the status quo remains. The more time I have to work Dick Wheeler, the more opportunities will exist for our firm."

"What about the economy? I heard on the news this morning that interest rates are rising. People cannot afford homes or mortgages, which means new home construction will drop sharply. Gas prices are rising, which will definitely lead to inflation. Energy rate increases influence all goods and services. The late seventies with gas rationing may not be all too far off."

"The economy is slowing somewhat, but Dick believes it is due to the media's manipulation of statistics, rather than an actual slow down of the economy. He told me, the other night," Alex noticed how he worked that in, "the projected economic indicators are rising. He wants the media to get off of the President's back, but you know how they are, the press only concentrates on the negative. It makes for better copy and higher ratings."

"What about the conflicts in the Middle East and Eastern Europe. Both areas are unstable. The President's foreign policy has not been firmly defined. They say his approval rating has slipped because of being a fence straddler. And if he doesn't take a position, any view, or a stance, then any foreign policy he tries to implement will lose its impact."

"Dick has told me about his concern. Between you and me, he's been feeling pressure to produce big gains for the President."

"Doesn't he work spin control?"

"Yes."

"He's missed some key damage control recently."

"It has resulted in a tarnished image for the President, and that has caused the press to be negative toward Dick too."

"Has he given you any sense as to any future plans which Lawton may have?"

"Dick told me he wants the President to concentrate on the issues here at home. He wants Lawton to stay away from foreign entanglements. No one is satisfied with action or inaction. You can't win. So he wants the President to become more isolationistic. He said Congress has been pushing a social agenda, which moves us from being global to isolationistic. He would rather have the President concentrate on social issues. Too much of our revenue goes toward unproductive ventures, especially when we spend money on foreign aid assistance and military might. For every dollar spent in our economy, in the private sector, we get two back. For every dollar spent on the military, we get nothing back."

"Does Dick Wheeler really think it is wise to turn inward? Expansion should always be on the minds of the American people," Alex said as he glanced at the dismal weather outside of his office Snow mixed with rain dripped down his window.

"He hasn't told me whether the President intends on turning inward, only that there seems to be this trend among the population, and Congress is feeling the same pull from their constituents to worry about matters within our shores."

"You can't be an island, especially in terms of today's technology," Alex said, playing the Devil's advocate.

"That's true, but you have to maintain the balance with the American electorate. The President is an elected official. If he wants to remain in power and have his party flourish, then he must be forced back to the middle occasionally."

"It may cause a shift in power if we don't concern ourselves with international matters, especially where our interests are at stake."

"What are our interests?"

"Truthfully?"

"Yes. How you personally feel. Not argument for the sake of argument."

Alex thought over the question. "The United States has a vested interest in the protection of its own shores, first and foremost. Next, comes protecting every citizen, no matter where they are in the world. Then, I suppose, is our own economic security."

"What's that?" Quinn asked.

"To maintain open and free markets for our industries to compete. To allow every citizen the ability to purchase the best product at the lowest price. You know, to allow the free market to establish price, based on supply and demand."

"Shouldn't the cost of labor be factored into that? If an industry is labor intensive, and certain countries have plentiful labor at low wages, then those countries should be the producers of those products that require more labor. Countries that produce technology, who can afford to pay higher wages and have an education work force, to sustain the increase in technology, should be concerned with technology. Countries which farm should produce food for the entire world to eat."

"Where is this scenario from?" Alex asked.

"Dick posed that to me the other night, while at the White House. He told me an underlying movement has existed, for some time, to force this country to diversify its resources and industrial base to other nations. He was concerned if we do, if we break down barriers, then we will lose our independence. He said NAFTA was only the start to make our nation dependent upon others."

"Why did the President support it?" Alex asked.

"I was of the impression Dick tried to have Lawton reconsider the treaty, or at least postpone the vote. The President was under pressure to support it. Dick argued this was just the beginning. He said he told the President if he supported the act, then our industrial infrastructure would become archaic. The industrial base of the Third World would grow. They would produce things with modern technology. We would be at their mercy for those products. He asked the President where we would be if they prevented trade with the United States"

"In a lot of trouble with not much room to do anything about it," Alex said. "It could even weaken our ability to defend our shores. Remember, our government converted industrial factories from the private sector manufacturing in World War II to produce weapons and supplies for our troops. That action allowed us to win. If we lose any more of our factories we'll lose the ability to defend ourselves. Power would shift to those Third World countries."

"That's how Dick felt. He said Lawton almost sided with him, but changed his mind at the last minute, after a closed door meeting with his Chiefs of Staff. Dick has shifted the focus of the administration to being concerned with becoming too dependent upon others, and not wanting to involve the U.S. in international disputes."

"I guess all we can do is wait and see how those things go."

They sat and looked at each other and around the room for several moments, until the silence became uncomfortable. Alex said, "Why don't we get started on the Ameritrend matter."

"That's what I'm here for," Quinn replied in his excited, nasal manner.

"Let me catch you up to speed, Quinn, if you haven't reviewed all of it yet." Alex picked up one thick red rope file and sort of dropped it on his desk with a thud. "As you can see, this file is pretty thick. This is one of seven files. This case is one of ten in the court systems throughout the United States. So, all things considered, there are probably over thirty red rope files, all just as thick, on the Ameritrend matters which we are handling."

"Incredible. How do you keep everything straight?"

"It's becoming somewhat of a burden, so I need more staff on the case. You volunteered. You get to be a part of this." He gestured toward the file. "You will get your fair share of work, believe me." He smiled. When Quinn said he would help, Alex knew he did not understand the depth and magnitude involved.

"Where do I start?"

"Always at the beginning." Alex thought of Laurel. "What I would like to do is to catch you up to speed on the matter pending before the U.S. District Court in D.C. That case is progressing the quickest, so I feel we should work up the file and start trial prep. We're looking for a late Spring trial date."

"Okay."

"I want you to take each of the red ropes, in order, review them, then we will sit down every Thursday at 3:30 and review the documents, looking at the history of the case. Within the next month, we can decide on the best approach to take." Alex looked at Quinn to make sure he was comprehending what he wanted him to do. "I'll dictate a memo on this, for your review and. . . ." There was a knock at his office door. "Just a moment, let me see who it is." Alex stood up and went to the door, somewhat perturbed Maura did not buzz him to let him know he was wanted. He opened the door. There, standing in the doorway was a Deputy Sheriff. Several attorneys and clerical staff were in the hall, watching and wondering what the officer wanted.

"Are you Alexander Westcott?" he asked.

"Why?" Alex replied, not wanting to admit he was, until he found out what was expected of him.

"I'm here to serve these papers for divorce."

"Yes, I'm Alex Westcott," he said loudly enough for everyone to hear, causing some to turn and carry on their business as if nothing was wrong. His heart felt hollow. He now realized there was no turning back. Laurel decided their relationship was over.

"Here you are." The Deputy handed him the Complaint for Divorce.

Alex took the papers. It was the first time he had ever been served. "Thank you," he said, not knowing what else to say. He felt foolish for saying thanks when he was handed an item which extinguished any hope he had for reconciliation. He stepped back into his office and closed the door behind him. He looked at the attorney's name on the documents. "Shit!"

"I'm sorry, Alex," Quinn said.

"That's not the worst of it."

"Why's that?" Quinn asked.

"Look who her attorney is," Alex instructed.

"Andy Vassily?" Quinn responded in astonishment. "I didn't know he did divorces."

"He doesn't. Not unless he wants to be an asshole. And believe me, he wants to distract me and this'll do it." Alex's voice was hinged with bitterness.

"What now?"

"How about us reviewing the files on Saturday at 10:00? I'll prepare an outline with a list of items I need you to work on. We'll take it from there."

Quinn stood up from the chair, walked to him and placed his hand up on his shoulder. Alex stood still, trying not to show he did not want to be touched. With his hand still on the doorknob, he opened it. "Thanks Quinn. I'll see you on Saturday."

"Saturday," came the reply as he left.

Alex closed the door quietly. He turned off his office light, preferring to darken the room, creating a womb like effect. He walked to his phone and paged Maura.

"Hello Mr. Westcott."

"Maura, please hold all calls and appointments. I don't want to be disturbed."

"Yes Mr. Westcott. Anything else?"

"No." Alex hung up the phone and looked down. He shook uncontrollably. He quickly sat down. The tears seemed to run right through him. All he could hear was the room filling with his heavy sobs followed by silence, as he held his breath so he would not hyperventilate.

"It's been done, I just got the call from my attorney."

"Laurel, are you sure you want to go through with this? Everything has been rather sudden, but perhaps you need more time to sort things out."

"William, I've thought so much about everything, I don't have anything else to think about. You know how I've been completely drained by this entire ordeal."

"Yes."

"You've given me the support I needed to make it this far."

"I don't know how much I've really done." Sniper felt some pangs of guilt.

"You've done more than you'll ever know." Laurel hesitated.

"What?"

"I was only wondering when you're going to be back in town," she whispered into the phone.

"I'll be back when I finish this investigation in D.C."

"When?"

"Two or three days. I'll be back as soon as possible." An intermittent beep could be heard in the background. "Laurel, I'm being paged, I gotta run."

"So soon?"

"I'll call you later tonight."

"I miss you."

"I miss you too."

Our greatest foreign policy problem is our divisions at home. Our greatest foreign policy need is national cohesion and a return to the awareness that foreign policy is something we are all engaged in as a common national endeavor.

Henry A. Kissinger
Secretary of State

CHAPTER NINETEEN
DECEMBER 23RD

He reached for the television remote on the nightstand, turning on the TV

"What are you doing?" asked Sam. "You're placing a damper on the mood."

Alex felt her naked body move over and press up against his. Her breasts touched the side of him. She moved her leg over his, running her foot down in a responsive caress. Her warmth radiated, enticing him.

Once served with the Complaint, Alex phoned his psychiatrist but could not schedule an immediate appointment. He then called Sniper, but he was in Miami on an assignment. He felt exposed, needing to talk to someone, so he turned to Sam. She was very receptive to his needs, meeting him at his house on the afternoon of the First, staying with him since. He was grateful she was there for him. Alex's perspective changed. He no longer felt lost, nor did he concern himself with the quest for an understanding as to the New World Order. Sam allowed, even demanded, that he to turn his attention to her. He was amazed by how well they hit it off and now, with Christmas fast approaching; they would spend it with one another. He felt young whenever she was by his side.

"I'm just going to take a look at the news, it's almost on."

"Oh Alex." Sam moved closer to him.

He did not think it was possible, but she did.

"Why don't you turn off that annoyance and let me take you away again," Sam said as she pushed her body on top of his. Sam nestled up to his neck, gently kissing and licking him, tracing her tongue from his neck to his ear. "I'm going to rock your world," she whispered.

Alex could hear every breath she took. Each one in succession aroused him more and more.

"I don't know if I can. I'm not as young as I once was." Alex never knew how great his sexual drive was until Sam was with him. She awoke his sleeping sexuality. Making love with her was unlike anything he ever experienced before. Every time was more intense than the one before. The effect was cumulative.

"You're only as young as you feel, and believe me, you are incredible. I want you again," Sam's words were wisps of air.

She exhilarated him all the more. The mere thought of her needing him made him want her all that much more. Alex wondered if he was becoming incessant.

"You are incredible. I always wish you were inside of me much earlier than this."

"No Sam." He pressed upward into her, grabbing her hips, caressing her back as he did. "You are more incredible than anyone I've ever been with. You bring me to higher highs." She moved her hips down to the top of his. The prurient tension was becoming greater. "I'm not a machine, damn it," Alex mocked. "I am just a man."

"You're much more than that, and you know it." Sam moved down. Kissing his chest, slowly moving down to his stomach. Alex looked at her, then to the television. The sound was low. The colors danced and reflected off of her skin in the darkened bedroom. The 11:00 p.m. News was beginning. He could see the headline.

"Chief Presidential Advisor Found Dead."

"Oh my God," Alex said in a suppressed tone.

Sam paused. Her eyes looked up at his, then she continued moving down his body. Alex half turned, then twisted toward the remote. Sam, reacting as if he was responding to her movements, continued. He increased the volume on the set.

"Tonight's lead story," the television anchor said in a pitch befitting a baritone singer. "The top advisor to President Lawton has been found dead in a parking lot off of the Parkway. Richard Wheeler was discovered around dusk, slumped over his steering wheel, dead of an apparent self inflicted gunshot wound."

Sam stopped, and then sat up in bed. She saw the look of shock on Alex's face, and then turned to watch the breaking story.

"We now go live to our Jim Reynolds, who is at the scene of the shocking discovery. Jim."

"Thanks Bill. I'm standing in front of a cordoned off parking lot by the George Washington Parkway. Both the District police and Secret Service have confirmed the body of top Presidential Advisor, Richard Wheeler, was discovered in his government issued car. He was pronounced dead at the scene of what authorities are saying was a self-inflicted gunshot wound to the right temple. Standing next to me is Loren Allen who made the discovery." Jim Reynolds half turned toward the camera. "Mr. Allen, how'd you discover the body?"

"I parked my car to go for a jog," he started in a thick New York accent. "I was out forty five minutes. When I returned, I noticed this car parked next to mine." He gestured back behind the yellow police tape, which cordoned off the area, toward some vehicles parked in a darkened lot, clothed in colors of reflecting sirens. "As you see, there isn't a whole heck of a lot of cars there, so I was cautious. I didn't want to be jacked, so I approached my car slowly, with my keys out. As I got closer," he gestured toward the automobile in the background, "I felt something was wrong. I saw some dark colored stuff on the driver's window and then I saw the driver slumped over the wheel, with a gun on the dashboard. It wouldn't take a rocket scientist to tell he was dead."

"What did you do next?"

"I ran to find someone with a phone, and stopped someone about one hundred yards over there." He pointed toward the camera. "Then I called the police. They came here and questioned me for over an hour."

"Was the car here when you started to run?"

"No."

"Are you sure?"

"Yea. Before you ask any more questions I want to tell my wife I'll be really late for dinner."

"Did you see anyone else around?"

"Nope. Just me."

"What happened next?"

"The police came first and blocked off the area, then Secret Service showed up and asked me some more questions. I knew it was someone famous when they got here, followed by all you guys."

"Did they tell you who it was?"

"Nope. I asked, but they said to answer their questions, so I did. I learned from another reporter."

Alex reached up and caressed Sam's shoulders, pulling her back and up to him so her back was against his chest. He reached over with his right hand and gently brushed against her breast. "This is incredible."

"I can't believe it either." Sam moved in closer.

The picture went back to the reporter, standing alone.

"I wonder how long they'll milk this."

"You know the media," Sam responded. "Probably for a while."

The portable lights were set up in the parking lot. The scene was flooded in a stark white light, creating an unnatural effect. There was a bit of a commotion going on behind the scene. The camera moved to Richard Wheeler's car. On the other side of the car was an ambulance, waiting to take the body.

"The authorities are going to transport the body to the Bethesda Naval Hospital. An autopsy is slated to be performed there in the morning."

Jim Reynolds paused as the camera focused on several people milling about, conversing how to handle the body's transit.

He placed his hand to his ear, and then faced the camera. "We have had word right now the authorities are treating this as a homicide. I have to preface that with this statement, as issued. There has been no indication of a struggle or any unforced entry into Richard Wheeler's car. The bullet remained in the automobile. It did not penetrate the driver's side window. I was informed it was from a nine-millimeter gun. One shot, apparently, was fired."

"Jim. Why are they treating this case as a homicide?" Bill asked.

He reached with his left hand and placed it against the receiver in his left ear, to hear the question better. "Bill, I was apprised that, as with any investigation of this nature, especially where someone has had such close ties to the President, the authorities will first treat this type of situation as a homicide before ruling it anything else."

From the television, Alex observed a figure encased in a white body bag. Four paramedics lifted it out of its position, in the car. The bag was limp, like a large sack of flour in their hands. The camera focused on the faces of the paramedics.

"Jesus," Alex said, sitting more upright.

"Are you all right?"

"My God Sam. What is he doing there?"

"Who?"

"Thomas Henry. That's him."

"Where?"

"Right there." Alex pointed to the face of a man behind the paramedics. "Do you see that guy there?"

"Yes."

"That's Thomas Henry. He's trouble. He was at Garrett Baird's the night I had my accident. And now this."

"Maybe he works for one of the agencies." Sam's reply was calm.

"I was told he was just visiting from out of town. I find it hard to believe he'd be there."

"Alex, that person is probably not even him. Lighting like that can play havoc on your eyes."

"Sam, I tell you it's him. I have his face engraved in my mind. I don't know if he's the lamb or the executioner."

"Thanks Jim for that late breaking news story. For those of you that don't know, or who have joined us late, the Chief Advisor to President Lawton has died of an apparent self-inflicted gunshot wound. Richard Wheeler. . ." There was a picture of him behind the news anchor, his hair was windblown, a forbearance of things to come. ". . . was the Chief Presidential Advisor. He was a boyhood friend of the President and had been asked to fill the position once the President was elected. Many would characterize his tenure as tumultuous. He recently came under fire for his handling of the President's exposure on the international front. President Lawton has issued a statement. He said, and I quote, 'Our deepest condolences are extended to the Wheeler family. Richard was a great friend, a trusted confidant and a true family man. He did his work admirably. He served his nation well. He was untiresome and diligent. We have all suffered a great loss with his passing'."

Alex reached over to the remote and placed the volume on mute. Sitting back, she placed her arms around his neck and kissed him on the lips in a seductive style. She then moved her face into the crook of his neck, closing her eyes as she did.

"Shall we continue from where we left off?"

"I don't know Sam, I'm kinda tired."

"Kind of." Sam emphasized the of.

"See, that's how tired I am. My words are even slurring together." Alex chuckled.

"What are you doing?"

"Nothing. Why?" Alex said timidly.

"I could feel you move in a jerky motion. Are you okay?"

"Fine Sam, just laughing to myself."

"About the slurring words?" She could feel him nod yes. "You must be tired. You're getting slaphappy."

"Yes I am," he replied, with hard affirmative emphasis on each word. They both giggled like kids. It was contagious. Each fed off the other. They laughed harder. All it took was for them to look at each other and soon they were laughing uncontrollably, tears were streaming down Alex's face. "There's a fine line between laughing and crying," he blurted out, as tears and drool fell on Sam's cheek, sending them both into hysterics. Alex could not remember the last time he laughed so hard. The phone rang, which only made matters worse. They both were laughing hard at the prospect of either of them answering it.

Sam said, "Aren't you gonna get it?" This caused them both to laugh harder.

"It hurts, it hurts," Alex forced out. "I think spit just came out my nose."

The phone continued to ring.

"It must be important," Alex said as he laughed. "Whoohoo." Alex could feel himself deflating, trying to get control to answer the phone. "Hellloo."

"Is Alex there?"

"Speaking."

"Alex are you all right? Did I catch you at a bad time?"

"Noo, not at all. What do you need?". Alex kept trying to compose.

"Did you see the news?" Quinn Colton asked.

"Yes." Alex was breathing in more of a normal manner.

"So you heard about Richard Wheeler."

"Yes."

"I talked to his wife after they discovered his body. She wants me to go to Bethesda with her, to identify his body."

"Really?" Alex took more of an interest. "Did she say anything else?"

"She said Dick was not depressed. She said she talked to him today and he was going over some reports. He told her demographics looked good and maybe now the media would lay off him, at least for the time being."

"That's interesting. Anything else?"

"Yea. She said someone killed her husband. They were planning on taking two weeks off as of tomorrow. She said he was looking forward to getting away."

"Maybe that's what he meant by getting away," Alex said.

"She also told me he did not own a gun. He never bought one. He didn't believe in them, especially with kids running around the house."

"Are you sure about this?" Alex asked.

"I'm just telling you what she told me."

"Why are you telling me?"

"I'm kind of nervous about it. My wife knows about Dick's death, nothing else. I can't tell her. I don't know if I should believe what I've been told, but if it's true, and he was killed, then if whoever did that to Dick finds out I know something, then something could happen to me."

"What can I do?"

"It's not what you can do, but the fact is just by you knowing, it could protect me. I don't want to tell too many people. They may think I am crazy, but I want a record made of what I was told."

"Consider it done."

"Seriously Alex. It's like Claudius from the Roman Empire. He recorded history, only he made two records. One was found and destroyed shortly after his death. The other was hidden and preserved for later discovery."

"I'm the later discovery," Alex rationalized.

"Yes. When the truth must be told, you can tell it. People must be ready to accept the truth before it can be embraced."

"It's a deal Quinn. Is there anything else I can do?"

"No. Everything else has been taken care of. Enjoy the holidays."

"Merry Christmas Quinn, to you and your family."

"Thanks Alex. I'll let you know what happens." Quinn hung up.

"Who was that?" Sam asked.

"Quinn Colton."

"Who?"

"You know the guy I work with."

"The one you can't stand?" Sam pushed her hand through his hair.

"Maybe I was too harsh on him, too judgmental."

"Why the sudden change of heart, Alex. Did the ghost of Christmas past pay you a visit?"

Alex laughed. "Don't make me start again."

"Well?"

"It's the predicament he found himself in. Dick Wheeler's wife called him and said it wasn't a suicide. She wants him to go with her to Bethesda to ID the body."

"Sounds gruesome. I'm sure every person who has suffered a loss goes through a denial period. That's probably what Mrs. Wheeler is doing."

"She claims her husband didn't own a gun."

"Maybe he bought it without her knowing."

"Well."

"Well, Alex, do you own a gun?"

"Yes, okay, I know where you're going."

"Wait, I am not finished. Did you buy your gun with Laurel's knowledge?"

"No, but."

Sam cut him off. "No buts. If you used that gun to commit suicide, wouldn't she have been surprised?"

"Do I need to answer that?"

"Yes you do."

"It's probably something she would have wanted me to do."

"Alexander."

He looked at her young beauty. "Okay, she would have been

256

surprised, and so would I."

"I didn't ask for any more commentary."

"You get it being with me."

"And being with me you get this." Sam stood up on top of the bed, her naked body washed in color from the television.

One day, I will wake up from this dream state and everything will be all over." Alex looked at her.

"How?" she asked.

"You'd be gone and I'd be alone here in a big empty house." He reached up to her hands with his. He pulled her close to him. "I'm doing this to make sure I'm not hallucinating."

She fell on top of his body. "This will prove that you aren't." Her being completely engulfed him. Sam kissed him slowly.

This time he could not resist her advances. "Hell, how much pleasure can one man experience."

Sam said, "You're on your way to discovering your threshold."

Every government is in some respect a problem for every other government and it will always be this way so long as the sovereign state, with its supremely self-centered "rationale" remains the basis of international life.

George F. Keenan
Economist

CHAPTER TWENTY
JANUARY 9TH

The change in seasons gave the drive out to Garrett Baird's estate a different appearance. Trees were bare and snow was on the ground. Everything had a cold, frosted feeling to it. Cars emitted white cloud wisps from their exhaust. Everyone bundled up to protect themselves. Spring seemed far away. Garret phoned Alex inviting him, along with a few other people, for dinner. He referred to the event as 'Men's night out,' promising ample food, satisfying libations and exceptional conversation. Even a good 'Cuban', in reference to the cigars. This party was Alex's foray into a new circle. Work was bogging him down, but he could not pass on this opportunity, networking into the system, the inner organization.

As he pulled up to the mansion's main entrance, two valets were there to open his door and park his car. Tonight's event appeared much larger than he anticipated. Alex got out of the Explorer, his only car after the MG was totaled. Laurel was getting a new one. She did not want the Explorer or much to do with him, for that matter. Apparently, she was holding off buying a new car until their divorce was finalized. There were no winners in a divorce. Jeremy and Christian were subjected to a life without their father, someone who had played a major role in their short lives. They were removed from familiar surroundings, exposed to losing friendships, spending the holidays without their family in tack. For Alex and Laurel, they had the same experiences only as parents and spouses. Jeremy was adjusting to the split better than Christian. Youth is much more resilient.

Alex found out several weeks ago that Sniper had been assigned in Miami, close to Laurel in West Palm Beach. He said he sees her once in a while, 'as friends.' He kept Alex informed of events in her and the boys' lives. Sniper told him, on the sly, that Laurel had been asked out, but she said no. Still, it hit Alex hard. He still did not want to share his wife with anyone. It was difficult for him to set aside fifteen years in a relationship, of companionship, growth, love and desire. Sam was great company, but they had no history with each other. Still, Alex did not want to seem hypocritical, 'Do as I say, not as I do' mentality left a bitter taste inside. He realized it was an obstacle he would have to overcome. There were still numerous times when he was with Sam he would think of his wife, so much so, he would not call Sam by her name for fear he would call her Laurel. Alex wondered what he would do if he could go back to when this all started. Hindsight was 20/20, and he knew that. The opportunity to make amends had long since passed. As it did, he found himself going through the grieving process. From denial to depression, and now onto acceptance. Sam was helping him along the path toward healing.

He got out of the car, leaving the door open for the valet. He gave an inquisitive look; unsure if was to receive a receipt to indicate which vehicle was his. Not that it mattered, all the cars there were much more expensive than his Explorer.

"You're set," came the unsolicited response. The valet closed the door and drove away.

Alex proceeded through the main entrance, beyond the imposing wooden doors, inside to the inviting dry warmth. One of the servants took his overcoat, folding it once over her arm, before heading in some unknown direction. Alex looked ahead. Garrett was there to greet him. His cigar, lit, was imbedded in the corner of his mouth. His left hand held a healthy glass of scotch.

"Alex. It's good to see you." Garrett said warmly. "I am delighted you are here to join us."

"Thanks Garrett. The pleasure is all mine. I appreciate being included."

"Not a problem. It's good to have the men over for a change. It gives everyone an opportunity to get to know the real person since no one must be politically correct. You don't have to put a guard up like when women are present. There's no need to wonder if anyone will be offended by what you say."

"You're lucky the government doesn't define this as a public place," Alex said.

"Why's that?"

"If you were, events like this wouldn't be allowed."

"Why not?" Garrett asked.

"Because you're excluding over fifty percent of the population. You know the government, they don't take to discrimination lightly."

"Alex, you're right. It's a good thing. Excuse me while I see to the help. Others are in the living room. Make yourself at home. Everyone should be here shortly. Drinks are being served there." Garrett quickly turned his attention elsewhere, leaving Alex alone.

Alex approached the living room where loud voices could be heard. The double doors were open, welcoming him to venture inside. The room was brimmed with warm light, boisterous conversation and smoke. In a matter of seconds, a waiter greeted him.

"Would you like a drink, sir?"

"Garrett wastes no expense here."

"Pardon me, sir?"

"Nothing. How about a Stoli on the rocks with a twist."

"Yes sir."

"Thanks." He looked around the room. A few faces were familiar, but no one he knew personally. As Alex mingled through the crowd, he felt out of place. The cigar smoke was bothering him. There were at least twenty people already gathered, all smoking and drinking.

"Would you like a cigar, sir?" A young waif of a woman asked, holding a box of cigars out for Alex's choice.

"No thanks. Believe it or not, I don't smoke."

"This is probably not your place then." She bowed before leaving.

"No it's not." He rubbed his eyes.

"Your drink, sir." The waiter held out the tray.

Alex relieved him of the burden, a glass one would consider to be more than a double. "Thank you. That's a real drink." Garrett was not kidding about the ample alcohol. As he approached a group of four men, Alex listened to their conversation about the economy, and then he introduced himself.

"You said your name was Alex Westcott?" a tall man, wearing wire rimmed glasses asked.

"Yes," Alex replied.

"It is definitely a pleasure to meet you. We all here owe you much gratitude. I've been wanting to meet you for some time, especially since you're the one who saved Garret's life."

"It wasn't anything, really." Alex tried to downplay his role. Shifting the conversation, "And your name is?"

"Jack Cutter. This is Wally Edwards, Truman Carson, Ken Campbell and Steve Walters." They all exchanged greetings.

"Certainly is quite a party. I hope I didn't interrupt your conversation. By all means, please continue," said Alex.

"We were just discussing the economy," Jack Cutter said. "What don't you tell us what your impressions are of the trade treaty?"

"Well," Alex paused, trying to remember what the acronym stood for. He straightened his tie, and then smiled. "If I can correctly recall, I think we've been trying to pass an amendment on tariffs and trade for fifteen years now. If we didn't want it back then, why bother right now? We would lose a lot of jobs if it occurs."

"How? The free market system must dictate what we pay for goods. If another country can make something for less, then we, as consumers, should be able to buy it."

"Look at it from a different perspective," Alex said. "What happens if we break down the barriers on trade, creating what appears to be a true free market economic system as to cars. If other nations supplement their automobile industries, through government controls and operations, research and development, subsidizing their goods, then as a nation, we'll lose jobs along with our automotive industrial base."

"If those countries want to subsidize their cars, then that acts as a boost to our economy."

"How?"

"Cause we keep more of our money here, forcing the exit of their currency through those subsidized cars, raising inflation there, while holding it down here. Consumers win even more." Jack Cutter responded.

"Remember that any gain is only for a limited duration," Alex explained. "After foreign competition penetrates our markets, effectively closing the automobile industries and jobs, then foreign companies can dictate the prices of cars, reap huge profits in the long term, thereby offsetting any losses they may have had in the short run."

"With a true free market system," Jack bantered, "Once we can produce those cars cheaper, then those industries will open up here. The same would be true of any industry competing in the global market."

"That will never happen." Alex coughed from the smoke.

"Why not?" Truman Carson asked. He was short, stocky, bald, with a cigar dangling from his lips as he talked. He had the rotund aspect of a banker.

"Because it hasn't happened yet. You can't name one industry we've lost which has started back up here. Look at televisions, motorcycles, shoes, even cars," Alex said.

"A true system would allow that," Carson interrupted.

"Only on paper," Alex countered.

"Beyond," he needled back. "There is much more strength in numbers. As countries pull together, they lessen the chance of catastrophe. Industries flourish, along with farming, retail and every other sector of the economy."

"Are you talking about the European Economic Countries?" Alex asked.

"Well, now that you mention it, their collective coalition has strengthened their power." The portly man blew smoke toward him.

Alex looked at him. "Are you sure? Their economies have not responded to their merger. There is a lot more dissention within each nation, each still wanting to retain some semblance of independence"

"It's only momentary. The dust must settle before you'll be able to see the magic in unification. How many independent nations can you have? Few I'd venture." Truman replied.

"Are you advocating a unified world?" Alex paused. "Like a New World Order? Where there aren't any borders or independence, even freedom?"

"A unified world would be better at production and the manufacturing of anything. Sort out the strengths and weaknesses of each area. Geography plays a role. Mountainous regions can't produce corn, but they might have valuable resources. It's a matter of being

263

logical."

"So our auto industry might be better suited in Japan and if it is, then that industry should go there." Alex said.

"Yes, or China, where labor is cheap," came Truman's reply.

"If we lose our auto industry, we lose not only highly paid jobs, but our industrial base. Without our industrial base, we become vulnerable to the onslaught of attack from other countries, economically and militarily. Without jobs, we become more socialistic, as we look to government to cure our ills, to take care of and protect us. An economy of that type will collapse from not having any money to pay for social, military and legislative programs we either need or want," said Alex.

"What's your alternative?" Jack Cutter asked.

"Take care of us first. We can't save the world. With the North American Trade Agreement, and our tariff and trade agreement, we bring the problems of other countries to our doorsteps. We allow their problems to become ours. Their homeless and impoverished become ours. They are strengthened and we weaken. It's that simple. You're only as strong as your weakest link. And, while it won't happen overnight, it is a gradual erosion, wearing away at our economic base. We will eventually tumble. The higher we are economically, the further away we may be, but when the body falls, the head hits harder than the knees or ankles."

"Alex. It is Alex, isn't it?" Ken Campbell asked.

"Yes."

"Alex, my boy, you are so naive. There really is no other term for you. I can just as easily turn that around by looking to England. They were the first nation to go through the industrial revolution. After which, they settled nicely into position as a post industrial leader. Their lifestyle is one of the best in the world. Their socio-economic ladder is stratified, which encourages further economic development. I would offer that as something to aspire toward."

"England? Are you kidding?" Alex laughed. Sensing it was a serious argument, he launched his attack. "Let's see. Where would you like me to begin. The British economy is not something to be proud of. They're suffering from high inflation and unemployment. Their social structure benefits the aristocracy. That's something either you are or aren't born into. You'll never have a chance to join the elite. Brains, wealth or initiative don't let you join." Alex paused, and looked at the group of men surrounding him, before he continued. "If they are so powerful, even after losing their industry, then why did they need us to bail them out of both world wars? And their economy, if it is so strong, why did they join the European Economic Community, a consortium of Western European countries. They joined together to compete in the world economy. It's obvious they can't do it on their own. Soon enough Europe will have one currency. Can you imagine that? How about us going on a one world monetary system to tie into the one world economy. It's closer than you realize."

"So what if it does happen?"

"I don't want to lose my diversity and individuality. Democracy and capitalism cannot be implemented worldwide. Someone will lose and it'll be us," Alex pleaded for understanding.

"Democracy can apply throughout the world. We are the living example and, with all that has been happening to destroy communism, it can work." Truman puffed smoke into Alex's face.

"Dictatorships, and Monarchies, benevolent or malevolent," Alex wheezed, "won't allow that to happen. Think they'll let others run their countries? I think not. Besides, a world economy would be incredibly difficult, if not impossible, to manage. It would force us to become even more socialistic. I believe no one here would want that to happen. It'll be interesting to see what Lawton does."

"The man has not changed his perspective. Rumor has it he wants to tighten the control over imports and restrain the free exodus of jobs from here. He just needs the right advisors," Jack said.

"Too bad about Richard Wheeler," Alex said.

"Yea. Why anyone would take his own life is beyond me. If you can't stand the heat, then get out of the kitchen," Ken Campbell said.

Alex looked at Jack Cutter. "What about the recently published reports which say he was murdered?"

"Bunch of Bullshit. No one ever wants to believe the truth. Look at all those people who believe in UFO's, O. J.'s innocence, that Elvis is still alive or there was a conspiracy with the murder of JFK. It's the way people are - they want to bury their heads." Jack replied.

"How about the President's staff rifling through Wheeler's belongings before Secret Service?" Alex asked.

"Alex, I'm sure they meant no harm, only preparing the President for the onslaught of news media. Besides, look at all the bad press Wheeler was getting over the past several months. Who could blame him for being depressed."

"You may have a point there." Alex shifted his stance.

"May I get you another drink?" the waiter inquired.

"No thanks. I'm still trying to finish my first fifth right here." Alex and the others laughed. "Now if you will excuse me, I need to find a room where I can breath for a few minutes. This smoke is getting to me." Alex left the blue haze of the living room. More people were still coming. He excused himself as he passed people in the hall. The cigar smoke seemed to follow him. He turned another corner, went down another hall, turned another corner, and found himself looking at his reflection in the glass doors to the library. He opened the door, walked in, and shut the door behind him. With the lights off, he proceeded to one of the tall backed chairs directly in front of the door and sat down with his back to the door. He closed his eyes which stung from the smoke. He could taste the cigar smoke in his throat.

"It's another one of those nights."

"Garrett, do y'all have the information?" Thomas Henry asked.

"Yes. I put together a memo."

"A memo?"

"Yes. Why? It tells everyone to destroy any information they may have."

"I'm surprised you prepared anything," Thomas Henry said in his southern accent. "After all we've been through. The last thing you'd want is any information to be leaked, no matter how piddly. Y'all sure it was a smart thing?"

"Nothing major." Garrett chewed down hard on his lit cigar.

"Where is it?"

"In the library. In a safe place."

"Let's go."

"What about my guests? I need to get socializing before anyone thinks something may have happened to me."

"They're all drinking and having fun. Don't think too highly of yourself," Henry replied. "Now show me."

"After tonight we won't be in contact," Garrett said.

"I know how to disappear."

"Just do it right."

Alex saw the shadows of two people walking down the hall, toward the library, reflect along the books across the room. He slid down a little in the chair. One of the doors opened slightly. There was a pause in their movement. He held his breath, feeling awkward being someplace he should not.

"As I told you, I have everything you need right in here, in a safe place." Garrett Baird said.

Alex got up and let Garrett know he was there, then he hesitated.

"Are y'all sure everything's in order?"

He remembered the voice. Thomas Henry. Alex wanted to turn and look, but he knew if they saw him move, he would be in even bigger trouble.

"Listen Thomas, this is not the first time I've been involved in something of this nature. The gauntlet has been passed and, after all I've been through, I think I can handle any situation I may find myself involved. Further, if you don't trust my judgment, then I don't want you involved. We can always do the script with the Service."

"That'll cause problems with the police and Senate investigations. Someone taking the heat. The unexpected always occurs and with today's technology an all the video cameras, it would be recorded. Bet your ass." Henry responded.

"True, but those problems can always be handled. Any investigation can show the involvement of only one person. Film and recordings can be touched up." Garrett paused, chewed on his cigar, and took a deep sip of scotch. "If presidents would only remain true to the course, to the creation of the New World through the United Nations, we wouldn't have to go through this."

"I've voiced my opinion. I don't want to see history repeat itself either."

"Neither do I Thomas, neither do I."

"I know my role well. I'll have no problem carrying out my responsibilities."

"You have been paid half of your contracted amount," Garrett Baird said.

"Yea."

"The remaining money will be transferred to your off shore account tomorrow."

"As requested."

"Is there anything you need to go over?" Garrett asked.

"No, I'm all set."

"Why don't we join the party for a little while, then you can come back here and get your material. By the way, your good friend is here."

"Who?" Thomas Henry asked.

"Alex Westcott."

"Really? Well he saved your ass," Henry laughed.

"Yes, wrong place at the wrong time, perhaps. Anyway, I only hope you don't screw up this assignment like you did with him. You'll be up against pros who won't be clued into what your intentions are."

"Listen Garrett, I'm a professional. He should have died in that accident. It was a one in a million chance he survived. Besides, I more than made up for it and proved my worth with Dick Wheeler."

"Yes. You did that nicely. It's too bad."

"What?"

"I would have sworn that would have gotten President Lawton in line. However, since he took more protectionist measures after Wheeler's death, I have no option but to go to phase two. You're it, once again."

"Not a problem."

Garrett closed the door, leaving Alex alone.

"Hey Garrett, do y'all want me to take care of Alex for you tonight?"

"No. That's okay. He's already taken care of himself. I expect no more problems from him. At least not for a while." Garrett closed the door.

"What do I do now?" Alex said softly. He could not call the police. Nothing had happened. He had no proof. It was not like he could say something would happen to President Lawton. Alex stood up and walked toward Garrett's desk in the back of the room, the floor squeaked, piercing the silence. Nothing was there. No drawers. The discussion mentioned having items in here for Thomas Henry to pick up. Now if he could just find some proof. Alex looked around in the dark. The light from the hall helped. Books surrounded him everywhere. The back wall's bay window let light reflect in from the main driveway. Off on the right side was the fireplace with two overstuffed chairs. The floor was hardwood, with two thirds covered by an oriental rug.

He knew he had little time to investigate the room. Alex estimated it would be five more minutes before he would be missed. Garrett and Thomas Henry were already looking for him. His other option, he guessed, was to try to get back to the room later in the evening, but by then it could be too late. Any information in the room would be lost once Henry left. Alex knew he would have to risk it and scour the room for any information he could find.

He got down on the floor and crawled under the desk. The floor squeaked as he did. He maneuvered onto his back, reaching up with his hands, feeling for a false bottom. It was solid, as solid as wood could get. Alex flipped back over and crawled from under the table toward the window.

"The books would be too obvious. That would be the first place anyone would look. Garrett wouldn't risk that. Maybe the fireplace." He went to the fireplace and looked inside, then he reached in and felt around. It was too grimy to put anything in there. Alex looked at his hands covered in soot. He needed something to wipe them on, so he walked back to the carpet. Its mosaic pattern was dark burgundy. If he wiped his hands on it before he went out, he would ruin the rug, so he flipped it up. "They'll never see the back side of this."

"What's this?" Alex looked again and saw there was a door cut into the floor, one foot by two. "Talk about a needle in a haystack." He pushed the rug back further, then grasped the handle and lifted. The door swung up and over so it laid back flat against the flooring. He looked inside. It was difficult to see, so he reached in and felt some papers. He lifted them out. There were four manila envelopes. From the light coming through the bay window, Alex saw that each had the same markings on them.

OP-86USA1-NWO-GO

Alex opened the first envelope. There was a memo on top. He read it.

MEMO

RE: OPERATION TARGET D.C. ONE

DATE: JANUARY 9

The definitive date is set for January 10th. D.C. One's itinerary has been obtained from Service. The eventuality is scheduled for 1600 hrs. at the main entrance when D.C. One is scheduled to greet well wishers.

All have been briefed as to job requirements and assignments. There will be no further questions answered after this packet has been received.

You must destroy this document and all materials within each packet. That means to burn them, then wash the remains down a sink with hot water for five minutes and follow with bleach.

There will be no further contact.

He started to sweat. He knew he had to go to the authorities with this, but he could not take the entire packet, or the operation might be called off. He sat and thought. "The only person to contact is Sniper," Alex said. He knew what he had to do - there was no choice. He gathered some information, folded it and placed it inside of his jacket pocket. He reached back in, felt around and pulled up a computer disk. He had no time to wonder about the contents as he placed it in his side pocket. He arranged everything else back as he found it, closed the lid, and straightened the carpet back over the floor. It was now time to get his coat and give his regrets for leaving so early.

Outside the kingdom of the Lord there is no nation which is greater than any other. God and history will remember your judgment.

Haile Selassie
League of Nations 1936

CHAPTER TWENTY-ONE
JANUARY 9TH

Sniper moved on top as she let out a slight moan. He maneuvered around so she was completely engulfed by him.

"Are you okay?" Sniper pushed her hair back, and then seemed to study her face, while stopping his upward momentum. He waited for her to situate herself.

"Ah," she hesitated. "Yes." Laurel paused, staring into his blue eyes. She ran her fingers through his blond hair. "I don't want this to end." She moved her hips, twisting down. "I've never been quite this. . ." She kissed his forehead.

"It's been a while." Their naked bodies interwoven. He caressed her breast. "Laurel."

"Yes?"

"You make me feel more complete, more than anyone I've ever been with."

She breathed heavily into his ear. Each breath becoming more labored as he gained rhythm. "I'm sure it's a competitive field."

Sniper grabbed her hips, pulling her up. "I can't get enough of you. All I want to do is to crawl completely inside, to become part of you."

"You are a part of me, beyond anything you'll ever realize," Laurel told him.

"God, I hope so."

"It's like I've been caught in a whirlwind." Laurel pushed back his hair as he came forward. "I mean I've thought about you and fantasized about this, but even in my wildest dreams, I never realized how intense we would be. I wish we could last forever."

"Me too."

"Why don't we do something about us?"

"What?"

"Let's move in together. There's been enough time since I've been down here," Laurel said.

"I don't think I could do that yet, not now, not to. . ."

"Shhhh. Don't say it. Think about what I am saying. I don't want you to answer, not yet. Remember, it would be best for all of us. I can't continue to lie to the boys. They're getting suspicious, at least Jeremy is."

"Let's break into this slowly. I want it to last, but I don't know at what cost."

Laurel pulled him closer. "I wouldn't push you. I just can't help but want to be with you and let the entire world know how I feel."

"I know. Believe me, I feel the same way," Sniper said.

"Are you sure I can't talk you into going up to D.C. with me and the boys tomorrow? We could make a week of it."

"What do you have to do in Washington?"

"I have my deposition scheduled for the eleventh and my attorney wants to brief me tomorrow, so, I'm, you know, ready."

"Alex is going all out, isn't he?"

"Yes, but it didn't help that I got Andy Vassily to represent me."

"Who's he?" Sniper asked.

274

"Alex's nemesis," Laurel explained. "I wanted to get him off of his game and I knew where his Achilles was."

"Remind me not to piss you off," Sniper laughed.

"Remember that. Now how about joining me in Washington?"

"Maybe."

That's all I get is a maybe?" Laurel lightly scolded him.

"Well, it's just that I seem to be preoccupied right now and if I were you I'd take the maybe. After all, it's better than no."

"Okay," Laurel hushed.

"Now where were we?"

He said his good nights and thanked Garrett for his hospitality and for including him in the evening, but he was under the weather, and felt he should go home and get some rest. Alex paid special attention to Thomas Henry, being cordial, without appearing like he knew anything. He briefly spoke to Judge Connally, who arrived as he was leaving. Nothing was out of the ordinary, including the Judge chiding him for missing the best part of the evening.

Alex was in his car, safe in knowing the Explorer would be much more difficult to run off the road than the MG. As he hurried home, he placed a cell call to Sam. He could only conceal a small amount of information on his person, but he also knew he had to take something to prove he was not hallucinating, left to bounce off walls.

The phone rang. Sam went over to his side of the bed and picked it up.

"Where are you?" She paused, swallowed hard. Her face turned a shade of pale gray.

"Yes." She nodded her head as she listened to the conversation.

275

"Yes. I understand." She started to shake. "I knew this might happen, at least sooner or later."

She listened some more, sitting down on the bed, wrapping the telephone cord around her index finger, kicking her legs, like a little girl whose feet do not quite reach the ground. "How long?" She tilted her head to the side. "Okay, right." She paused. "I know already." She frowned, and then pushed her hair from her face. "Yes. I'm just so sorry." Softly, she hung up the phone, then went into the bathroom and started the shower.

"Time to call Sniper. Come on Snipe, you've got to be home." One ring, then another. "Where are you?" Third ring, fourth. "I'll give you six rings, then I'll try from home." Five. Click. There was a second of silence. "Hello Snipe?"

"Hello, this is William Weylyn. I'm not here but if you leave your name, telephone number and a brief message, your phone call will be returned." Beeeep.

"Shit," Alex said, letting his subconscious take control. "Hey, Snipe. It's me, Alex. Look. I need to talk to you tonight. As soon as possible." Alex breathed deeply, thinking what else he could say.

Click. "Hey Alex." Sniper sounded as though he was rustled from sleep. "What do I owe this to?"

"I hope I didn't catch you at a bad time, but I found out something which will blow your mind."

"Where are you calling from? You seem to be going in and out."

"I'm in my car, heading back to Old Town," Alex responded.

"What's up?"

"I have some information you need to handle. It concerns Lawton. There may be a conspiracy to get to him."

"What? When?" Sniper took a sudden interest. "You're not trying to run a game?"

"No. This is not something I wish to be involved with, let alone have any knowledge of. If I could just forget about it, I would."

"When?"

"Tomorrow at Four. It's scheduled to happen outside of the White House. They have the President's schedule."

"Who does?"

"I. . . get. . . detailed."

"Bad connection Alex, where?"

"He's. . . supporters by. . . gates."

"You're breaking up. Say it again."

"Damn cell transferors. I said he's to greet supporters by the. . . gate. In time for the national news. They're using it to try to. . . his support."

"Who's involved?"

"Thomas Henry, you know, I've told you about. . . before."

"Yea. I know him, but I never would have expected this from him."

"What Snipe? I didn't hear you."

"Nothing, I just didn't think this could be possible."

"You. . . check it out yourself. You have. . . in the Secret Service, look at the. . . schedule. You'll see if I'm right without. . . suspicions. You've got to do something. If I go public, it won't happen, but if it doesn't happen, then I risk losing all I have left in my life. And I'll tell you. . . Sniper, I've already lost all I. . . I can handle."

"You've got it, Alex. I'll handle it from here."

"Thanks."

"Alex, do you have any supporting documents?"

"What?"

"Supporting papers. Do you have anything?"

"I have some things."

"What?"

"They're documents which. . . and they outline tomorrow's event. I took them from the house."

"Can you get them to me?"

"Sure. How?"

"Do you have access to a fax?"

"I have one at the house. I'm heading there now, I can fax them right away."

"Good. I want you to fax them to this number, then destroy them."

"Hold on, I need to. . . this down." Alex reached for his pen from his inside breast pocket, then held the phone in the cradle of his neck, as he leaned over to write on the newspaper on the passenger seat, pulling it over to the center console. "Go ahead, I'm set."

"It's (202) 634-5124."

"Got it."

"Alex, I'll be the only one who sees anything you send. If everything is as you say it is, after I review and confirm all of the information, I will have a car placed outside of your house, keeping an eye on you for a few days. Okay?"

"Thanks. Listen, I hope I'm wrong."

"Me too, but you can't be too careful." Sniper paused.

"Remember, trust no one, not even Sam."

"Come on, I don't think I have. . . to worry about. I'm. . . a speck."

"You do know how to screw people, after all you are an attorney."

They laughed. Alex respected the levity, plus Sniper seemed to relieve him of this burden. "Thanks for your help. You're friendship is much. . . . I'll see you later"

As Alex continued on toward his house, he tried to phone Sam to tell her about all he stumbled onto. "Damn!" The line was busy.

The road blurred as he sped along, lost in thought, becoming fixated upon something, but not knowing what. The fixation was deep in the subconscious. Alex was now on auto drive as he turned into the driveway, stopping outside of the garage. He looked around, wondering how he got home. He retraced the route through a hazy memory, before he turned off the engine. Alex looked down and shook his head, then reached over and grabbed the newspaper, which jarred him back to reality. "I've got to fax the info," he said loudly, as though he were waking himself out of a deep slumber. He opened the door, stepped down and closed the door.

Alex looked up and down the street, but there were no cars present. He hurriedly walked around the garage, to the side entrance, and unlocked the door, pushing it open, and then quickly closed it behind him.

"Alex?" Sam's voice came from upstairs.

"Yes, it's me. I got home early. I didn't mean to surprise you."

"I wanted to make sure. I just got out of the shower," she said. "Why don't you come up? I need to be dried."

"It's tempting, but I have to make a call. I'll be up in a few minutes," he said.

"What?" Sam asked.

"I have to fax some documents."

"Can't that wait?"

"No, it really needs to be done," replied Alex.

"You're delaying some amazing pleasure."

"I won't be long, believe me." Alex took his topcoat off and headed into the library. He took out the documents he had taken, carefully unfolding each, placing them, one by one, on his desk, smoothing them out, so he could fax them. He reviewed the four items.

The first document was the memo, outlining the details of the plot to go after the President.

The next item was a letter from the Secret Service dismissing Garrett Baird from duty.

Garrett Baird   December 18, 1964

Special Operations

Department 1920-A

United States Secret Service

Washington, D.C. 20010

Dear Garrett:

You have been a loyal member of our department for several years now, which makes this the most painful choice I have ever had to make in my capacity as Director. After long discussions with President Johnson, he has concluded it is best, for all concerned, that you leave the Service.

The United States government is much indebted to you for your years of service. You stood your ground and performed your duties beyond reproach. It is unfortunate you were in the wrong place at the wrong time. What more can be said. The Warren Commission exonerated you from any wrongdoing. Our agency has done the same through its own internal investigation. You know how I feel, but my hands are tied.

You will be leaving many friends. Your severance pay will allow you time to seek new opportunities, and I am willing to help you in any way I can, now and in the future.

Sincerely,

William Mayer

"Why would someone who is hailed as a hero, be taken from duty?"

"Who are you talking to?"

Startled, Alex turned quickly to the door. Sam was wearing a silk robe, draped over her. Her hair was still wet. Her naked body could be seen when she moved. She did not try to conceal herself. She never did. Her openness and comfort with her body made Alex desire to be with her. She was consuming him. He was incapable in stopping her from having her way. "God do I want to be with you right now."

"What's stopping you?" she purred.

He gestured toward the papers sitting on his desk. "I've got to fax these out."

"And that's more important," Sam said as she opened more of her robe. "Than this?"

Alex closed his eyes, inhaling deeply, then exhaling slowly. "I want you more now, than I can ever recall. You are truly beautiful."

"Beauty is fleeting, so you better hurry."

"Sam. Look." He was at a loss for words. "Just give me three minutes. Go upstairs, get ready, and," he paused. "Don't get started without me."

"Hurry or I may just have to." She turned, letting her robe drop at her feet, leaving him with a final view of her naked body as she headed upstairs.

He turned his attention to the fax. "Well old buddy, you'll just have to sort through this without me. I have more important issues to take care of." Alex stacked the papers, quickly scribbled a cover sheet to the attention of William Weylyn, and placed the bundle in the machine. He picked up the newspaper and dialed the number Sniper gave him, then pressed start. Beep ba beep bo beep.

"Just like a tune," Alex said as he heard the numbers chimed out by the machine, followed by Eeeewooooop click eeeewooooop. The documents were being fed through the machine. After each was sent, he ripped the page into small pieces. Once the items were transmitted, he gathered the pieces, took them to the bathroom and flushed them down the toilet. He went back to the library, grabbed his suit jacket, turned off the lights and headed upstairs.

I represent a party which does not yet exist: The party of revolution, civilization. The party will make the twentieth century. There will issue from it, first, the United States of Europe, then the United States of the World

Victor Hugo
Philosopher

CHAPTER TWENTY-TWO
JANUARY 10TH

Bolting straight up in bed, roused suddenly from a deep slumber, Alex was sweating from a strange dream. He was being chased through a field by an angry mob. The faster he ran, the slower he would go. The crowd was gaining on him. They wanted to hang him, but he did not know why. He kept running as fast as he could. When Alex looked ahead, he saw a small white picket fence, and as he approached, it transformed into a brick wall. It kept growing in height, getting taller and taller. Suddenly, Alex was not in the open field, but in a darkened alley. Skyscrapers were on either side, the giant wall in front. Christian's face appeared on the building to his left, Jeremy's surfaced to his right. Alex stopped. The crowd grew in size, but they did not move toward him. On the wall, directly before him, looking down, was Laurel. She had an angry glare. Then, as she looked past him, toward the commotion, a look of contentment came across her face. Alex turned. Towering over him was Sniper. He held a club above his head and swung it down. Just as it struck, there was a bright flash.

"Umm. Are, are you all right?" Sam asked sleepily.

"Yes, I had a strange dream, that's all. Go back to sleep." He got up from bed, moving away from her naked body. He leaned over and kissed her as he left.

"Don't leave," Sam said into her pillow, her voice muffled.

"I'll be right back." He looked at the bedroom clock, which shone a pale red 2:18. He walked over to one of two chairs in the bedroom, which served as a respite for clothes, put on some sweatpants and a T-shirt. He grabbed his lap top computer in its case, by the bedroom door, and went to his suit coat and grabbed the computer disk. Then he went into the guest bedroom.

Alex sat on the bed. He kept the lights off, fumbling with the clasps, as he opened the case, taking out his laptop computer and turned it on. The screen projected a dim white light across his face. After a few seconds, the prompt appeared.

C:>

Alex typed.

A:\

On the screen, it presented the A prompt, so he continued.

A:>WP51

He felt around in the briefcase, and pulled out the air card. He hit the ALT button on the keyboard, pressed O for Options. Alex accessed his firm's computer. He would modem the computers together to communicate. The computer made some clicking sounds and then was connected.

He opened up New File, and typed. He entered into the file system at his firm, and pressed:

ALT ENTER M;

then

ALT ENTER F S;

The room was dimly lit with the eerie glow of the screen. Alex placed the disk into the computer. He typed:

ALT ENTER F M S E MERGE ALL

The program was being downloaded onto the main file.

COMPLETE

Flashed on the screen. Alex turned the computer off, sending him into darkness. He shut the top to the computer, leaving it where it was and went back to the bedroom. He glanced over to the clock, but it was not on. "Strange."

"What?" Sam asked.

He reached over to the light on the nightstand and turned the switch. Alex rotated the switch three more times, but there was no electricity.

Sam stirred more. "Is everything okay." She sat up.

"I think we've lost power," Alex whispered.

"I didn't hear a storm or anything. You know what a light sleeper I am."

"Did you hear that?" Alex's heart pounded.

"No. What are you talking about?"

"There. There it is again. You had to hear it that time."

"I think I did hear a creak or something."

He went over to the window. A non-descript vehicle was parked across the street. The shadow of a person was inside.

"See anything?"

"Nothing," he replied. "Let me see if I can make a phone call." Alex went to the telephone, picked it up and dialed, then stopped.

"What's wrong?" Sam asked.

"The phone's dead." He set the phone gently into its cradle, and opened the nightstand drawer. Alex felt the cold steel of the 9mm Smith & Wesson. He kept it there after Laurel left, no longer having to worry about the boys getting a hold of it. He picked it up.

"What's that?"

"My gun. I have to see if everything is all right. Don't panic, but throw some clothes on. And don't leave this room until I get back."

"Are you crazy? How is your gun going to help?"

"It is known as the great equalizer."

"Maybe you're overreacting." Sam got out of bed and searched for something to wear.

"Better safe than sorry."

"Why don't you put it away before someone gets hurt?"

"I'll be okay. It's probably nothing."

I'm going with you," she replied.

"No." Alex looked at her naked body. "I'll be right back." He walked out to the hallway, closing the bedroom door behind him, careful not to make any noise.

With his back to the hallway wall, he slowly inched his way along. Alex tightly gripped the gun in his right hand. He got to the top of the stairway and looked down, trying to see. Everything was dark. The moonless night did nothing to enhance visibility. He did not see the red dot, at first, as it slowly moved up the stairway. As the light was on his chest, Alex dove to his right. The first shot grazed the side of his left arm. The second shot shattered a picture hanging on the wall behind him. The flash lit the stairs, but there was no sound, not until the picture came crashing down. He landed on his side and rolled onto his back, up against the hallway wall, as far from the stairway as possible. Alex looked at the bedroom door, which was still shut.

He took a quick inventory of himself. He still was holding the gun. There was no pain. Little blood flowed as Alex felt the wound on his left arm, just a slight sting as he pressed against it. His endorphins raced through him as he crawled back toward the stairs. If the intruders made it to the second floor, he and Sam would be history. Alex kept his nose to the carpet as he carefully measured his progress back.

Approaching the stairs, while crawling, inching along, he turned his head to the right. He pointed the gun toward the stairs. Alex's chest was pounding; he was sweating profusely. Blinking a few times to get rid of the stinging sensation, allowed him to focus. The step creaked.

"Come on mother fucker!" Alex shouted as he blindly aimed the gun over the first step and quickly fired four shots. The sound startled him as it shattered the choking silence. The spent cartridges went up and over his head and bounced off of the hallway wall behind him. There was a groan, followed by the noise of someone staggering down a few steps, before tumbling to the foyer floor.

Alex rolled back up against the wall, propping himself, waiting for someone to come up the stairs. "Come on, there has to be more than one person," he said quietly. He felt nauseous. He took a few deep gulps, and then held his breath while tightening his abdomen. It was a calming technique.

After thirty seconds, he crawled over to the top of the stairway and looked down. A shadow of a figure, dressed in black, was sprawled at the bottom of the stairs. His head was turned to the left. His right foot was propped up against the first step, with his left leg angled in underneath his right knee. The image looked grotesquely deformed with the moonlight peering in through the front door window, adding more shape to the crumpled mass.

The person moved slightly, letting out a groan. Labored breath could be heard. Alex looked around, but did not see or hear anything. He slowly rose and proceeded down the stairs, one at a time, getting closer to the body, with each step. Alex got to the first step, then kicked the leg off of the stair. A gun was close to his hand, so Alex kicked it away. There was a slight moan but no movement. He kneeled over and placed a hand on the chest. The heartbeat was faint. Alex's hands were wet and sticky from one of the wounds.

Alex lifted the hood up, then off. He stared in disbelief.

"Shit!" Alex half screamed, half yelled. "You God damned son of a bitch!" Alex kicked him in frustration and anger.

A loud cry came forth with the kick.

"What were you trying to do?" Alex asked

Michael Connally's breath was elongated. "Come here," he panted. The Judge was in pain.

"Why?"

"It's too late, Alex."

"What's too late?"

"Our lives," he gasped.

"I'll get out of this," Alex responded.

"No," he panted. "We all have our stations. . . in life, each of us take different. . . ways to get there."

"This is not my calling!" Alex threw the hood down by the Judge's feet.

"Well. . . this was my life, my calling. I had certain orders and I followed them. This is what life is all about."

"Bullshit!' he screamed. "You sold out to a system."

"You do what benefits you." Michael Connally struggled to maintain his focus. "You have to serve your cause. . . your beliefs. If you don't, well then you. . ." he grimaced. "May as well be dead."

"Why me?"

"You didn't know when to leave well enough alone."

"Was I blind to all of this? Why didn't I see this coming?" Alex pushed his hand through his hair. "Especially from you."

"Not blind," Connally said. "Too competitive. . . . Too inquisitive." Gasping, Judge Connally's breath became shallow.

Alex mumbled, "What did I ever do to deserve this? It must be a

288

dream"

Judge Connally looked at Alex, then past him. He started to say something, but fell silent. He slowly closed his eyes.

Alex pushed his hand through his hair. He then fell back against the front door, grasping his right shoulder as he did. He saw a bright white flash as the bullet went through him. Then he saw the flash of the gun from the top of the stairs, followed by its retort. There was no pain, only shock. He looked up, wondering who was there. He pointed his gun up the stairs. He felt the next shot strike him in the lower ribs. He immediately gasped for air. His body was shutting down to prevent him from feeling the pain. He looked up the stairs and saw Sam descend slowly, with a gun in her hand.

"Huh? Wwhat?" he stammered as Sam came closer. He slid down the door, leaving a trail of blood. "Sam? Why?" he choked out. He lost feeling in his right side as he tried to find the gun.

"Alex. You bastard. I loved you. I really loved you. I could have spent the rest of my life with you. Instead you have to go and fuck everything up." A tear trickled down her cheek.

Alex looked at her while she was talking; he was in a dazed trance. Shock was setting in from the wounds.

"You see, I don't have a choice here."

"We all have choices Sam. . . and we both made ours."

No! Either I stay alive, or both of us die. I don't want to die."

"How about me?"

"You were already dead. That decision was beyond my control."

Alex looked at her. Sam's features were becoming distorted, melting together. He tried to gather the remaining strength to devise a way to save himself. "Self preservation is so strong," he said. "We all want to survive."

"Don't you understand?" Sam asked. "You found yourself involved in something that was too big for you or me to handle. You had no control. No one would support you. If you would have left everything alone, then you. . ." Sam hesitated, "We. . . would be fine right now. But they knew what you have been questioning all along. You've been watched and undermined and plotted against and injured. They even saw what you did at Garrett's. That's when they had to react."

"How?"

"How what?" Sam said.

"How did they find out so fast?" His voice was becoming hoarse, allowing him to hear each breath he took, which was more intense, labored. He tasted blood with each swallow. It was thick, coagulated, which made speaking difficult.

"Who do you think you're playing with? Neophytes? These people have power, connections, wealth, and technology. You name it, they have it. They've been at this a long time. No one is going to stand in their way. We are a one world government and it's only a matter of time before you and everyone else realize it. Garrett Baird's house was a completely monitored circuit. His library was wired. Every move you made was recorded."

"Why didn't they get me there?" Alex coughed up blood. Some came from his nose.

"There were too many people around. It would have caused too much of a disturbance. They figured they'd let this one ride out, here, where it would be easier to manage and clean."

"I guess they didn't think this would happen." Alex half smiled. "How would they cover this up?" Alex could feel the gun in his hand. There was a sense of heaviness to it as he slowly tried to pick it up. His eyelids felt thick. He was becoming tired, cold. He knew the signs of shock.

"I didn't want to be here tonight. I didn't want to see what would happen to you. I gave my body and soul to you. Why did you have to make me do this?"

"How did you get involved?" He closed his eyes.

"At Dumbarton Oaks," Sam said. Her hand shook as she continued to point the gun at him.

"How?"

"They believed your research was going to lead you there after Wilson's house. I was backup, you know, just in case. I didn't know I'd fall in love with you though. I hope to God you don't hate me and that you can understand."

"Sam. . . . I don't hate you," he breathed deeply. "I was pulled into an. . . obsession."

"I begged you not to go tonight. I had a feeling something was going to happen."

"I know I'm going to. . . . Sam? Come here," he struggled to say.

She approached cautiously.

"If you love me, finish it," Alex said.

"I can't."

"Sam. . . . Listen. . . . if you don't, I will kill you." He struggled to pull the gun up to his thigh and aim it in her direction.

"You couldn't."

"This is not the time to ask what I can or can't do." His breath was labored. "I'll give you to five."

"I can't. Not anymore. I've had enough."

"If you don't do it then someone else will. . . . Please just take care of it. I'm in pain. I can't catch my breath. . . . Just do it." Alex looked up at her, his vision was blurred. "Don't you hear them?"

"Hear what?" Sam asked.

"Helicopters."

"No."

"They're coming. I can hear them. One."

"What?" Sam said. "How many?"

"Two. Three." He struggled to bring the gun up higher. "Four. Five."

Sam kept her gun aimed at Alex as she looked around, then toward him. "God No! Please, Alex!" she shouted.

What is at stake is more than one small country. It is a big idea, a new world order, where diverse nations are drawn together in common cause to achieve the universal aspirations of mankind: peace and security, freedom and the rule of the law.

George H. W. Bush
43rd President

CHAPTER TWENTY-THREE
JANUARY 11TH

Quinn Colton slowed his pace as he ran down the sidewalk back toward his home. He was almost done with his five-mile route. His sweatshirt was soaked, but it was a feeling he enjoyed. He wiped the sweat from his forehead with his sleeve before reaching down and picking up the morning's Washington Post from the front porch. It had been some time since the paper landed in an easy access area.

"Thank God I don't have to make another call to the main office. Hopefully there won't be any more reprisals," he said aloud, without a care who heard.

Over the past several months, Quinn had talked to himself as a way to relieve the stress and anxiety he was having. His therapist said, "Let go of your inner self. It matters not what others think but how you feel about yourself. It will free you from your anxieties. Express and you will be free." He was told exercise would be a great way to reduce stress reduce and high blood pressure. Quinn refused conventional treatment, not wanting to medicate, and instead developed a holistic approach to life. Wearing a watch even seemed uncomfortable.

He breathed deeply. "Remember to let go of your inner self." He would repeat this as a means of self-control. After the incident with Dick Wheeler, he took an eight-week sabbatical, desiring to spend more time with his family, to get himself together. His work output was slipping and the firm's Board of Directors pointed out, at his last review, that if he did not increase both his hours billed along with a higher percentage of cases won or resolved to the client's satisfaction, he would no longer be a partner at MacClennan, O'Brien, Dougherty & Ernest. He would become one of many other attorneys trying to eke out an existence on the cold legal streets.

It was early morning. The sun had not risen. Everything was quiet, dark and peaceful. The calm before the storm of the day's activities. The perfect time to run.

Quinn limited himself to read only the morning paper. He no longer watched the news before going to bed, nor did he listen to talk radio. He opted to forego the frustration and aggravation those charged shows caused. He kept abreast of world events, but he no longer had to be up to the minute current. Mornings were the time to read and then he would have all day to work off any stress from events he had no control over.

As he closed the front door and went to the kitchen, Quinn poured himself a cup of coffee and sat at the table. His wife and kids were asleep and would be for another hour. The quiet of the early morning was his time, a time he savored, to relax and be by himself. He wiped more beads of perspiration from his face, then unrolled the rubber band from its tight grasp of the Post and placed the band on the table, next to him. Quinn unfolded the paper in his ritualistic manner, smoothing it out. He would read one section at a time, from beginning to end, then place the paper back together in the same order he found it. The bold headline grabbed his attention.

"Jesus," he said.

PRESIDENTIAL ASSASSINATION ATTEMPT FOILED

President William Hamilton Lawton survived an attempt on his life yesterday, while shaking hands and saying hello to well-wishers and school children standing outside of the east gate to the White House. It occurred at about 4:00 in the afternoon.

President Lawton had addressed the National Association for Fairness in the Media, when, as he was traveling back to the Oval Office, to finish working on his United Nations Address, he noticed a group of children outside of the East gate. They were in Washington D.C., on a class field trip from Greenfield Elementary School in Raleigh, North Carolina. They arrived too late to tour the White House and were hoping to glimpse the President as his motorcade drove past.

Presidential spokeswoman Michele Stratmore-Carey briefed the media. She said the President, while in route, was informed about the school children waiting for him to appear. President Lawton made it clear he wanted to talk to them, letting them have something to remember about their stay in Washington. Little did he know, they would become part of an event which they will remember for the rest of their lives, to pass onto their children and grandchildren. William Lawton was elected as a populist president and had, over the past several months, voiced to his staff he was becoming too removed and protected from those who supported him. He did not believe his inaccessibility was helping his credibility.

Reports indicated a troubled individual identified by Secret Service as Thomas Patrick Henry, of Lubbock, Texas, tried to assassinate the President. He was standing in the back of the crowd, behind the group of children wearing a long overcoat, which was not unusual, considering the cold weather Washington had been experiencing of late. Thomas Henry reached into his coat and pulled out a semi-automatic rifle. With the children positioned in between the President and Henry, Secret Service did not have time to react, nor could they without endangering many young innocent lives.

Unknown to Henry and Secret Service Agents, FBI Special Agent William Weylyn was standing behind him. "I knew I had to react quickly. I was there with a friend of mine and her two sons. I just happened to be in the right place at the right time. Nothing more. I saw this man in front of me pull out an assault rifle from his coat, bending over as he did. He was using the children for cover. I knew there was nothing I could do, besides taking him out. I identified myself. He kept going down into a combative stance. I had no option but to pull my gun and shoot. I fired three times. He fell to the ground. I jumped on top to prevent him from taking further action. At that point, I held up my badge so Secret Service would know I had the situation under control."

Secret Service moved in quickly to calm the situation. At first, they did not know who fired the shots. The event was described as pandemonium. Children were screaming and running in every direction. The President was hustled into his limousine. After twenty minutes he returned to the crowd and held and calmed many children. He had all of the Greenfield Elementary children brought into the White House. President and Mrs. Lawton entertained them for a couple of hours.

President Lawton issued the following statement: "My wife and I wish to express our deep appreciation to Agent William Weylyn, who happened to be in the right place at the right time. His actions went well beyond the call of duty. His astute attention and reaction to the events that played out before him saved not only my life, but also those of many innocent children. My family, Mrs. Lawton and I thank him for his outstanding act of heroism. He is a true American hero."

The gunman, Thomas Henry, has been characterized as a loner. His family had not heard from him for several months. He had a history of leaving for extended periods of time, without contacting them. His absence did not alarm them. His father, Robert Henry, said, "We are saddened by the loss of our son. He had some problems, but we never expected him to try something like this. There was never an indication he would try what he did. We are thankful no one else was hurt. I'm sure Tom is with his Maker, at peace. For that we are grateful."

Secret Service has put together this composite of the gunman. He left Texas in October, traveling to California, then Florida, where he purchased the assault weapon in November. He had been in the D.C. area since December 15th, staying at several area hotels. He is believed to have acted alone. His car was found four blocks from the White House. When searching his car, police found a note indicating he intended to assassinate the President and that he expected to die after he succeeded. They have not released the full contents of the note. Other ammunition and assorted guns were found at the car, along with pornography and drugs. It is believed he lived a dark, lonely life, and wanted to prove his existence. Police would neither confirm, nor deny Henry was on drugs, which may have also precipitated the attack. Continued on page A3

Quinn turned to the third page. Much of it was taken up by pictures of the event. All of it was captured on Secret Service videotape. There was one picture of William Weylyn, with an unidentified woman and her two sons standing next to him and the President. "If I didn't know better, I'd swear that's Alex's wife." He looked at the various pictures, saw the President addressing the United Nations, and then read the caption below the picture.

BUSINESS AS USUAL

President William Hamilton Lawton continued with business as usual, four short hours after the assassination attempt on his life. He addressed a specially convened session of the United Nations, outlining his goals with respect to "developing that parliamentary body into a stronger military police force, increasing World stability, ending Global bloodshed, famine and discrimination in any form."

Quinn turned the page. He almost missed the article, but something drew him to it. There it was in the lower left hand corner of page five.

ATTORNEY KILLS JUDGE THEN SELF

Attorney Alex Westcott of the law firm MacClennan, O'Brien, Dougherty & Ernest, burst into Judge Michael Connally's chambers early yesterday morning, killing him. He then turned the gun on himself. He shot himself in the head and was pronounced dead at the scene. Initial investigation showed Westcott was distraught over a case the Judge was hearing. Judge Connally issued a ruling against Westcott's client, Ameritrend Chemical Company, which incensed him.

"Jesus Christ, No!" Quinn shouted. He slammed his hand down on the table, shook his head, and peered back to the paper.

A review of all public records indicated Alex Westcott was having difficulty in his personal life. He was arrested for drunk driving in October, after being involved in a single car accident. In December, his wife of 15 years filed for divorce. All of these factors may have contributed to Alex Westcott's strange behavior. Unnamed sources say he was trying to sort through various personal problems through the aid and advice of a Psychiatrist. When reached for comment, his treating physician was not in and has returned no phone calls.

"Bullshit! They don't know what strange is. If there was ever someone who had his act together, it was Alex."

William Dougherty, senior partner at Mr. Westcott's law firm indicated "Alex was having both personal and professional problems. We were all concerned with his increasingly bizarre behavior, so much so we recommended he seek professional help, which he did. Apparently it was too little too late."

"Why is Dougherty trying to undermine Alex's existence?" He picked up the paper and held it closer to his face. "What a puckered asshole."

The story here appears more tragic. Alex Westcott left behind two young sons, who are now without a father. Michael Connally, in addition to Annie, his wife of 25 years, is survived by two adult children. Judge Connally has left behind an impressive legacy. He was the youngest judge ever appointed to the Federal Bench. He was well liked by his colleagues and attorneys who practiced before him.

"Liked?" Quinn shook his head in disbelief. "Name one attorney, besides Westcott, who even had any rapport with the son of a bitch."

He was an avid outdoorsman, active in many activities, hunting, camping, rock climbing, skiing, and his personal favorite, hockey. Judge Connally and Alex Westcott had a similar family history. Both of their grandfathers served in the U.S. Congress and the Senate. Judge Connally's father was also a Senator from Texas, who retired in 1982. Senator Andrew Westcott was from Colorado, whose term ended when he died in a plane crash in 1945.

Quinn read and re-read the article in total denial. He did not feel the warmth of the spilled coffee. It formed a river of brown mud, swirling and flowing from the overturned cup, across the table, then down on his lap. At first, it streamed off quickly, cascading like a waterfall, and then the flow trickled down to a steady drip.

Among the natural right of the colonists are these: first, a right to life; secondly, to liberty; thirdly, to property; together with the right to support and defend them in the best manner they can. Those are evident branches of, rather than deductions from, the duty of self-preservation, commonly called the first law of nature.

Samuel Adams
American Revolutionary Leader

CHAPTER TWENTY-FOUR
JANUARY 14TH

"I'm glad that most of our employees could be present for this meeting. The senior partners believe it is imperative to have input from everyone, not just the attorneys, and that's why you all are present." Bill Dougherty looked around the crowded room. "Contrary to rumors, the firm is not falling apart at the seams. We are open and ready for business, but we have to have everyone behind it, or we will disintegrate. Let's open the room for discussion, and let's keep this informal. Everyone here will have an opportunity to talk."

"Mr. Dougherty, how much longer are the police going to be here?"

"Good question Gary." He paused. "As you know, we have fully complied with the FBI and District of Columbia Police Department. I've been told they will be gone before the middle of next week."

"Are you sure, they've been quite disruptive. We can't meet with clients here and it's becoming a great inconvenience."

"Yes, they are a nuisance. The partners have decided to push their investigation as fast as possible, which is why there have been so many investigators here. We are well aware of how they've scoured the firm, but they are paying special attention to Alex's office and its belongings. So that should keep them from being too noticeable."

"What about our clients?" Harrold McGeorge asked.

"Mr. McGeorge is rightly concerned. For the time being I would suggest we reschedule appointments, take them out for lunch, dinner, or even meet at their offices, but once we get this over we can then get everything back to normal."

The door to the room opened. "Excuse me, I hope I'm not too late." The murmur grew louder.

"Quiet, please," Dougherty strained. "Quinn thank you for coming on such short notice. We're discussing the direction of the firm. Please sit down." Quinn moved to the back wall.

Maura said, "Mr. Dougherty, I believe that I can speak for most of those present when I say the investigation has disrupted the everyday balance which existed here before Mr. Westcott's death. They've questioned everyone - what he did, with whom he socialized, what cases he was working on, even whether he was seeing anyone. Every aspect of his life has been looked into. I've probably been grilled more than most people, since I was his secretary, but now I'm tired. Excuse me for saying it, but this just bullshit."

Dougherty slammed his hand down on the table to quell the noise. "People, people. We're all a little ragged and tattered from all of this, but I would ask you to remain focused."

"First things first," Maura continued. "Before I decide to stay here, I feel it's important to find out what you, the partners and everyone else believe about Alex. I for one don't believe for a second he would ever act this way. It just doesn't seem right. And if he did this, then I will go my own way. It won't be too difficult to get another job someplace else."

Sheldon Gage glared, then responded, "Perhaps you should think things through. Maura, the stigma of what has happened here runs deeper to you than to anyone else. You would be a marked person in this environment."

"People," Dougherty strained to be heard. "People, I will not stand for any accusatory tones. We have to remain focused and above any petty bickering. I hope that's understood, right Gage?"

Sheldon Gage did not reply, only sinking lower in his chair, tilting his head down, away from the stares.

Dougherty said, "As for your question Maura, as to where I stand, I would have to agree with you and I would hope and expect the same from everyone here. Alex would not react like this, but logic precipitates and prevails. In law we are taught to be objective, to review all of the facts and figures before we make any decision. I cannot help but believe what the authorities say happened, happened."

"I don't agree." Everyone turned and looked to Quinn, who was leaning against the wall. He stepped toward the table, looked around the room, and continued. "With all due respect, I knew Alex Westcott; he was a friend of mine and he wouldn't do any of this which he's accused of. Remember, the dead cannot defend themselves." He paused and looked at the entire firm's staff, seated and standing. "Maura's right. We're losing our focus. It is wrong to assess blame here, any type and on anyone. What we all must focus on is that we have seen a tragedy, but we need to adjust. I cannot let all of my hard work and drive turn to dust and blow away. I've, no, we have traveled too far together to believe this is true and to let an event of this nature destroy our livelihood."

"Well then, what do you suggest?" Dougherty asked.

"Remember that you called this emergency meeting to see what effect Alex's death and the resulting publicity would have on the firm."

"True," Bill Dougherty responded.

"With that in mind, we have to present ourselves as a cohesive unit, a unified front. No one strays from the party line, and if anyone is uncomfortable, jump now. We need commitments from those who are

302

truly dedicated in making this work. If we have that, then we can ride this storm," Quinn said.

"Why should we bother?" someone chimed. "It's too late now."

"It's never too late." Quinn's voice rose. "Think logically. While Alex was a partner, his name was not on the letterhead," Quinn stressed.

"He's still associated with us in the press," MacClennan reminded him.

Quinn countered, "He oversaw many files which have been quite lucrative for the firm and, quite frankly, we shouldn't give them up. Another factor to consider is no one in the legal profession cared for Judge Connally's judicial temperament or legal rulings."

"True, true," O'Brien said.

"Yes," Dougherty responded.

"I've been called back to work by Mr. Dougherty, on behalf of the partners, and I am ready. I'll take it upon myself to get all of Alex's files, including Ameritrend, in order. Billing will only apply to work in progress along with future work. If any client is not satisfied, then they can seek legal representation elsewhere."

"I'd suggest that we take a vote on this measure," Dougherty said. "Are there any other comments? Sensing none, all those who want out, leave this room now. You'll be compensated one month's salary and given high recommendations." No one moved. "Good, good."

"I'd like to take Maura on as my assistant," Quinn said. "She knows all of Alex's clients and files better than anyone here. I'm going to need to file motions to adjourn hearings and extend deadlines, so I can get up to speed."

"I'd be happy to do that Mr. Colton," she replied. "The one thing you'll have going for you is that Mr. Westcott was meticulous. All of his files are extremely organized. Whatever you need, I'd be glad to help."

"One more thing," Quinn said. "We need to present a cohesive front. There cannot be any leaking of information to the press or the police. Let them investigate and see what they can find on their own. Alex was one of us and he'd be as protective of our privacy as we should be of his. Let's face it, he wasn't the type of person to explode. This wasn't the person we all knew and respected."

The heroes of the world community are not those who withdraw when difficulties ensue, not those who can envision neither the prospect of success nor the consequence of failure—but those who stand the heat of battle, the fight for world peace through the United Nations.

Hubert H. Humphrey
U.S. Senator

CHAPTER TWENTY-FIVE
FEBRUARY 21ST

"Good morning Maura, and how are you today?"

"Just fine Mr. Colton. The adjournment on that mediation is all set. Your messages are on your desk."

"I'm going to finish reviewing the files on Ameritrend, then go for my workout at lunch." Quinn walked into Alex's old office, which he had taken over. This day did not differ from any other. He was guaranteed he would receive a bonus on a quarterly basis for returning to work. Since Alex's files were taboo and no one wanted to handle them, his price went up. Quinn's stress outlet was working wonders for him. He ran and lifted weights every day, usually around lunch. People complimented him on how good he looked. His productivity went up, as did his self-confidence.

Maura helped him to master the computer, through long hours of training. Quinn had some difficulty, but he was capable. He had to go through all of the items on Alex's computer, through the directories, files and sub files. He sat down at his desk and powered up the computer. It kicked to life, with clicking and scanning noises, until the screen, full of color, came to view.

WELCOME TO THE MAIN MENU

Good Morning . . . Please Enter Your Selection

1. FIRM TIME AND BILLING

2. SPREADSHEET

3. WORD PROCESSING

4. DOS UTILITIES

5. MISCELLANEOUS

F1 Menu Maintenance   F10 Exit to DOS

February 21   8:17:58 am

Quinn looked, and then pressed 3. The screen changed.

WORD PROCESSING

Please Enter Your Selection

    A. Grammartext

    B. Read Plus

    C. Legal Net

    D. Works Processing

Press [Esc] Key For Main Menu

February 21   8:18:02 am

    He stroked D, which placed him into word processing. "Success," he said. Looking over his options, he did not know what to do next. "How about open existing files." Quinn punched the keys. The screen showed a variety of Directories from which to choose.

    DIRECTORIES

    AMERITREND

    AMBOLYN

    ANDERSON

    BALIN

BASTIN

He worked the cursor so that it was over AMERITREND, and pressed ENTER.

FILES.WPS

112073

112174

112275

112376

112477

Maura informed him that was how Alex kept track of his dictation and that it was not important. He pressed CONTROL R. "That isn't what I wanted to do." Quinn looked at the screen. "Well, I may as well try this one".

REDROWEN

He highlighted the file, then pressed ENTER. The computer clicked, made a grinding noise, appeared to power down, and then back up. The screen flashed. He cautiously looked at it.

C:\SYSTEM ERROR

C:\CONTINUE?

He typed Y, then ENTER

C:\INTERNET

"This is going better than I thought," Quinn said as he typed Y, then ENTER.

C:\PASSWORD

He hit ENTER, again the computer hesitated. There was a dial tone, then pulse tones were emitted. There were several high-pitched squeals, followed by a click. "Maura, maybe you should get in here," he called softly. The monitor changed to a colorful image.

ENTER PROGRAM

Quinn did not understand what this program was doing. "Maura," he said louder as he pressed ENTER.

PROGRAM ENTERED AS REDROWEN

CONFIRM

Quinn pressed ENTER. The program came on the screen. He looked, pulled his chair closer. He read. "Maura!, Get in here!"

"What? Is everything okay?" she said.

"You tell me. Look." Quinn moved away so Maura could see the screen.

I'm Alex Westcott. It's January 10th about 2:20 a.m. If this program has been accessed improperly, by someone other than me, and others are reading this, then probably the worst has happened.

I don't know what or how I'll be portrayed, but I've had some premonitions about something happening real soon. I've met people who could make any saint seem like a sinner, and I have no doubt I'll be cast in the same light. All I ask is for anyone who reads this, please keep an open mind, look at all of the facts.

If you are reading this, it means my program has been accessed without the proper password. I encoded this program to be accessed only through my password. If it was diverted, then a send program would transfer this file onto the Internet for all to read. It's been red flagged to draw more attention to it.

An acquaintance, who is probably a better friend than I will ever realize or perhaps know in this life, told me whenever I am in doubt, note everything more than once, and inform others. That's what I'm doing. Here is my story.

ABOUT THE AUTHOR

Michael J. Balian is an attorney in Rochester Hills, Michigan. This is his first novel, which was written 20 years ago. He has dedicated himself to going through his book bank to complete more of the stories he has in his head.